CW01430120

The Trouble With Titles
Copyright © 2024 by Nina Jarrett. All rights reserved.
Published by Rogue Press.
Editing by Katie Jackson

For more information, contact author Nina Jarrett. www.ninajarrett.com

THE TROUBLE WITH TITLES

INCONVENIENT SCANDALS
BOOK FOUR

NINA JARRETT

ROGUE
PRESS

To my mom, a single mother who built a life for three children against the odds.

Thank you for everything you have done for us.

PROLOGUE

"Psyche, of all mortals, is too beautiful to belong to earth."

Lucius Apuleius, *Metamorphoses*

* * *

SUMMER 1810, LONDON

*T*he sun was low over the rooftops, igniting a glorious spread of oranges and pinks, while above the stars twinkled in the darkening firmament as if to mirror the joy in his heart.

Simon was home.

He walked across the back lawn to where he would find his lovely Psyche awaiting his arrival.

More than eighty years ago, the Aldritch brothers had built two freestanding townhouses side by side, after they had made their fortunes, sold off their businesses, and invested in property to join the gentry as newly minted

1

gentlemen of leisure. And one of their first actions was to build monuments to their splendid success. The result had been two matching buildings of great beauty, with colonnades, ornate porticos, and statuary upon the roofs, all within verdant gardens. Yet it was the walled garden shared by the two homes which was the true jewel of their commission.

Forty years later, when Simon's father, Lord Blackwood, had purchased one of the properties, it had been with the stipulation that the garden would continue to be shared by the owners of each household, which some astute legal work had ensured. Lord Blackwood had gladly paid a small fortune for such a magnificent testament to the architectural arts, agreeing to the hidden garden between the connected properties.

The baron had come to regret the agreement. Much to his chagrin, in 1792, when Simon had been a babe toddling in the nursery, the adjoining property had been sold off to a common tradesperson. Not just any tradesperson—heaven forfend—a tradeswoman!

Simon knew the year of this terrible event because his father would speak of it often, lamenting the decline of the neighborhood. Personally, Simon thought that Eleanor Bigsby was beyond compare. The widow had moved to London after her husband died and had purchased a struggling artificial stone business. She had not wasted any time, building it into the preeminent stone manufacturer in England. Weather-resistant neoclassical statues, architectural decorations, and garden ornaments of great artistry had raised the enterprise to new heights under her leadership, with a client list boasting both King George III and the Prince of Wales. She held the only Royal Warrant for such a business.

Simon picked up his pace when he saw the archway leading to the secluded domain.

In his estimation, Eleanor Bigsby's greatest accomplishment was not her empire of moulded stone, but rather the twin daughters she had raised as a lone parent while conquering the high commerce of London.

He entered the garden, pausing to take in the exceptional beauty of the towering columns and lush vegetation that encircled the magnificent stone urn filled with a profusion of flowers. Along the border of the hidden area were silent sentinels—Roman gods and goddesses watched on as Simon rushed forward to greet the ravishing creature of grace seated on the bench positioned below the urn.

"Madeline!"

Her head rose, and her face lit with joy as she leapt to her feet. "Simon!"

They rushed into each other's arms, and Simon took in her beloved features. Madeline Bigsby had a delicate, heart-shaped face, a slender upturned nose, enormous eyes of lustrous amber, and arching eyebrows of honey brown to match her silky hair. She was dressed for dinner, ravishing in her silk evening gown, and he had dreamed of her often in his bed at Oxford.

More than dreamed, if he were honest.

He lowered his head on impulse to brush his lips over hers in a moment of heady passion, before composing himself. Just a year apart in age, they had been meeting in the hidden spot for as long as he could remember. Growing up next door to her made returning to London an event to look forward to. He thanked his good fortune that his father disdained the country and had rarely traveled there since his epic quarrel with Simon's older brother Peter, who had died many years ago. Lord and Lady Blackwood preferred the comforts

London offered to rusticating, so he required his stewards come to London to meet him. Simon had no complaints because it had meant more time spent with Madeline.

"You are taller," she exclaimed in her sweet voice, thrilling him to his very toes. It was wonderful to be home after months of letters. To hold her in his arms and breathe in the scent of orange blossoms, which he liked to imagine her bathing in. Simon grunted as he pictured such an event. Madeline was a young lady, so she favored modest bodices, not least because of the men she worked alongside, but her creamy skin … He believed he would be unmanned when he eventually saw her naked.

"I put on muscle since I was last home."

Madeline's eyes dropped to his shoulders in shy appreciation as she squeezed his biceps. "I can tell," she whispered.

Simon shook his head to clear his thoughts, stepping back so they might sit. He could not continue to be a gentleman unless he unhanded her.

"How was your day?"

Madeline sighed heavily, twisting her fingers in her lap. "I wish Henrietta was interested in working with me at Bigsby's. She has gone off to be Uncle Reginald's private secretary, so it is official. I am to run Bigsby's when Mama retires while Henrietta plays hostess to the political elite."

"You will be excellent in any role you choose," Simon replied. It was true. Madeline was a gifted young lady of great intelligence.

"If I were choosing, I would continue to sculpt new pieces and work with the craftsmen! I have no wish to contend with the business dealings. Mama is imposing, but even she has to address the prejudices of small-minded men who think a woman's place is at home. I will learn to manage them as she does, I suppose … but it is not what I enjoy. I enjoy working with the craftsmen."

Mrs. Bigsby, indeed, cut an imposing figure—six feet tall with a firm jaw and determined nature. The thought of Madeline, who was far more dainty at five feet two inches, filling her mother's shoes in negotiations with clients and vendors was difficult to picture, but he knew she would find a way to do it if she willed it so.

"Then I shall learn the business dealings. When we wed!" Simon declared it in a cheery tone and, for a moment, they both considered the perfection of working side by side in the future as man and wife.

Eventually, the content expression on Madeline's face faded as reality set in. "Lord Blackwood will never allow it. One of his spares engaging in trade?"

Simon shut his eyes, the illusion rushing away like clouds dispersed by a tempest. "And Eleanor Bigsby would raise some objections, too, I believe."

They sat in silence, contemplating the future while watching the last rays of sunlight disappear. Mrs. Bigsby was not petty, in Simon's estimation, but Lord Blackwood's continuing campaign to wrest their communal garden from her had antagonized Madeline's mother beyond civility. His father had even attempted to blacken her reputation and drive clients away from her business, but the King's patronage had muted the effects of such endeavors, serving to fuel the feud between the two neighbors. Neither were willing to give up their beautiful homes or the landscaping gem that unified them in mutual animosity.

"I brought you a gift," Madeline announced. She reached into a basket on the bench beside her, then turned to present him with a small figurine carved out of stone.

Simon took it, careful with the fragile piece. "Did you make it?"

Madeline nodded, her pink lips stretching into an angelic smile that made his heart clamor with excitement.

Simon peered down at the wondrous work of art. It was exquisite—the detail of muscled arms and legs, the strands of hair, the gaze of the masculine figure staring out across the distance, and the quiver of arrows slung over its broad shoulders. In its curled fist was a bouquet of flowers carved in intricate detail. Madeline might be a proper young lady, educated by the finest tutors and business minds in London, but she knew about the human form. She had to in order to apprentice at Bigsby's Stone Manufactory.

"Eros."

"Gazing at their garden of flowers."

Simon chuckled. "Because he and Psyche found their happiness?"

Even in the gathering darkness, Simon could perceive that Madeline's eyes had grown misty. "I do not know what the future holds, but this will always be our place."

Simon reached out to take hold of her gloved hand beneath his. "We will find a way to be together, fair Madeline. I swear it."

* * *

MADELINE WATCHED Simon walk away into the night, his lean form cutting a fine figure as he exited the garden. Their garden.

He must have been about done increasing in size because he was no longer the boy she had grown up with, but instead a man of six feet with broad shoulders and narrow hips. His almost-white buckskins accentuated the musculature of his legs, reminding her of the statues that were carved at the manufactory by talented artistes. Earlier, she had thrilled at the intense blueness of his eyes as he leaned in to kiss her and had shivered at the slight scrape of stubble when he had released her.

Would there be a time in the future when they could court?

It seemed an impossibility given the state of affairs between her mother and the baron.

Brushing her fingers over her lips where she could still feel the impression of his mouth brushing over hers in a fleeting kiss, Madeline gazed up at the star-studded heavens and fought back the feeling of dread that had been plaguing her these past months. Simon was adamant their future would be together, but he was so young. He had not even reached his majority yet, and she was a year younger than him. So much could go wrong in the next few years to drive them apart until they gained control over their lives.

Gathering her things back into her basket, she made her way inside.

As soon as she opened the terrace doors to enter the library, she knew her mother was in the room. Mama had a magnetic presence, one that filled spaces and attracted all eyes to her. As Madeline's eyes grew accustomed to the light, she looked about but could not find her.

"It will end in unhappiness." The pronouncement came from near the fireplace, which was empty, the warm nights of summer not needing the intrusion of its heat. After the initial fright, Madeline deduced her mother must be seated in one of the plump wingback chairs that dominated the room.

"Perhaps he will convince the baron," Madeline replied.

Silence followed her words, which even to her ear did not sound confident. Finally, her mother responded. "For your sake, I hope this is so. But you should prepare yourself, daughter. It may not come to pass."

"Simon will find a way. He loves me."

"The baron is a cruel man who does not consider the happiness of others, Maddy. He is persistent in his grievances, and it is unlikely he will relent on the subject of *class*."

Eleanor Bigsby's tone was bitter as she emphasized the subject of their neighborly feud. Madeline could not protest; the baron remained unwavering in his rigid views on proper breeding. It would not help that Madeline herself was now involved with the trade that raised his ire so.

* * *

THE NEXT DAY, 1810

"You are to stay away from that chit next door, you hear?"

Simon had been summoned to his father's study for a setdown. It was not the first time, and he was resilient, so it did not perturb him. This had become a ritual—a litany about the terrible Bigsbys each time Simon returned home. It had not deterred him in the past, and it would not deter him now.

"I need a response, young man!"

Simon had learned that it did not do to quarrel with the old man. It was impossible to change his fixed ideas, and any attempt prolonged their altercations. "I heard you."

Lord Blackwood was a man from a different era. Now in his seventies, he had buried two wives before marrying Simon's mother twenty years earlier. Isla Campbell was a Scottish viscountess with a healthy appetite for status. She had been a girl of Madeline's age when she had wed the baron who had children older than herself. Imagining it was enough to make Simon nauseous, but it was the way of the noble classes.

Which was why he had a father who was a full two generations older than himself and an older brother who could have been his father for their age difference.

"It is your duty to marry well, and that Bigsby chit is a distraction. Dreadful bloodlines. You must focus on your studies. There are courtesans whom you can visit, but that Eleanor Bigsby will cry foul and trap you into marriage with her daughter just to spite me if you continue to meet with the flibbertigibbet alone!"

Simon bit back a retort. Debating made matters much worse, so he held his tongue.

His father slammed his hand on the desk, but it was rather ineffectual. The baron had not aged well. Too many years of cigars, rich foods, laudanum, and alcohol had worn him down to a hollow husk of his former self. He was emaciated, his wrinkled skin as pale as a whitefish with the translucence of aged glass. The wisps of hair he had left were white and sparse, and his bald pate was rife with blue veins visible beneath the skin. Lord Blackwood was a cautionary tale that convinced Simon to take care of himself lest he follow in his father's footsteps.

Simon repressed a shudder at the thought.

"Duty is important," he commented when he noticed his father was awaiting a response.

"Look here, son. I know I have told you this before, but you are a man now and you must face the future. It is obvious John will not have heirs, which means there is no longer any doubt that you will one day become the Baron of Blackwood."

Simon straightened up, a frown on his face as he considered this fresh declaration. He had not thought about it, but his much older brother John was now in his forties and remained childless. His wife was in poor health. After fathering two stillborns, John did not display any interest in pursuing another attempt at siring an heir to the Blackwood title.

Peter Scott, the baron's second son, had died in Italy

when Simon was still a babe in the nursery. Simon had no recollections of his older brother, and it was entirely possible he had never met Peter, who had returned from his Grand Tour to quickly fall out with the baron in an epic storm over a young Italian woman before returning to Florence. War with France had broken out, making it difficult to reestablish contact before Peter had died from a fever fifteen years ago.

Which left Simon as the young spare, something he had not thought about. The declaration that he was not merely the spare, but was to be the future heir to the Blackwood title, was disconcerting.

The baron sat back with a pleased expression, evidently having noted Simon's reaction. "John has made it known that he will not attempt to have children again. You will be the future Lord Blackwood when your brother leaves this world."

Simon was not sure how to feel about that. Until now, he had always imagined that in the future he would marry Madeline, with or without his father's consent. Odds were that it would be without Lord Blackwood's consent, so Simon had always thought he would follow her into trade as they had talked about the night before. In the morning light, learning he had no choice in his future path, Simon felt the pressure of expectations pressing on him. A thundercloud threatening torrential rain to wash away his choices. How would Madeline feel about his revelation? Would she consent to be his wife if she was to become Lady Blackwood? What of her work at Bigsby's?

There would be much to discuss when he met her in their garden after dinner.

"Which is why I have instructed the servants to lock up the house during dinner. You shall not go to the gardens tonight to visit that Bigsby chit. She is not fit to be the future Lady Blackwood, and that mother of hers will not allow her to serve as your mistress. Your wife will bear my grandchildren, and she must elevate the family bloodlines, which is why … your connection is severed." The baron's tone was triumphant, his wrinkled face pulling into the caricature of a smug smile.

Simon jumped to his feet. "I am a grown man! You cannot lock me in the house!"

He had no intention of allowing the baron's interference to stand in his way. His father's declaration was outrageous, but it would not stop Simon from seeing Madeline. Nevertheless, he amplified his visceral reaction to the news in order to convince his father that his ploy would prove successful. It would make it easier for Simon to sneak out later that night if the baron believed he had won their little conflict.

Arguing ensued for another ten minutes before Simon found his cue to exit and departed the study. Entering the dim hall, he found his little brother, Nicholas, who must have been eavesdropping on their contentious conversation.

"When did you arrive?"

Nicholas was several years younger than him and had not yet had his growth spurt. The lad was half Simon's size, with a spindly body but large hands and feet that declared he would be a tall chap when he eventually grew into them. The boy's blue eyes were wide as he stared up at his brother, his dark brown waves of hair in need of a trim lest he be mistaken for a fop.

"Deuce it, Simon! How do you find the courage to be so outspoken with the old man?"

Simon laughed, bringing his hand down on his brother's shoulder to lead him toward the library, where their father would not overhear their conversation.

"Father will always bang on about duty and rules and

proper behavior. It is important that you know what you want, and the rules be damned."

Nicholas shook his head in disbelief. "But … he is so … mean!"

"He is a bitter old man, so it is important that you do not care what he thinks. Be brave. Be your own man. Follow your own path. Father will never allow you to do anything interesting if you pay him mind."

His brother considered his advice, apparently mulling it over with careful thought. "I want to be like you. You are never afraid and everyone likes you. Father is always complaining about the state of the world, and the commoners next door."

Simon drew up, irritated at how his father's behavior might affect a young boy's perspective. "There is nothing common about the women next door. They are all exceptional, every one of them. Mrs. Bigsby boasts wealth to rival our family's, and she earned it through ingenuity and hard work. It is Father who is common with his obsession about bloodlines and appropriate conduct. Nay, do not pay heed to his sour concepts of right and wrong. You must seek your own path, Nicholas Scott!"

Nicholas nibbled on a fingernail, clearly thinking, then dropped his hand, raising himself to his full height. "I promise to be brave like you."

"Good lad." Simon reached out a hand to tousle his brother's hair. They were the youngest in the Scott home by far. It was important they stick together. "How was Eton?"

Nicholas groaned, his shoulders slumping before he dragged his adolescent body to flop onto a settee. "Latin is so difficult!"

Simon chuckled, following suit to take his own seat and catch up with his brother. He and John were the only family Simon enjoyed spending time with, so it was a pleasurable respite to provide advice for Nicholas's troubles at school.

After he left Nicholas to spend time with their mother, the day proved uneventful. Long and boring, but finally the sun was setting. It was time to join his Psyche in their garden of flowers.

Simon peered out from his window on the third floor, enjoying the wash of colors on the horizon before leaning out to consider the trellis that was attached to the wall near his window. It was a good three feet from the ledge he leaned from, but it was fortunate that his bedchamber happened to be on the side of the house that had a sturdy vine climbing the wall. The moment his father had announced the house would be locked, Simon had decided he would use the trellis to climb down. Madeline would be waiting for him even now in the gathering night.

Reaching out an arm, he grabbed hold of a wooden slat and shook it to test its strength. It was sturdy and fastened to the wall securely. Simon climbed out onto the stone ledge that passed beneath the windows. He had considered climbing down in his stockings but decided to wear his riding boots to protect him from the sharp stems sure to poke out of the branches of ivy. They were well grown, as thick as his forearm, and had been creeping up the wall for more decades than he had been on this earth. It was sure to be uncomfortable to descend. Much easier to scale when he returned than to climb down, was his guess.

Grabbing hold of the trellis, he committed, allowing it to take his full weight and soughing in deep relief when it held. He began to gingerly make his way down, surprised by how much it worked the muscles in his shoulders, back, and arms. It took longer than he expected, until he was a few feet from the ground. Using the wall to push off, he dropped down, bending his knees as he hit the ground to dissipate the shock, and then rose up to straighten himself, brushing twigs and leaves from his clothing. When he knew he was all together, he strode along the side of the house to the hidden garden, careful to duck down under the stone balustrades so no one would see him from one of the windows.

Entering the secret garden, he saw Madeline jump to her feet with joy. She must have been wondering where he was—

A terrible scream rent through the evening, causing Simon's heart to beat painfully within his chest.

His jaw dropped in horror as his mind attempted to process what was happening. Madeline stared back at him with a flabbergasted expression.

Within a second, he recognized the voice.

"Nicholas!"

He turned on his heel to race back to the side of the house that his window faced, and as he turned the corner, his worst fears were realized. Far beneath his window was the crumpled heap of his little brother, a tiny pile of clothing and limbs, and Simon knew—he knew exactly what had happened.

Rushing forward, he dropped to his knees beside his lifeless brother and ripped off his own gloves. Checking for a pulse, Simon almost fainted with elation when he felt the flicker beneath his fingertips. Sitting back on his haunches, he assessed his brother's condition, noting that the boy's leg was twisted at an odd angle.

"It is broken," announced Madeline, who had approached behind him.

Simon was fighting back tears, guilt wrenching his gut. "You must go home. I must take care of him."

As he gently scooped Nicholas up in his arms, her soft touch brushed over his shoulder, but by the time he was on his feet and turned around, Madeline was nowhere to be seen. But Simon had no time to consider his Psyche at that moment. Nay, he must take responsibility for his negligence.

His brother weighed almost nothing, still but a child, as Simon made his way with care to the front of the house. Taking most of the boy's weight with one arm, he managed to knock on the door, which was opened within a few moments by their butler, Walter MacNaby. MacNaby was a most proper upper-servant, with a round face and a ready smile, but the moment he saw Nicholas, his blood drained to leave him pale.

"Send for a doctor," commanded Simon, stalking past the retainer. As he reached the staircase, his mother was coming down.

"MacNaby, did you hear that dreadful scream—"

Lady Isla Scott was an ageless beauty of not quite forty years of age, with dark brown hair and striking blue eyes which spotted the limp form in his arms.

"Nicholas?" she shrieked.

Simon watched in despair as she swooned, crumpling into a heap on the stairs, but was helpless to catch her while he had his brother sheltered in his arms. He leapt forward to use his legs as a barrier lest she tumble down.

"Mother?"

Lord help him if the baroness was injured, too. Simon had much to answer for as it was, and he did not need any more added to the substantial burden of culpability he was fighting off as he took care of his current duty. He must see to his brother, and there was no time for his emotions.

Roderick, one of their footmen, appeared in the hall, breaking into a run to bound up to the baroness. He assisted her to sit up, her expression dazed. Simon took it as his cue to run Nicholas up to his bedroom, which was next to Simon's on the third floor.

Placing the boy into his bed, Simon removed his shoes

and breeches, leaving his small clothes in place as he carefully rolled his stocking off the injured leg. Hissing in anguish, Simon stepped back to stare at the limb with a hand clamped over his mouth lest he cast up his accounts at the overwhelming shame of what he had done. The break was bad, bone poking through the skin, and Simon had no knowledge of what to do to help Nicholas while he awaited the doctor's arrival.

Behind him, the sound of someone entering the room startled him from his misery.

"What is this?" demanded his father, his alarm clear.

"Nicholas fell from … the window." Simon knew his secret departure was about to come to light, but he could not quite bring himself to admit the truth.

"I do not understand … the window is shut?"

Simon swallowed. The time had arrived faster than he had expected. "My window."

"Why would he fall from your window?"

"He … was … following me." Simon knew it. He had encouraged Nicholas to be more like himself. The boy must have come to visit him in his room and seen the window Simon had left open. The window he had left open so he might sneak back in. And Nicholas had decided to be brave, so he had followed Simon to join him on an unknown adventure. But he was a small boy who had misjudged the distance to the trellis.

Lord Blackwood grunted, approaching the bed to reach out a trembling hand toward the leg. "Is he …" For the first time in his life, Simon witnessed his father overcome.

"He lives yet. MacNaby has sent for a doctor."

The baron nodded, his eyes moist as he stared down at his youngest son. Simon wished the old man would rage at him, blame him for what he had done in leading his little brother astray. Lord Blackwood must have realized what had transpired, but instead he plopped down on the edge of the bed and panted in shock, as if his emotions were attacking his aged body.

The next few hours were a blur. The doctor arrived, his face grim as he examined the boy. Eventually, he set the leg. Nicholas mumbled a little when the bone was pushed back in place but did not awaken despite what must have been agonizing pain. Once the leg was set, the doctor stepped out into the hall to discuss the situation with Lord Blackwood. Simon joined them.

"There is bruising on the boy's head, but little that can be done. It is a matter of time before we know his condition. The hope is that he awakens in the next few hours. If he does not … there is no method to predict head injuries, I am afraid. It is a matter of time."

His father nodded at the news, his expression distant. "What of the leg?"

"A very bad break. It is certain the boy will have a limp, but it is the head injury that worries me most. With a situation like this … you should prepare yourself for the worst, my lord."

Simon's stomach clenched into a tight knot, but he kept his wits about him, noting the doctor's instructions with great attention to detail, including the administration of the laudanum he provided. He was battling with a dark tide of emotion threatening to drag him under, but he had to be present and take care of Nicholas, and he could not afford the luxury of lamenting his role in his little brother's downfall. His tiny brother who looked up to him.

His mother arrived to see her youngest boy but became hysterical when she saw he had still not awakened, so Lord Blackwood led her away. "Come my dear, perhaps a little laudanum would do your nerves some good."

Some hours later, in the early hours of the morning,

Simon sat alone beside Nicholas's bed to keep vigil. His brother was pale and vulnerable beneath the covers. Full of life and energy just hours earlier—Simon would give anything for the boy to open his eyes and say something.

He thought about how he had encouraged his little brother to break the rules and buck authority and, without warning, his guilt resurfaced as he bowed his head to weep, his shoulders shuddering with the force of it. If Nicholas died, it would be his fault. He had done this!

I am a selfish bastard.

Wiping the tears from his eyes, Simon got down on his knees, clasping his hands together to pray.

Please, Lord! I am sorry for my hubris! I promise to do my duty if you allow Nicholas to live!

CHAPTER 1

"When you opened your eyes, you saw love itself, and now you have lost it."

Lucius Apuleius, *Metamorphoses*

* * *

JULY 19, 1821

"*N*icholas, I wish to speak with you."

Simon's tone was hostile, but it had been two days since he had last seen his little brother.

Not so little anymore.

Nicholas topped Simon by an inch, but he appeared taller yet. His form was lean—too lean. His habits of carousing for days on end, and barely eating, were evident and, in Simon's opinion, the youngest Scott was abusing spirits.

Simon had attempted to have his allowance curtailed to limit his habits, but John had been insistent that Nicholas was a young buck sowing his wild oats. John was now the master of their household, so after some heated debates, Simon had relented and agreed to abide by the new baron's wishes. This did not mean he was not seeking other avenues to address the crisis that was forming in front of his eyes—clouds were building on the horizon, and it was only a matter of time before the storm burst.

"You shall have to join me in the library then, old chap."

Simon experienced a flash of guilt as Nicholas limped down the hall. Striding to catch up with his younger brother, he entered the room to find Nicholas at the drinks cabinet pouring a port.

"It is eight in the morning—a little early for drinking?"

Nicholas shrugged, then limped over to a settee to drop down and nurse his drink in an insolent sprawl. "It depends on your perspective. For you, it is the start of the day. For me, it is the end of a very late night."

Simon could not help it. He rubbed his face as he tried to find words—new words—that would somehow penetrate the cloud of alcohol that buzzed around his brother's head. And perhaps laudanum, too.

In his estimation, his family relied too much on both, not to mention rich foods, and they suffered from the ill effects. Simon made it a point to take care of himself and not fall into such bad habits, but being surrounded by relations in a perpetual state of inebriation took its toll on his peace of mind.

"Nicholas, I am concerned for your health. Your leg has been stiffening up, your limp more pronounced. I wish for you to see the physician that has been recommended—"

"Not this again! I am well and have no need for such things. I am an idle buck of the noble class with no chance of inheriting or making something meaningful of myself ... Unless there is a lucky change in my circumstances."

Nicholas waved his crystal wineglass at the lame leg, which caused a physical sensation of regret to wash through Simon. "I shall live fast and expire young while I hold on to my Campbell good looks."

Framed by the claret red wallpaper and bookcases, the morning sun filling the library with light, Nicholas appeared ghastly with his pale features and reddened eyes. "Where were John and Mother off to so early?"

It was a transparent change of subject, but Simon was at a loss for words. Attempting to talk to Nicholas when he had been out routing for as long as he had was pointless. Best to attempt this conversation when his brother had some sleep and some food in his belly.

"The coronation is this morning."

"Ah! That explains those puffy breeches."

As Baron of Blackwood, John was garbed in antique dress per the specifications laid out by the College of Arms at the King's behest—a tight-fitting doublet with shining buttons. Gold and white breeches formed a puffy skirt, which stopped at the upper thighs to reveal a long expanse of white-stockinged legs. Heeled shoes along with a red velvet cape lined with ermine.

"Quite. The monarch had some ridiculous notions about what is to be worn by the lords. I am quite heartened to be a mere heir rather than suffer the indignity of what can only be classified as costume. It is unlikely there will be a coronation of such *grandeur* again." Simon's voice was laced with sarcasm. He appreciated art and beauty, but this morning's ceremony seemed more of a pompous spectacle. Their mother, the dowager Lady Blackwood, had been tittering in glee at his older brother's ensemble when they had left for Westminster. The ladies were not afflicted with such silly adornment.

Nicholas chuckled, downing his port to smack the glass

down on a side table. "I predict there will be humorous prints for sale come morning!"

It was not long before Nicholas limped up the stairs to find his bed. Simon went off to take care of baronial business. John might be the baron, but his health had been declining since their father had died eighteen months earlier, so it was Simon who had taken over managing the vast estates held by the Blackwood title. The work would not complete itself, and it would be better to keep his mind occupied until evening when he would need to deliver some unwelcome news. Tomorrow he would sacrifice much in the name of duty, and he must sever his ties to the past if he wished to claim he possessed any integrity as a gentleman.

* * *

MADELINE TOYED with her apple and potato pie while her twin and Mama discussed the coronation over dinner. As private secretary to Uncle Reginald, Henrietta Bigsby was privy to information about the cost and organization of the ceremony held earlier that day, but Madeline was finding it difficult to participate, so she just listened while they chattered.

"Uncle Reggie says that Parliament provided one hundred thousand pounds! Can you believe such a princely sum for one event?"

Eleanor Bigsby tutted, her expression scandalized. "It is wasteful."

Henri leaned forward, tapping her finger on the white linen tablecloth for emphasis. "That is not all. A further one hundred million francs came from French war reparations!"

Mama gasped. "That is a fortune!"

"Altogether it is close to two hundred and fifty thousand pounds! Uncle Reggie says it is twenty times more than the last coronation. Such outrageous extravagance! No members of Parliament will speak out about it publicly, but plenty at Commons are complaining in private. One could build a palace for such a sum. Or fund fifty foundling homes for the orphans of war."

"Did Uncle Reginald attend the coronation?"

Henri shook her head, her honey brown hair glowing from the golden light of sunset. "Uncle Reggie could not obtain an invitation, but Lord Gwydyr invited him in to visit the Abbey last night to witness the preparations. The King's procession arrived while he was still at Westminster."

"It is a pity he could not witness it firsthand."

"He managed to secure a seat to watch the banquet. There was a temporary gallery built within the hall. I look forward to hearing about it tomorrow."

"You did not meet with him today?"

"Nay. We spoke last night when he returned home from Parliament, but he had to leave for Westminster early this morning."

Henri had been at their great-uncle's home the past few days to assist him with coronation-related duties. Visiting dignitaries, political soirées, and other functions had resulted in all hands on deck at Parliament. It was the first they had seen of her sister since the prior week.

"That is not all. Uncle Reggie says there are plans afoot to build out Buckingham House into a palace. Both Commons and Lords are anxious due to the King's expensive tastes."

Madeline pushed her plate away to sip on her watered-down wine. She did not know why her thoughts were plaguing her so. Last week she had enjoyed the pinnacle of career success, impressing even her mother, who was the premier titan of moulded stone in all of England. But it had been some time since she had wielded a chisel to craft *objets d'art* which would act as templates for stone statues and ornaments to adorn the monumental buildings of the realm. She spent her days engaged in the business of manufactory, rather than the artistry she had once loved so.

All she could think about was that soon she would turn nine and twenty. She had made no definitive decision that she did not wish to wed one day. With time marching on, the decision to wed would soon be beyond her control. Talk of the coronation did nothing to distract her from the frustration of lonely nights. If she did not marry, she would never know the joy of her children.

Madeline was approaching a crossroads, but she did not know what she wanted to do about it.

She wished she could discuss the subject with Henri, but her sister had no interest in it. Henri enjoyed her work with Uncle Reginald, and never discussed courtship or settling down. Madeline had often wondered what her sister would do when Uncle Reginald finally left this world. He was getting on in years, so eventually she would need to make a change when their great-uncle … was no longer around to employ her.

Thinking of death did nothing to lift her desolate spirits, and soon she picked up her fork to poke at her pie once more until dinner was over.

After dinner, Madeline wrapped a shawl around her shoulders and headed to the walled garden. She would enjoy the evening sky, she decided. It was not at all because she hoped for a visit. Simon appeared less frequently with every passing year. Sometimes weeks would go by without him making an appearance. She knew there was no possibility of courtship between them, that his unfailing commitment to familial duty this past decade would never flag, but it was a secret joy when he did join her in their garden. It reminded her of happier times, when the future had held such potential, she could scarcely grasp the magnitude of her joy.

Madeline soughed heavily at this admission. Considering the darkness of her thoughts, perhaps it was time to stop visiting the garden. Perhaps it just held echoes of her youth and had become the source of unhappiness.

Entering through the archway, she was startled to see that Simon had arrived before her. She could make out the shape of his head, his broad shoulders, and the white cravat that practically shone in the light of the waning moon.

He rose to his feet as she approached, and she noticed he had grown a neat beard since she had last seen him. Close cropped, it framed his angular jaw.

"Simon!"

"Madeline," he greeted. "You look lovely this evening."

Tears prickled her eyes at the polite words. She had been his Psyche, but she was no longer the girl he had worshiped. His manner was distant, as it had been these last few years. Visiting with an old friend who was no longer the person she had known only caused the disappointment of fond memories. Their conversations had grown stiff—stilted—and Madeline would return to the house feeling hollow. As if she had brushed past a delightful aspect of her childhood only to find it lacking from her adult perspective.

She nodded, and they took their seats on the bench. As always, Simon sat on the far edge as if he were afraid to touch her. Madeline revisited her thoughts about whether she should be spending her time in the walled garden. Perhaps it tethered her to the past—a place which could not be revisited. Perhaps she had clung to old dreams for far too long. Perhaps she should venture forth to meet some young men while there was still an opportunity to wed and bear children instead of reminiscing over lost love.

"How have you been?"

The polite question was a stake through her heart, and Madeline had to repress a gasp. Ever so proper. Ever so correct. She remembered the bold, irreverent young man he had been before Nicholas's fall. She missed the old Simon so. It made her quite resent the Scott family for their sobering influence over him.

If only—

She cut the thought off. There was no patience left for 'if only'.

Mama would be pleased if I brought up the subject of courtship.

Mama had hopes for her daughters, which she made known, but she had always given them space to make their own determination. As much as she wanted heirs to their empire of industry, as a leader, she believed if a person was forced into something, it would lead to incompetence and misery.

Eleanor Bigsby had often pointed out that Madeline was the future of Bigsby's Stone Manufactory and she must learn to exercise free will if she was to follow in her mother's footsteps. Browbeating one's heiress would not result in developing a strong, confident woman who could overcome the male-dominated trade they did business in.

These notions served to highlight the lack of free will she had been demonstrating in this aspect of her life. Madeline realized she was on the brink of a decision, and that this might well be the last night she visited here.

"I have been well."

Simon nodded, seemingly satisfied by the appropriate response. Once they had talked freely as equals, but now they behaved like acquaintances with little in common. She could no longer hide from the truth—waiting for him in their walled garden every night … had become depressing.

It was time for her to gather the remnants of her pride and end this ritual. And the obvious course was to make a declaration. Which meant she just needed to find the words to tell him she would no longer be here waiting for him in their garden of flowers.

"I shall not be visiting our garden beyond this evening."

* * *

EARLIER THAT DAY

Simon was not having a good day.

This morning his attempt to talk to his younger brother had failed. The layabout had gone to sleep, risen when John and their mother had returned from the coronation, and used the distraction of their lively discussion to disappear into the early evening before Simon could speak with him as he had intended.

John had returned home in a fine funk, grumbling to Simon's mother about an encounter at the ceremony. Simon was forced to listen when he joined them in the family drawing room to get his brother's signature on important documents.

"That little coxcomb, Lord Filminster, sat next to me. I haven't seen him since attending Oxford, but the first thing he did was to offer his condolences over Peter's death! My brother died more than two decades ago! Why would he not mention our father, who expired a mere eighteen months ago, or the death of my own wife just three years ago?"

Isla Scott made soothing noises to calm the baron down. "He sounds like a rotter, but do not let it upset you, dear. It will make you unwell, and the night is just beginning."

Simon's mother was an attractive peeress a mere nineteen years older than himself, and several years younger than John. If one were not aware of their relationships, she could have been mistaken for Simon's older sister. Her dark brown hair was still glossy without signs of gray, her oval face barely lined, and her intense blue eyes could pierce armor at fifty feet. A beautiful woman who had aged like a fine wine.

"Isla, it was not just that. He asked me about my heir without a by your leave. He was always an obnoxious fop with vulgar manners. The years have not improved his character."

Isla's eyes had flared in disapproval. "That is rather rude."

"Heaven forfend." Nicholas had entered the room, leaning against the doorframe with a nonchalant air. "How did you respond? Did you preen about Simon's brilliance?"

The facetious questions grated on Simon's nerves. He narrowed his eyes, noting that his brother had donned an overcoat, evidently heading out for another night of carousing.

"Of course! I informed him of Simon's brilliance in orchestrating the modernization of our estates after Father turned over the reins years ago. A fine heir, indeed. You will never guess what he had to say to that!"

Isla leaned forward, handing John a cup of tea. "Dear, you must calm yourself."

The remonstration had put Simon on the alert. John had not been well since their father died, and the coronation was sure to have exerted him with so many hours of ongoings. Worse, the baron was off to dinner with friends to celebrate, which Simon considered ill-advised, but his brother had been excited about it for weeks, so he had not the heart to dissuade him. John was aging beyond his years, a cloud of wispy, fair and gray curls forming a halo around his head, while his face sagged with pouchy flesh. In that moment, his complexion was more ruddy than usual, and he was heaving slightly as he drew breath. The unusual activities of the day were wearing him down.

"Perhaps you should stay in tonight," Simon had suggested.

"No!" John straightened in alarm. He must have realized the sharpness of his tone, relaxing back into his seat with his tea. "Tonight is important. I shall rest before I head out."

"Drink your tea, dear. It will help," Isla coaxed, a benign expression on her face. Her irises were mesmeric in the late afternoon light, and Simon pushed down a surge of irritation. It appeared his mother had enjoyed a little laudanum at some point during the day, her pupils pinpoints in a constellation of riveting blue. Her reliance on her tonics was yet another cause for concern.

Just then, Molly entered the room dressed for dinner in a muted mourning gown of lavender velvet, which offset her rich brown hair and hazel eyes. "Oh, hallo. What are we about, then?"

Simon rose to his feet. He was still not accustomed to the young lady's presence in their home. Molly Carter was the niece of his father's second wife. Not a blood relation to the Scotts, but a valued member of the family just the same. John was now the trustee of her estate by a bizarre mix-up in her mother's will which had stated John Scott, clearly meant to be their late baron, but with no specification, the solicitors had played ignorant to assume it was the son rather than the father. Which meant, in effect, Simon, who was managing all affairs related to the Blackwood title.

She was a practical young woman, especially when compared to the eccentric Scotts, and Simon enjoyed her calm presence. However, he had yet to form a comfortable relationship with her. "Molly, please join us."

Her lips had quirked into a smile, and she took a seat beside Isla, who busied herself pouring a cup of tea to hand to her step-niece.

"John was informing us of a rather irritating baron from Somerset whom he sat beside at the banquet."

"Just so. What did your friend have to say to Simon's

genius?" asked Nicholas, a smirk on his face as he poured out a port. Simon had been well aware of the jab aimed in his direction, but ignored it.

"The little upstart had the temerity to imply family disloyalty!"

This was followed by a cry from the expressionless Isla. "What?"

"He asked if I was aware that Peter had married before he left England? Had I taken the trouble to seek out his offspring, or was I following in my old man's footsteps to manipulate the heir of my choice?"

At these words, for just a moment, Simon woolgathered. If Peter, the brother he had never met, to his recollection, had sired heirs … that would mean Simon would be free to pursue his own path. With Madeline.

If only …

The thought of it had his heart leap with excitement before he scolded himself for foolish whimsy, refusing to complete the thought that would lead to frustration at his circumstances.

"What a cad," Isla proclaimed. "Your father was committed to duty. The baron would have brought Peter's children into our home and raised them as his own even if they diminished the Scott bloodlines. If there had been any progeny. It is a ridiculous accusation!"

John bobbed his head. "I do not trust the little weasel not to spread lies. You are to steer clear of him, you hear?" The baron had peered about with an expectant air while he waited for each member of the family to assent to his request.

Molly stared back in mild confusion when it came her turn. "Whom am I to avoid?"

"The Baron of Filminster."

"Oh. Certainly, I shall avoid him."

Simon buried a smile, hearing the irony in her voice despite the polite response. Molly was in mourning for her mother, so she did not get out and about much. John's intrinsic understanding of what her day consisted of as a bereaved, unwed young lady was deficient.

Shortly the family adjourned, Simon managing to solicit the much-needed signature from his brother. Isla was to dine with friends, and John was off to a separate, but similar event.

Simon had turned to find Nicholas, only to find he had disappeared without so much as a goodnight, frustrating Simon's intention to corner his little brother before he left for the night.

Shaking his head in aggravation, Simon held out an arm for his step-cousin to escort her to their lonely dinner. Molly smiled, locking arms with him, and they walked down the hall.

"Are you enjoying your stay with us?"

Molly giggled. "We have years ahead of us in this household. Must you remain so formal?"

The question gave him pause. He had not considered his studious nature might be viewed as too proper. It irked him, but then he had become rather serious over the years. He could not recollect the last time he had burst into genuine laughter. Doing his duty was killing his humor by a million tiny increments, and he hated it. But not as much as the duty he would fulfill come tomorrow.

"I apologize. It is not directed at you. Being dutiful is a habit that is hard to relinquish, I confess."

"How about we enjoy our dinner with no talk of duty, then? Just two cousins sharing repast?"

Simon forced a grin. Considering his plans for later, there was no joy to be found this evening, but he would make an effort to provide Molly with convivial companionship.

Which he did for the coming hours until he noted the sun was setting and it was time to do his duty yet again.

Leaving his step-cousin in the music room, he headed out to the garden to wait for Madeline. His stomach was tight with tension, and he dreaded what he was to do.

I do not wish to deliver bad news.

But it was more than that. Tonight, he buried his last links to his past. To the man he had been and the dreams he had held. He had put it off as long as he could, but John's health made it imperative that he take care of his obligations. It was time to close the door.

He waited as evening cast shadows upon the ground, kept company by Greek gods and their feminine counterparts, savoring the sense of freedom that the garden had always represented. An oasis from the solemnity of real life. A place he could still hold on to the fantasy of a future shared with his Psyche.

It was more painful than he had thought it would be.

The sound of gravel crunching beneath slippers had alerted him to her arrival, his heart leaping when he caught sight of her. She was ethereal in the ghostly moonlight.

"Simon!"

"Madeline," he greeted. "You look lovely this evening."

She dipped her head in acknowledgment, but she did not seem pleased at the compliment. He sensed she was melancholy as they took their seats on the bench.

Simon sat on the far edge, as was his custom lest he be overcome by the impulse to bolt from his rigid life where his responsibilities would rise to suffocate him if he considered all he had lost.

"How have you been?"

Madeline had fidgeted as if uncomfortable, not speaking for several moments as the silence stretched on. When she responded, there was an undercurrent of disappointment. "I have been well."

Simon nodded, not paying much attention as he summoned the will to say his piece.

"I shall not be visiting our garden beyond this evening."

* * *

SHE DID NOT REPLY for some time, and Simon was afraid he would have to repeat the awful declaration to cap his terrible day.

"I ... see."

It was all she said, and Simon's discomfort grew in the pursuant pause until he was compelled to explain himself further. "I have negotiated a marriage contract with Lord Boyle to marry his daughter."

"He is a viscount."

Her remark did not require a response. They both knew it was the primary motive for such a match.

"Which daughter?"

"Olivia ... the eldest."

"Do you admire her?"

Simon rolled his shoulders. The question was ... discomposing.

"I barely know her, but it will strengthen the Blackwood title. Elevate our connections and increase our influence when I wed the child of a respected viscount. Strengthen our bloodlines, which was my father's wish. It is—"

"Your duty." Madeline completed the sentence for him. "You have not visited our garden in some time. Did you come to tell me this?"

Simon bowed his head to study his boots, his legs stretched out in a languid position which did not reflect his state of mind in the least. "I wanted you to hear it from me, not read it in the news sheets."

Madeline rose to her feet, making to leave. "I thank you. Felicitations, Simon. I wish you great happiness in your future endeavors."

The impending loss of what could have been overwhelmed him. He was not ready. Reaching out, he caught her delicate hand in his. He was selfish—an utter bastard—but tomorrow he faced the gallows, and he was not quite ready to say goodbye.

"These are my last few hours of freedom. Would you … spend them with me? Perhaps we could speak openly as we did in our youth?"

He missed that simpler time shared with her, when he had been a bold youth without the weight of expectations weighing him down. When they had planned their lives together. How different things might be if he had not caused Nicholas's accident.

Madeline cocked her head, considering his words until she relented and seated herself. "One last conversation before we say goodbye."

His heart resumed beating in his chest, and Simon resolved to savor each second of their last night. He made a conscious effort to cast off the mantle of solemnity which was his character of late and, after an awkward start, they talked and laughed together about the mishaps of youth until well past midnight.

Finally, she checked the time. "I have work in the morning." Her tone was regretful as they rose to their feet.

Simon raised a finger to brush back a lock of her silky hair, taking his time to view her features in the silvery light for the last time. Leaning down, he brushed his lips over her soft mouth. He should not have done it, but he could not help himself as he ended this chapter of his life. It was a token to hold in his memories as they bid farewell.

Stepping back, he gave a little bow. "Farewell, lovely Psyche."

Madeline gave a tremulous smile, hesitating for just a moment, then headed toward the arch to disappear from sight.

Simon watched his goddess walk away, his thoughts bittersweet. He was losing his best friend to be an honorable husband to Olivia Boyle. To be fair to his future wife, he would have to do his best to find peace within his arranged marriage, but he could not help thinking he would never see Madeline naked upon his sheets, as he had often dreamed of during his years at Oxford, or feel her soft curves pressed against him.

He hoped she would find a good husband to appreciate her.

CHAPTER 2

"The pain of their separation was felt deeply by both, though neither could bridge the distance between them."

Lucius Apuleius, Metamorphoses

* * *

JULY 20, 1821

*T*heir carriage drew up in front of Lord Boyle's townhouse, and Isla made a sound of displeasure. In the afternoon light, Simon's mother appeared almost supernaturally beauteous in her deep blue pelisse, her eyes strikingly vivid even in the dim interior.

"I know your father would be most pleased at the match you are making, and I am all for the improvement of our connections. If only it did not mean spending time with … them."

Simon was aware that the odd noise, and complaining,

were in lieu of frowning. Isla Scott did not frown. It marred the face with lines, and she would not tolerate such indignities.

"They are an influential family which ranks above us."

"I am aware, and the match is most pleasing. The Boyle girl is the same age I was when I wed, and the family is known for producing progeny. She should provide strong, healthy heirs." Isla contemplated this fortune with a contented look, which was hard to read, for she would not smile. Smiling was as ill-advised as frowning, she liked to say. "But … do they have to be so silly?"

Simon smiled despite himself. It was an accurate description, and he had lain awake at night thinking about the future with Olivia. The custom of married couples maintaining separate bedchambers, at least amongst the nobility, was something he appreciated given his circumstances. He would have somewhere to retreat to.

Duncan, their strapping head footman, knocked politely on the carriage door before opening it. He stepped aside so Roderick could attach the steps that would allow disembarkation. This was an important day for the Scotts, and John had insisted on pomp, instructing their senior footmen to accompany Simon and his mother.

The two servants stood on either side of the front door, Duncan lifting the knocker to bring it down with a resounding thud. Soon it opened, and Simon and Isla swept in to find Lord Boyle in a state of agitation in the entry hall.

Thin, tall, and attired in a champagne gold suit embroidered with frolicking cupids, Lord Boyle was quite a sight which caused Simon to grow giddy while he attempted to clear his vision of the monstrosity.

"Terrible, terrible news, I am afraid. I should have sent word to postpone our meeting, dear boy!"

Simon gritted his teeth, tearing his gaze away from the

nauseating cupids swimming in front of his eyes. "Lord Boyle, allow me to accompany you to your study while my mother takes a moment to rest."

Lord Boyle shook his head of shaggy gray-blond hair. "Of course, Lady Blackwood. Please, my footman will show you to the drawing room where the ladies are enjoying tea. Such terrible news! I am afraid everyone is most upset."

Simon persevered through the sorrowful lamenting, steering Lord Boyle into his study. He might not have spent much time with Miss Boyle, but he had acquired considerable experience in managing her high-strung father over the past weeks during their negotiations. The truth was … Lord Boyle's finances were not ideal. The nobleman had intended a very good match for his daughter, but when the time had come for her Season, the coffers had been a bit bare. Perhaps because he spent outrageous sums on his ostentatious garments.

Consequently, the lord was forced to allow a match inequitable in his estimation. The Scotts might be a rank lower, but they had proved excellent stewards for their holdings over the past two centuries. The coffers were overflowing, which Lord Boyle was in need of.

Thus, Simon had maintained his course through their numerous excruciating meetings. Finding the man in a state was not a welcome development.

Despite his tenuous finances, Boyle was reticent to commit quill to contract, sending notes off to his solicitor for every minor detail they agreed to before he would discuss the next inane demand. It had taken months to reach their current agreement.

Ushering his prospective father-in-law to take a seat, Simon walked over to the drinks cabinet.

"What would you like?"

"A brandy, dear fellow. I must settle my nerves after such unfortunate news."

Simon dutifully poured a drink into a crystal tumbler and brought it over. Lord Boyle accepted it, taking a sip before holding it to his chest with a worried expression.

Gritting his teeth to stay his torment, Simon took a seat and relaxed into a languid pose. It was time to learn what fresh delay the neurotic gentleman had unearthed.

"What news, Lord Boyle?"

"You have not heard? The entire *ton* is speaking of it!"

Simon shook his head. "I have been with a steward from one of our estates all morning."

"A peer has been found murdered! Here in London. His skull bashed in by his own statuary in his private study. His inner sanctum! What is the world coming to?" The alarmed tone and general demeanor of the viscount made it clear that there would be no contract signed today. Perhaps he had been a close friend of the deceased?

At best, all Simon could accomplish today was to calm him down in order to set a new appointment.

"That is dreadful. Who is it?"

"The Baron of Filminster. An odd little coxcomb from Somerset whom no one has seen in twenty years."

Not a close acquaintance, then. Simon could swear Lord Boyle made a sport of seeking out issues to be upset over.

A bell rang somewhere in the recesses of his mind. Had he heard about Lord Filminster recently?

"Who would want to kill him? Do you think it is the start of an uprising?"

Simon restrained a roll of his eyes.

Certain members of the privileged class, gentlemen of a certain age, were petrified of a revolution such as the one in France three decades earlier. Lord Boyle and his friends must have been terribly shocked when the French monarch had lost his head at the guillotine. Lack of understanding or skills in leading his own people would explain part of Boyle's financial woes. The lord had long since lost touch with the common man … if he had ever had such contact at all.

Simon had to respond out of politeness, to mollify the viscount so he could arrange a new meeting.

"It sounds to me like an act of passion. Who is the coroner investigating for the crime?"

Lord Boyle leaned forward. In a low voice to announce the melodramatic intrigue, he whispered what he knew. "Word is that his son might have … compelled his inheritance."

Simon considered the revelation with antipathy, as one who could not relate to this notion. His looming inheritance, the Blackwood title, was an anchor around his neck, dragging him into the pits of despair in his nightmares. He would do anything to avoid such an event, so he might follow his own path. Alas, duty was why he was here now—to wed the lord's daughter so he could fulfill his obligations to his family. Certainly not to himself.

"That is not all. Rumor at my clubs is that the heir is not the baron's boy. The mother was betrothed to the baron's older brother, who died before the wedding."

Simon wanted to shake his head in irritation. He did not abide gossip, a character trait he would not expose to the simpering Boyle who loved it. The fact that his own plans were delayed because of some unrelated event that Boyle had already confessed had no bearing on his life, other than to serve as a source of aristocratic melodrama … This entire affair continued to be frustrating.

Worse, despite his lack of momentum, Simon was still required to perform a visit with Olivia and her family before he left. The thought of insipid small talk and dainty biscuits made his head ache.

Lud. He knew where he had heard the name before. Just last night, he had agreed to avoid the baron from Filminster when his brother had complained about his behavior at the banquet.

What a bizarre coincidence.

It took a further half an hour to calm the anxious Boyle, assuring him there was no uprising from the lower classes to prepare for, before they joined the ladies in the drawing room.

Olivia Boyle had the light blonde hair of her father and a fondness for pink bows. One topped her coif now, so large it could have been mistaken for a hat. The sheer size of it dwarfed her head. Miss Boyle was an attractive creature, quite proper by polite society standards … and rather flighty.

"La! Mr. Scott, we did not expect you to visit us!"

Gritting his teeth was becoming a habit.

Miss Boyle was seated next to his mother, who did not stop herself from rolling her eyes in his direction. One of the few facial expressions that she allowed herself because there was no risk of forming wrinkles. The problem with Miss Boyle was, she was proper without judgment. She had assessed that feigning surprise at his visit was the correct gambit, despite Lady Blackwood being seated at her very side, sipping on their fine tea and looking bored, which disproved Miss Boyle's declaration.

But, to be fair, his mother always appeared to be as stoic as a china doll. Simon knew she was bored because of their conversation in the carriage and his ability to read the minuscule shifts of her expression after years of experience. Her habit of adding laudanum to her day assisted with her aversion to lines on her face. A mixture of opium and alcohol, she claimed she needed it for female disorders, but Simon suspected it was more of a beauty treatment.

Laudanum helped her to remain composed because emotions were aging.

Simon noted he was focusing on his mother in an effort to avoid the young lady seated at her side. It was difficult to stop himself from comparing Miss Boyle to Madeline, but he must refrain from such disloyal ideas.

He bowed in greeting. "Lady Boyle. Miss Boyle, you are ravishing."

It was true. She was a pretty girl with a slim elfin face, a little button nose, and large blue eyes framed by lush blonde lashes. The perfect foil to his own darker appearance. It was the contents of her head that were … questionable.

"Oh, Mr. Scott! You are so kind."

Simon seated himself on a spindly, rose-pink chair with a gilded frame. The entire room was decorated in pink and gold, causing his ballocks to retreat in protest.

It was his sincere hope that Miss Boyle would not attempt to cultivate her parents' sensibilities in the Scott home—their extravagant tastes were difficult on the eyes. Perhaps his mother could rein her in and teach the young lady about elegance. Simon's eyes fell on the cupids dancing across Lord Boyle's clothing, prompting him to say a silent prayer.

"I was just telling Lady Blackwood that we went shopping a few days ago! I found a pair of kid gloves in the perfect shade of pink! Are they not beautiful?" Miss Boyle held up her hand for Simon to see. He leaned forward to peer at them before smiling in response.

"They are." They were not. A peach-pink color, which suited her, so that was not the issue. It was the well-to-do couple, attired in the style of a century earlier, embroidered in intricate detail, which made him wish he was riding in the park. Anywhere but in this pompous parlor of pageantry. He longed for the rich red walls of his study, with neat white trim and skillful paintings of Italian masters within gracious frames. Visiting the Boyle home brought out his priggish inclinations. He supposed he was something of an art enthusiast—these rooms assailed his senses until he was dizzy from distaste.

"Have you and Papa reached terms?"

He smiled. "Of course."

"So we are betrothed?"

Lord Boyle coughed into his hand, his eyes darting away to stare sightlessly into the center of the room, which contained nothing but a pink and gold rug on the floor.

"I am afraid not. Your father assures me that tomorrow we shall be so."

"Oh, Papa! What is it this time? I so look forward to informing my friends that I am to marry!"

Lord Boyle tugged on the cuff of his sleeve, unable to face his daughter's disappointment. Lady Boyle scowled at her husband. Apparently, she did not adhere to Isla's strict code of living frown-free. "Lord Boyle! Olivia was hoping to inform Miss Simmons she is to wed. That little chitterling has been lauding it over our dear girl that she is betrothed for weeks now!"

Simon kept a straight face, but Lady Boyle had a habit of misusing jargon. He thought it likely she had meant to say chit, but instead had referred to the innards of a pig. He heard his mother's sharp intake of air, her sole reaction as she sipped on her tea. When he looked over at her, he could see the mirth dancing in her eyes as she stared back at him with a challenging glint. He quickly glanced away lest he burst into laughter.

He decided it was time to remind himself why this was a good match, while the sound of the Boyles' unbecoming family squabble continued on for several minutes.

Olivia is lovely.

From a good family.

Her eccentric tastes will mellow within the elegance of Blackwood House.

The lady is young and will form a more interesting personality over time.

As a married woman, away from her parents, she will find her own voice.

As I grow to know her, she will turn out to be quite delightful.

His tension eased. This was not what he had envisioned his life would be, but duty demanded a reckoning, and Simon had vowed to obey. His family was counting on him to do the right thing.

When they finally left the Boyles', Simon shared his assertions with his mother on the drive back home. It took some time because the streets were congested, and Simon appreciated the opportunity to air his thoughts. He found himself desirous of reassurance.

His mother bestowed him with a rare smile, leaning forward to pat him on the knee until her face fell back into its customary benign expression. "It is true, dear. It is fashionable for young ladies of the *ton* to appear empty-headed. Once they wed, their true personalities are revealed as they mature. I hear Miss Boyle possesses quite a musical gift, which implies discipline, so I know her strength of character shall come to light after you wed."

"What of our attachment? The young lady seemed more concerned with boasting to her acquaintances than our connection as husband and wife."

"If you are honest, Simon, you are more concerned with duty to the title than the young lady's heart."

He grimaced. "True, but I intend to work on building a genuine marriage."

"And I am sure she will be committed, too." It was Isla's last word on the subject. She folded her hands neatly in her lap and put her head back to doze off while the carriage trundled on.

* * *

MADELINE CHECKED her pocket watch as her carriage pulled to a stop in front of her home. Her footman opened the door to set the steps in place. As she was alighting from the dim interior, she caught sight of Simon with his mother walking up to their front entrance. Madeline paused, watching him for a moment as he disappeared inside. She had been thinking of her daily routine on the drive home, of how much she enjoyed the walled garden. But the memories and hopes it evoked were troubling.

She wondered if there was some method to continue her respites there without associating the secluded oasis with the past and with Simon, and she believed she had come up with just the thing. A test of her developing theory was in order.

But, for tonight, she was going to deliver the news to her mother that she was willing to consider courtship. Perhaps Mama could engage a matchmaker while there was still a possibility of Madeline being able to bear children. She knew Mama would be pleased. Legacy was important to her and, with no sign of interest from Henri, Eleanor Bigsby was facing a future without grandchildren unless Madeline pursued marriage. The clock was ticking, and the process of finding the right man would be complicated, given a wife's lack of legal rights and that the endurance of the manufactory must be assured for decades to come.

Entering the house, Madeline located the news sheets and headed to the library for a read. Soon tea was brought in, and she perused the articles. It was too soon for word of Simon's betrothal, but she found herself committed to skimming all the headlines despite herself.

She was just finishing her cup when Henri entered.

"Good evening."

"Oh, excellent! I am in need of a cup." Her sister walked over to flop onto the settee beside her, then poured out her tea and added milk and sugar.

Settling back with a blissful sigh, Henri took a cautious sip to verify the temperature and put it on the table to cool down. "Did you hear the frightful news?"

Madeline's brow puckered. She could hardly claim she did not want to hear the latest *on-dits* while holding news sheets. Gossip made her weary, and she rarely read them except for the stock and business news. She could not admit to the embarrassing truth—that she was scouring the small print for an announcement about Simon Scott and Olivia Boyle.

"Has something of import happened?"

"A baron was found murdered. This morning! He had not visited London in more than twenty years, but he was here for the coronation. All of Westminster is talking about it."

Madeline squashed a surge of irritation. In her opinion, Henri was far too enamored with the celebrity of Parliament and high society. She supposed it was appropriate—her sister acted as a social hostess for their great-uncle Reginald, who had been widowed nigh fifteen years ago and displayed no inclination to remarry. It was just that Madeline found it dull. Perhaps exposure to the Scotts next door had made her weary of class distinctions. However, a significant portion of their clients fell into the categories of people her sister and Uncle Reggie dealt with, which had led to orders for Bigsby's, so she could hardly dissent.

Nevertheless, she needed to consider her idea about the walled garden. She found her peace there, away from the family business and social gossip.

"Which baron?"

"Lord Filminster. People are saying that the coroner suspects that his estranged son did it to hurry his inheritance. They have not spoken in years, but the son lives here in their London townhouse."

Madeline considered this surprising turn of events. A nobleman murdered? Such a heinous act was unheard of.

"Well, then … I hope the heir *is* guilty, or his reputation is being destroyed without cause."

"I did not think of that. It would be terrible for him if he is innocent."

Nodding in agreement, Madeline hoped that her sister would reconsider her propensity to gossip. Henri spent far too much of her time with people who were willing to ruin the credibility of their acquaintances for their own entertainment and, perhaps, from hidden envy of the people in question.

CHAPTER 3

"He tried to live without her, but every thought returned to her face, her voice, her touch—Eros found no peace away from Psyche."

Lucius Apuleius, Metamorphoses

* * *

AUGUST 31, 1821

Simon entered the breakfast room to find the entire family gathered in the throes of aggravations.

"I am well, I tell you!" John was shouting, heaving as he struggled to breathe. "Give me my damn coffee!"

"You must stop the coffee, dear. It is not good for you. Roderick, bring Lord Blackwood a pot of tea." Isla waved toward the baron with a voice that did not brook argument. This, however, did not deter Simon's older brother. Simon could have foretold it. He had spent years attempting to persuade his family to pursue healthier habits, to no avail.

"I do not want tea! Duncan, bring me my coffee!"

The head footman froze, then threw a glance to Roderick, who was collecting the teapot. The second footman was frozen, too, as the two servants stared at each other in an *impasse*. Who were they to obey—his lordship or the dowager baroness?

Checkmate.

Simon folded his arms to watch in amusement. Which of the footmen would break first?

"Roderick," prompted his mother.

He had the teapot hovering just an inch above the sideboard. In response, he completed the motion, lifting it to spin on his heel and walk over to the table where he placed it in front of the baron.

John shot a glare at Duncan, whose expression was contrite but helpless. "My lord, your doctor ..."

"Grow some ballocks, Duncan! Are you not a Campbell?" The footman's chagrin was palpable. He was a good sort. Duncan Campbell had taken care of John for many years, even acting as the baron's valet when his own man took ill. Which was far too frequent in Simon's estimation. The valet was either a dreadful weakling, or he preferred to stay abed.

Molly offered to pour the tea which earned her a bark from John, who was in a fine state, his skin mottled with fury.

Nicholas paid none of them mind, staring down into his own coffee as if he were nursing regret from a hard night of drinking. He must have been too weary to leave, despite the loud quarreling sure to be driving a knife through his inebriated brain. "Could you please lower your voices?"

"Why are you here?" barked John in a belligerent tone. "Should you not be out drinking with your friends?"

Simon grimaced. The mood was decidedly foul. It

happened from time to time, and he never knew what set it off because he was inevitably the last to arrive.

"Hungry," was the singular answer from Nicholas, who must have just returned home. He continued in a plaintive voice, "Even an insignificant spare must eat."

Bloody hell!

Simon wished to turn and leave. His little brother was preparing to spew the multiple reasons he was a victim of circumstances which were never amusing to overhear. Complaining about his situation was a common habit when he had over-imbibed. Simon preferred the supercilious version over the self-pitying Nicholas who blamed all for his circumstances. He suspected his brother's moods were a barometer of what particular spirits he had abused his body with in the past twenty-four hours. Perhaps wine brought out his humorous, if sarcastic, character, while brandy, the miserable defendant of terrible harms visited upon him.

It was a theory, at least.

Molly checked her timepiece, muttering something conciliatory he could not hear, and scraped her chair back to depart. Simon did not blame her. Tensions were rising, and soon Nicholas would break into a dramatic tirade about the unfairness of it all, or John into a rousing speech about being respected in his own household, while Isla interjected her drugged benevolence with platitudes that exacerbated tempers. If he had to hear his little brother complain, it would renew his shame at what he had done to contribute to his injury.

Simon gestured to Duncan, who appeared relieved to stride over. The tall footman, with brawny shoulders and a handsome, square face, doted on the baron and must have been feeling terrible to be the object of his disappointment. "I shall take my breakfast in the study."

The servant nodded, turning to collect a tray together while Simon headed down the hall.

* * *

MADELINE HAD FOUND a new routine these past weeks, which suited her. She had rearranged her schedule to rise an hour earlier and breakfast in the walled garden. She would enjoy her meal and a book, which was how she had discovered a wonderful new friend.

Hearing the crunching of gravel as someone entered the secluded space, she lowered her book and grinned. "Molly!"

Befriending the pragmatic young lady from next door had been a happy consequence of changing her routine. She was an amusing and intelligent companion with whom to begin the day.

It took a minute to note that under the shadowing brim of her bonnet, Molly's expression was unhappy.

"What is it? Has something happened?"

Molly approached to settle on the bench beside her.

"I enjoy living in London, for what little I see of it. But the Scotts are … there is something amiss in the household. Lord Blackwood's health declines at a rapid rate, and his physician is useless. I swear that the doctor is naught but a drug peddler. Yet the baron does nothing to improve his own health while Isla overindulges in her laudanum. Not to mention her lack of facial expressions. It is unnatural!"

Madeline made a sound of commiseration. "It was similar with the late baron—their father. I think it is the same Dr. White whom Simon would complain about. He suspected White was over-medicating the old man." It was not her habit to speak of her former love, but Molly needed to air her grievances, and it had slipped out in a moment of sympathy.

"It is so frustrating! I have yet to encounter Nicholas sober, and I have been residing here for five months! The only dependable person in the household is Simon, but he is both aloof and—" Molly sought a word for what she wanted to communicate. "—glum."

Madeline dropped her gaze to stare at the book in her lap. She knew the change that had been wrought in Simon Scott over the years, but it was depressing to contemplate. "He was not always so."

Molly paused, shooting her a worried glance which Madeline caught from the corner of her eye. They had not spoken about the former relationship between Madeline and Simon, but Molly was perceptive, and it was clear that she had surmised something from their prior conversations ... and the specific person Madeline avoided mentioning.

"I am sorry to burden you with this. It is just ... the quarrels have been intensifying. The coronation sparked something off because our meals have grown increasingly strained since that time. I cannot think how that event would create trouble. I just recall that the baron was in an ill humor after the ceremony."

"Things will settle down, and you are always welcome to take a respite at our home if you need to."

Molly reached to pat Madeline with a grateful smile. "I appreciate I can visit with you. I count the days until I am done with this mourning period. My mother would hate to think of me so listless on her account."

"Dear friend, I assure you, I need you just as much as you need me."

It was true. Usually they discussed books they had read, or Molly asked questions about her work. Their burgeoning friendship had been the distraction Madeline needed as she made plans for her future.

She must do something to help her new friend. Something to lift her companion's spirits. Madeline tried to think of activities suitable for a young gentlewoman that would not be considered improper during her time of grieving.

"Perhaps we can go visit a bookshop together? I could ask Mama to escort us."

* * *

SIMON STARED at the contract on his desk. Lord Boyle had finally signed it, sending it with a footman just minutes earlier. All that remained to make the betrothal official was for Simon and John to put their signatures to it. He and Olivia Boyle would be tied into a single legal entity. The culmination of his duty to the Blackwood title.

He was finding it difficult to draw air in his lungs. The walls seemed to be moving closer, and his starched collar and cravat conspired to strangle him. Scraping his chair back, Simon stood up, unable to tear his gaze from the neatly written contract. The desire to run was overwhelming. He wished he could bolt off to the walled garden. So he could breathe. But, alas, the garden was out-of-bounds because he was … about … to be … *betrothed!*

He could think of nothing other than the horrible truth. He was to wed the wrong woman. When he signed the contract, Madeline would be lost to him forever. Any hopes he had that he was only dreaming this suffocating life, that he would wake up to learn he was still a student at Oxford, and that Madeline was still his intended, slipped away as the pages taunted him with their cruel intentions.

Simon realized he needed to take a respite before his panic turned into hysteria. Leaving the contract where it lay, he stalked off to request his overcoat. Soon he was slipping on his gloves, donning his beaver, folding the morning news sheets under his arm, and heading out the door to a nearby coffeehouse. He sat alone, recovering from the shock of receiving the elusive paperwork from Boyle by reading his sheets and sipping on a mug of coffee. The tightness in his chest gradually eased as he took his time to enjoy some time alone.

Just as he thought he might survive the day, a sense of unease gripped him. He had the sensation he was being watched. Simon raised his head to flick a glance around the establishment as the feeling grew. Across the room, at a corner table, sat two gentlemen. They did not appear to be watching him, but he found it odd that they had kept their hats on. Even their overcoats were on and buttoned up despite their being inside on a warm day. Stroking his beard, Simon considered if he was imagining it, but then the smaller one of the pair, whose soft features spoke to his youth, flickered unusual silver-gray eyes in his direction.

Simon made up his mind. There would be more privacy at his clubs, so there was no need to analyze if he was being watched, preferring to trust his instincts in case someone had noted his trappings of wealth and was planning to fleece him.

He rose, tossing some coins down on the table, and headed out the door, casting a surreptitious gaze back to see if anyone followed him out.

Through the window, he saw that the odd pair in the corner had risen to leave. Simon narrowed his eyes, picking up his pace. He veered at the next corner to enter St. James's Street. His club was nearby, and scoundrels who intended him harm could not follow him in to that guarded dominion.

Inside, he went to the library to find a book, realizing he had left his news sheets behind in his haste to put distance between himself and the men that might be pursuing him.

Settling on a leather settee, he ordered some coffee and stretched his legs out to enjoy the quiet of the oak-paneled room. His nerves were on edge, and likely the entire thing had been a figment of his imagination brought on by the stresses of what awaited him on his desk. Be that as it may, he still needed to calm himself, so it was a pleasure to relax in the cool interior. Thankfully, regardless of how trying his marriage turned out, Olivia and the Boyles' annoying chatter would never find him in this hallowed retreat.

CHAPTER 4

"As he flew away from her, Psyche called after him, but her cries could not reach his ears."

Lucius Apuleius, Metamorphoses

* * *

OCTOBER 1, 1821

"*T*hat is when I told Miss Simmons that as a lady to marry a handsome future baron, I outrank so she must enter behind me!" Olivia's voice grew high-pitched and mirthful as she completed her story with a giggle of triumph.

"Brava, daughter! Well-done of you!"

Simon shot a glance over at Lady Boyle, uncertain if she was serious in her congratulations or being facetious. His heart sank. It was genuine pride.

His spirits dropped even further than they had been. The Boyles were visiting for a Sunday meal after joining his family for church services, and Simon was considering going down to the local docks to join any merchant ship setting sail. He would be a hardworking deckhand, dodging scurvy and terrible storms rather than eating at the dining table with this ridiculous family.

There are things to like about her. She is ... a pleasing songbird.

Or, at least, rumor had it. Simon had yet to hear her sing because he found an excuse to keep their visits short each time they met.

His mother was seated across from him, barely touching her meal, with a vacuous expression as she stared over his shoulder into the distance and fanned herself. Perhaps Simon should try laudanum himself, as it evidently got Isla through these encounters.

"It is quite the social advantage, being the betrothed of a handsome future baron!" Olivia's shrill voice was grating on his nerves. They had been at lunch for a good half an hour, and the conversation had been dominated by the joys of a woman betrothed.

"I could have secured you a viscount if you had but waited," Lord Boyle replied with a sour tone, still put out that he had had to settle for Simon.

I wish you had.

"Do not be silly, Papa! Lord Clutterbuck was the only viscount who displayed any interest, and he is older than you! No, a handsome future baron is quite sufficient to make Miss Simmons ill with envy!"

Simon had become aware of Olivia's habit of stating everything as a dramatic declaration. One could hear the exclamation mark that punctuated the end of every sentence. It was one of the most irritating idiosyncrasies he had cataloged as he sat in silence. Thus far. One did not have much opportunity to speak when the Boyles were talking about themselves, and he was not inclined to contribute to the inane bickering.

"That is correct, Lord Boyle! That fire ship was quite put in her place!" Simon cringed at Lady Boyle's interjection, and even Isla roused a little with an astonished blink. Molly was sitting beside his mother, and choked. She put her fork down to compose herself. Simon gritted his teeth lest he burst into laughter. He did not know what the viscountess had intended to say, but it could not have been a *fire ship*—a terrible insult which referred to a wench with venereal disease.

Next to him, John was not so composed, breaking into a wheezing cough so he might cover his smile and disguise his amusement. Simon raised his wine to hide his own grin as he grappled with the threads of his self-control.

Then the hilarity was over as Olivia brought the conversation back to what really mattered. "It is true! Miss Simmons is well aware she has lost our clash of wills and that I have emerged the victor ... because of my betrothal to a future baron!"

Simon's spirits plummeted again as he fidgeted in his chair at the uncomfortable warm weather. The aspect of himself that he disliked the most was that his future had been chosen for him, and he was on a path that the fates had set upon him in the manner of mythological gods conspiring to shape his destiny into one of tragedy and denial. The fact that Olivia harped on about his lack of free will served as a constant reminder of his discontent.

Mother said her personality will mature.

He was regretting his commitment to duty, but it was too late. A contractual betrothal was as good as married, except for the final step. Almost impossible and financially ruinous to end. There was no doubting Lord Boyle would sue them for every penny of the Blackwood fortune if they attempted to break the contract. Nay, Simon's matrimony was a *fait accompli*.

A wedding was being planned for late October, and with each passing minute, the sensation that he was drowning in a circumstance of his own contrivance increased in teeny tiny increments until he was a heartbeat away from hysterical panic.

He had heard tell of a form of torture they practiced in China. *Lingchi*, or slow slicing. A victim was executed by a thousand cuts so that he suffered greatly until he eventually expired.

Dabbing a handkerchief over his face to counteract the heat of the day, Simon felt he had stumbled into a form of intellectual *Lingchi* in which he was sliced by a thousand bacon-brained comments until, at last, his ability to think intelligently would leak out his ears to leave him a gibbering fool.

Did all members of their class consider the minutia of precedence to be of such vital importance?

Sometimes his mind would float away so that he was sure he was living in a waking dream, but, unfortunately, he would never awaken. This was his life now. Soon they would all be united by matrimony and … and … *Dear God, perhaps laudanum is not such a terrible idea after all?*

* * *

MADELINE WAS READING in the walled garden, enjoying a tea in the shade and fanning herself to dispel the unseasonable heat, when she heard hurried steps approaching. Looking up, she found Molly entering through the arch with a hunted expression.

"I had to escape the house," she offered as her explanation, dropping onto the bench with a heavy sigh. "I used you as an excuse, I am afraid. I did not know if you would be here, but I claimed I had made arrangements in order to leave our lunch."

"I do not mind."

"It is the Boyles. Lord Boyle is a blunderbuss. His wife is a bufflehead who throws words about without a sensitivity to their meaning, and Miss Boyle ... she is obsessed with her station. Every sentence ends with a mention of her betrothal. I actually imagined stabbing my palm with a knife just so I might have an excuse to leave mid-meal."

Madeline bit her lip in sympathy, her thoughts on Simon, who would hate such an interaction, despite his adherence to duty. He enjoyed intelligent conversation and fine things. When she had begun to sculpt artworks for him more than a decade earlier, he had become quite enthused, asking detailed questions about the craft. Conversation such as Molly described would pain him to his very core.

It is not your concern.

"Then I am glad you thought of using me as an excuse instead," she murmured, diverting her thoughts from the gentleman she must forget.

A crunching of gravel had both women turning their heads back to the archway in surprise. Simon appeared in a fine, blue wool coat and gray trousers. Madeline's heart leapt at the sight of him, drinking in the sight of the beard she had yet to see in proper daylight with a direct view. It suited him, the blue of his eyes ever more vivid because of it.

"Oh! I apologize. I was ... seeking a moment of respite."

Molly rose to her feet. "Are the Boyles still here?"

Madeline remained seated, suppressing a smile at her friend's alarmed tone.

"Are you bringing them to the garden?"

"Uh ... no. They are taking their leave as we speak. I ...

should be … there." With that, Simon spun on his heel and was gone.

Madeline suspected he might have hoped to see her, knowing this was where she liked to spend her Sunday afternoon. The presence of Molly must have frightened him off. She wondered what he had wanted to say.

* * *

SIMON WAS NOT sure why he had gone to the garden. His feet had led him there after pacing the walkway to the side of the house. Perhaps a moment with Madeline would restore his sanity. Or, if she had not been there, he could have sat on the bench to find his bearings and capture the happiness of his youth for just a fraction of a second.

Striding back to the house, he remonstrated his faithless behavior. He would never cheat on his betrothed, but he had been desperate to recapture the calm pleasure of Madeline's presence. They might no longer be prospective lovers, but this did not alter their long history of friendship.

The worst part about his reaction to his betrothal was he could not air his concerns so he might appease his misgivings. John thought the match to Olivia both appropriate and amusing. Isla thought it the natural state of affairs for a future lord. Nicholas was always drunk. Which left Madeline as a confidante who could understand the torture he was experiencing as a result of complying with his duties. She would have listened to him gripe, then made some suggestions to help him gain perspective. A good friend who would have made his situation more palatable, somehow, despite any disagreement she might have.

He gritted his teeth at his selfish nature. She was Molly's confidante now, not his. Which was as it should be. Molly must be bored in their home, and Madeline was the perfect companion to enliven her day. Madeline deserved a friendship with someone of equal footing instead of with him and the burdens he bore. The possessive feeling that sprung up at finding them together was uncalled for, and must be beaten down.

As he approached the house, the butler, MacNaby, appeared in the doorway leading into the main hall. "Sir, Lord Blackwood has requested you join him in the study."

"The study?" Simon worked out of the study. John rarely entered it unless there was a large amount of documentation to sign.

MacNaby bobbed in acknowledgment. "There are some unexpected guests. His lordship had them shown into the study for privacy."

The butler turned and disappeared before Simon could clarify. Unannounced guests on a Sunday afternoon? It seemed rather untoward. Pulling out his handkerchief, he dabbed his face dry. It was a hot day, and venturing outside had been a mistake.

Entering the hall, he stopped in front of a mirror to check his collar and cravat were in order. Tugging his cuffs, he strode toward the study, then paused in the doorway to swivel his head about in surprise.

MacNaby had understated the guests. Several gentlemen were gathered, seats having been brought in from the library. The windows had been opened to allow for a cooling draught, and some of the men were standing near to the windows in a bid to find relief from the heat. If they were anything like him, they wished to remove their wool coats, but it was not the done thing.

Taking stock, he realized he did not know any of the gentlemen present, but he recognized the huge blond Viking who was unmistakable. The Duke of Halmesbury. Next to him, with his arms folded as he peered out at the garden, it appeared to be the Earl of Saunton. The rest of the men were strangers, but there was a young lad with them with his hat still on, standing in the corner and staring back at him with unusual silver eyes that seemed vaguely familiar. Simon could have sworn he had seen those fascinating irises somewhere in the past few weeks, but he could not bring it to mind.

John rose from an armchair, his posture weary, and Simon experienced a pull of anxiety. His brother was pale, gray, and flushed all at the same time. He should be resting after so much exertion from the day, which he confirmed by signaling Simon to speak on his behalf.

"What is this?" The question was directed at the duke, the highest-ranking peer present and, as such, the leader of the assembled men.

Simon counted five.

His Grace swung his head around, his gray eyes assessing him. "Mr. Scott?"

"That is correct, Your Grace. What can I do for you?"

John broke into a paroxysm of coughing, hacking into a handkerchief and prompting Simon to rush over and coax him back into his seat. "Gentlemen, perhaps you could state your business and we can set an appointment for another day. Lord Blackwood is in need of his rest."

His Grace approached, pausing a couple feet away to address him. "I am afraid this cannot wait, Mr. Scott. This is a matter of … *mortal* importance."

There was a pause.

Mortal?

That seemed unduly ominous.

"They have news, Simon. Of Peter. We must hear them out."

Simon glanced down at his brother, whose breathing had

eased and who was looking up at him with worry on his face. "Are you sure? They can come back another day."

"I need to hear what they have to say."

Simon nodded, and His Grace took it as his cue to make introductions.

As he had thought, it was Lord Saunton he had spotted at the window. To his surprise, a younger gentleman was introduced as Lord Filminster, which was a name that had come up a few times in recent weeks. Presumably the son who had inherited the title from the murdered baron, but Simon did not ask. Then he was introduced to a coxcomb with hair in startling contrasting tones and a luxurious suit that could have been dreadful but had turned out to be a creation of sartorial genius. Sage green with a gold brocade waistcoat. Too lavish for Simon's tastes, but the buck had a flair for it which Lord Boyle could only hope for. It turned out to be Lord Trafford, whom Simon had heard about—he had been something of a disreputable rogue until the news sheets had reported he had wed last month.

The duke gestured to the corner. "And this is ... Mr. Gideon. He is ... brother-in-law ... to Lord Trafford." Halmesbury seemed hesitant in introducing the lad, who bowed his head politely but said nothing. His beaver was still on, as it had been when Simon had entered.

They took their seats, Simon first ringing a bell. Duncan entered and Simon ordered tea for his brother, whose well-being still had him worried. Glancing about, he asked if their guests would care for some, too, but they shook their heads, and Simon did not wish to encourage them to remain longer than necessary. Despite their polite demeanor, there were undertones of resentment in the room. John needed to retire to his rooms to recover from his outing to church, and the interminable meal with the Boyles.

"We represent several lords, and I have been authorized

to speak with you by the Home Secretary in the interests of keeping this discussion unofficial."

The duke's voice was calm, but Simon's unease was rising. He could not think what was of such import that these peers would interrupt their day of rest. The single notion to enter his head was that John had mentioned something months ago about the late Filminster raising the subject of Peter's issue. But, surely, it could not be that?

"This morning we received confirmation from Florence that Peter Scott sired two children with his wife, Mrs. Bianca Scott, before his death." The duke paused. "*Male* children."

Simon jumped to his feet in bewilderment. "What?"

John gasped, clutching his chest, and began to pant. Simon immediately forgot about the incredible news, rushing over to his brother in alarm. The baron waved him back, concentrating on his breathing. After a few minutes, he had recovered, the guests waiting in silence. Then he gestured to Simon, a cue to continue the discussion. He looked back at their guests, who were waiting with an expectant air. All except the youth, Gideon, whose silver-gray eyes were scrutinizing his brother with unwavering interest.

"We have … nephews?"

Despite his need to focus on the answer, to ask discerning questions, and to ascertain if any of it was true, it was as if his thoughts were floating away. He listened to the revelation from a far distance while he sorted through a variety of reactions. Two nephews! That meant he was relegated to third in line to inherit! He was not the future Lord Blackwood, but rather it was some boy living in Italy. Which meant …

Am I free?

Heady elation followed this thought until a second intruded to bump him rudely back into reality.

He was betrothed to Olivia Boyle.

An act that could not be undone.

He was to wed Miss Boyle despite this turn of events. He might not be the heir, but his duty still bound him. She could not be deserted without ruining her, and he would never do that to a lady vulnerable to censure. He was in the seventh circle of hell, and there was not a solitary reason to be there if he had no obligation to the title.

"Misters Marco and Angelo Scott are making plans to travel to London to meet with you," the duke responded, oblivious to the turmoil raging in Simon's mind.

"I shall ... expect confirmation of ... this news." John's panting declaration drew Simon back to the present, his gaze returning to his brother, whose pallor had worsened.

The Earl of Saunton leaned in to speak to the duke in a low voice. The duke nodded, eventually responding to John's request. "Perhaps we should finish this conversation tomorrow, Lord Blackwood? I had heard you were not well—"

"Is there more to be discussed?" John's voice was firm.

The duke's eyes flickered back to Lord Saunton before he turned to look at Mr. Gideon, who was still standing apart in the corner of the room with those silver-gray eyes fixed on Simon's brother. Mr. Gideon, noting the silence, shot a glance to where His Grace was waiting and gave a slight nod of authority.

"There is ... more," replied Halmesbury.

Simon was perplexed. It appeared that the duke had just deferred to a lad who could not have been more than fifteen or sixteen, from the soft features and lack of stubble. The brother-in-law to an honorary viscount. Why the blazes would such a high-ranking peer obey the direction of such a green youth, whose gaze had focused on John once more?

"There is evidence to suggest that the late Baron of Filminster was murdered to conceal knowledge of your rightful heir."

"What?" John straightened up in surprise, then an expression of horror crossed his pallid face. "Are you ... accusing one of us?"

The duke looked at Simon. This meeting had ventured into territory that was wholly inappropriate.

"We would like to know where you were the night of the coronation, Mr. Scott? At around midnight?"

His jaw dropped in amazement. They were here to accuse him of a heinous crime! It was beyond the pale! He would set them to rights so they could take their condescension and barbed indictments to be on their way.

Smiling with smug satisfaction, he declared, "Of course. I was in the walled garden with—"

Simon shut his mouth, realizing too late the trap he was in. Their families might be aware that he had been alone with Madeline on countless occasions, but he could not state such a fact to hostile opponents without them inferring the worst possible—they would conclude Madeline was his mistress!

He would ruin his dearest friend because the caper-witted denizens of the upper classes would never accept a public friendship between a common tradeswoman and the son of a baron. There was no possibility he would ever risk her reputation. Madeline might not be of the gentry, but the Bigsbys were a well-respected family who relied on business from polite society. Such scandal could destroy them.

Simon licked his lips. "I was with—"

The night Nicholas had fallen from his window had been the worst experience of his life, but if he dragged Madeline into his muddle, it would rival that event, so he scrambled for an alternate alibi—and reached the awful conclusion that he would have to refuse to provide one. Which meant this accusation could expand into an official investigation. Had the duke not mentioned the Home Office?

"He was with me. We drank wine in the moonlight in our walled garden to celebrate the ceremony, although the moon was waning so visibility was compromised. Nevertheless, it was a beautiful night."

All heads spun to the open door where his mother was framed, and Simon could have wept with relief at her intervention. Isla must have realized his conundrum after he had announced where he had been, guessing that Madeline was the alibi which had caused him to falter.

With deep gratitude, Simon agreed. "I was ... with my mother, Lady Blackwood."

CHAPTER 5

"In her dreams, Psyche still saw Eros, but the reality of their separation was a cold and lonely awakening."

Lucius Apuleius, Metamorphoses

* * *

As soon as their guests had left, suspicions over Simon's false alibi obvious, John demanded they discuss the news. Simon was still reeling at the questions that unknown heirs posed, but was forced to sit in silence while his family gathered to discuss what had happened.

Molly was the first to arrive, removing her bonnet with an expression of alarm. Being summoned to the study was an unusual occurrence, and it was clear she was worried. Nicholas was roused from his sleep, and it took twenty minutes for him to finally appear in a state of dishevelment as if he had dressed in a hurry.

They remained in the study, on the extra chairs that had

been brought in, and John informed them of the news. It was, he had reasoned, imperative they hear about it before scandal broke in the news sheets or amongst the *ton*.

After his mother's heroic intervention, she had settled back into an opioid daze. Simon would have checked on her, but he was in somewhat of a daze himself, albeit for different reasons.

"So some Italian brats are now in line ahead of me? I am no longer the spare, but the damned third spare? How could my circumstances have worsened even further!" Nicholas's plaintive tone would have grated on Simon's nerves, but he thought he might be in a slight state of shock because he did not feel much of anything. Logically, though, it was *he* who was most affected, not Nicholas. The meaning of his life, his adherence to duty, had all been for naught. He had sacrificed everything he had wanted for himself and was now betrothed to a girl he did not know, or particularly like, in the pursuit of family unity. He knew what he would do if he had been a free man. Return to Madeline and beg her to forgive him for his neglect.

But I am not a free man.

John thumped the desk where he was still seated. "Can you think of no one but yourself?" Simon thought for a moment his older brother was addressing him until he noticed John was glaring at Nicholas. Simon experienced a moment of sentimentality that John defended him so, which was quickly set straight when his brother continued speaking. "What of me! I have to bring some European clunches into our family home as honored guests! We have no knowledge of their breeding or education! Do you have any notion of the crisis that this has created for me?"

Simon drummed his fingers on his knee, attempting to keep himself together as best he could until he was left alone with his thoughts. John had not always been so self-absorbed. It was a characteristic that had come to light after he had become ill, and Simon could understand that his brother had not the energy to think of anyone else when he was so sick.

"Your father would be so ashamed at such a development," proclaimed Isla without any sign of emotion. "He so wished to elevate the family bloodlines, and these accusations are deeply insulting."

Simon did not think the statement helpful, but he was inclined to be charitable, considering his mother had stepped in to help him with an alibi. He was still rather taken aback at the decisive action she had taken to protect him. Isla wandered through life in a soporific state, so the fact that she somehow noted what was taking place in the study and presented herself on cue had been the singular fortune Simon had experienced in recent weeks.

He could not credit that he had been accused of murder. What alarmists their guests had been. What on earth could lead them to make such an assault on his character? The baron must have been killed by someone in his own household, considering the news sheets had reported his death to be late evening while he was in his study. Their family was distantly acquainted with the murder victim at best. Perhaps Filminster had caught his steward altering the account ledgers for his own gain and been bludgeoned for his troubles?

The bickering continued, each Scott insisting they had been the most wronged by the earlier visit. Simon held his tongue, contemplating his predicament as the drama played out without his intervention. He was jolted from his wool-gathering when Molly suddenly sprang to her feet.

"I appreciate all that you have done for me, I do! But I feel compelled to point out that Simon is the one most affected by this news, and I find these unattractive remarks to be self-serving and selfish!"

He blinked, taken aback at the demonstration of support from the relation he barely knew, watching as Molly turned on her heel and stormed from the study. Simon wished he could follow her.

* * *

MOLLY HAD BEEN SUMMONED AWAY by the head footman, Duncan Campbell, so Madeline was left to read her book in the afternoon light. She had her parasol crooked up, along with her bonnet to shade her eyes, but the glare on her page was making it difficult to read. Putting her book down and fiddling with the parasol to see if she could angle it to cast shade on her lap, she then picked up her novel to continue reading.

It was not a well-advised choice of book, but she had a yearning to read *Waverley*. Simon's family hailed from Scotland, but Madeline did not know much about their northern neighbors. The descriptions of towering mountains and reflective lochs had captured her imagination. Not a thoughtful cure to her blues about Simon's recent betrothal, but engrossing nevertheless.

Buried in her story of highland drama, she did not notice the passage of the sun across the sky until she was startled from her bemusement by a shadow cast across her peripheral vision. Flinching in surprise, she raised her head to find Molly staring at her in a state of agitation.

"Simon needs you."

Madeline frowned in perplexment at the dramatic announcement. Molly had struck her as a level-headed young lady, so it was odd to see her in a state of obvious disquiet. "I am afraid that Simon and I no longer visit with each other. We have not in quite some time."

"He has just received news ..." Molly shook her head, her face displaying turbulence. "His family can think only of themselves. They care not for his distress. Heaven forfend any of the Scotts pay mind to another member of their clan." She stopped, cocking her head at this pronouncement. "Except for Simon. He never speaks of himself. I think him to be quite selfless. I almost wish he would lose his temper and assert his own rights."

Madeline squinted, closing her book and putting it down on the bench. Molly's assessment was similar to her own. Simon had been a well-balanced and considerate individual until the night of his brother's accident. That event changed him. He had been by his brother's side for weeks, obeying the physician's instructions and doing everything he could to help Nicholas recover. From that time on, Simon had been obsessed with caring for the family, speaking of duty each time she met with him, which had become less frequent over the years until he had announced his betrothal to another woman. Madeline accepted that she had lost him a long time ago, but it had been difficult to let go of her past hopes.

She should be protecting herself from further loss, but it was difficult to ignore a plea for help. If she did not assist him in a time of need ... there was no one else he could turn to for support.

Madeline realized Molly was speaking again, probably because several moments had passed without response.

"I am sorry to burden you, but Simon and I are not close. He is so aloof, and I do not know how to offer my help. I think he needs someone who knows him better than I."

He had not been reserved in their youth. Madeline suspected the aloofness was a defense against his abandoned dreams. If he dared to consider his own desires, she thought, he would come undone. He was the rock that held the Scotts together, and she did not believe he received any benefit for his efforts.

"What has happened?"

Molly walked over to collapse on the bench beside her. "His older brother, Peter, the one who died?"

"What of him?"

"He had sons! An heir and spare. Which means …" She did not complete the sentence, the announcement hanging in the air as if a cannon had been shot.

Madeline gasped as the realization hit her. "Simon will not inherit!"

"Just so. But it is worse than that. That baron who was murdered, Lord Filminster—it is believed he was killed to conceal the heirs."

* * *

EVERY ASPECT of his life was up in the air like hundreds of leaves swirling in a blustering wind.

Except for one.

Despite the revelations, Simon was still required to marry Olivia Boyle, a fact which made the walls move to box him in.

As little affinity as he had for his betrothed, she was an innocent debutante whose reputation would be sullied if he left her unprotected against high-society scandal. The demons of the *ton* would eat her alive if he were to break their engagement, not to mention there would be rumors that they had lain together due to the nature of betrothals. As he contemplated the regrets he had for his decisions over the last ten years, the one comfort he could cling to was that he had tried to do what was right. But, unfortunately, what was right was to honor his commitment to the viscount's daughter or else ruin her within polite society.

Simon realized that, for the first time in his life, he did not know what the future held.

In his youth, he had been committed to following his Psyche into trade. Bigsby's Stone Manufactory had been a temple of possibilities to his youthful self.

Then, after his brother's accident, Simon had pursued his obligations with the knowledge that if he were to be the baron, he would be the best damned baron he could be. He had spent his time learning and improving the holdings of the Blackwood title, despite his interests lying in a different direction—where artistry and business blended together into a stone empire.

Now … now he had no notion of who he was and what he was to do with himself. The one thing he knew was that he was a man of honor who must hold on to his integrity despite the fearsome storms of life.

He tried to calculate some way out of the muddle, but—

A light knock sounded on the study door, which was shut after John had left and Simon had shooed the rest of the family out. Simon gnashed his teeth in aggravation before tempering his impatience to call out.

"Come in."

The door swung open, and Molly popped her head around. "Oh, good. You are here."

She disappeared again, leaving the door wide open to bedevil Simon. He jumped to his feet to cross the room when an unexpected figure appeared in her place. Simon stopped in bewilderment.

"Why are you here?" he cried.

"Because you need me," Madeline replied in a pragmatic tone.

She swung the door closed and approached him where he

had halted in the middle of the room, stopping to peer up at him with concern. "Molly said you were in need of a friend, so she helped me sneak in through the garden to see you."

Simon stared down at the face of feminine perfection and thought about how he would have been free to court her if he had not signed that poxed contract two weeks earlier. Instead, he would have to settle for … friendship.

"I am …" He shook his head, grinding to a stop as words failed him.

"You are free to follow your own path. It will take a minute to work out what that is, but you are a resourceful man who will work out a new plan."

"Unfortunately, that future will include—" He could not bring himself to complete the sentence.

"Your future will include Miss Boyle."

Simon bobbed his head, relieved she understood without an explanation. Molly had been right. He needed to speak with someone who understood him. Someone he should have never deserted, who cared for his happiness and from whom he should have sought advice this past decade.

"It will."

Madeline reached a hand to touch his forearm in sympathy before remembering herself and letting it drop back to her side. "You will make it work."

She said it with such assurance, despite his abandonment of her a decade earlier. She had never wavered in her support, though she must have disagreed with his decisions. Madeline was the best kind of family, though they would never reach that destination together.

"I do not deserve you … um … your help." Simon caught himself. He was betrothed, so he could not reveal his desire to return to their previous understanding without being an utter cad to Olivia.

"We are friends, are we not? We might remain apart, but I

am here when you need me." It was so sweet. Madeline had always been constant, one of the traits he admired about her, but the truth was …

I do not wish to be friends.

Which was why he must stay away from her. He was not the kind of gentleman who could have a wife while pursuing another woman. As it was, he was afraid that he would not be able to prevent himself from yearning for his Psyche in their garden of peace and moonlight.

But he intended to find a way to remain faithful to his marriage irrespective of his feelings, which meant he should listen to her advice while he had the opportunity to do so. Future interactions must be avoided, so this was his chance to hear her thoughts.

"What do I do?"

Madeline's lips curled into a smile. "If there is one thing I am confident of, it is that you will find a new plan. You are resourceful, Simon Scott. This is a temporary setback."

Simon drew in a deep breath and with it came some sense of peace in the midst of his psychological tempest. "I shall contrive a new role for myself. One of my own choosing."

Her amber eyes glowed in approval. "You shall."

"What of Miss Boyle?"

Madeline's smile faltered for a fraction of a second until she recovered. "You will find a way to make it work because that is the kind of man you are. A true gentleman through and through. She … You …. The two of you will discover what you have in common and grow closer over time. Perhaps one day"—she swallowed as if the sentiment caused her composure to sway—"fall in love."

Simon stared down into her beautiful face, tempted to lean down and brush his lips over her soft mouth, but he willed himself to hold on to his integrity. Despite the swimming confusion in his mind, Madeline's contribution was calming the despairing beast within, and he could almost imagine that he would be happy in his new life with Olivia Boyle at his side if he stayed true to his honor.

"You are a good friend, Madeline Bigsby."

"Will you be all right?"

He nodded. "I will find a way."

CHAPTER 6

"Her first task was to sort a huge pile of mixed grains—millet, barley, poppy seeds—before nightfall, a feat no mortal could achieve."

Lucius Apuleius, Metamorphoses

* * *

OCTOBER 2, 1821

The family physician was in John's private rooms when Simon joined him to force a serious discussion of developments from the day before. Dr. White was a friendly old man about five feet high, with a balding head framed by a thick fringe of white hair, and he sported a luxurious mustache. His thick eyeglasses pinched either side of his head in their tight embrace, and … Simon eschewed treatment from him.

There was something glib about White's manners, and his

propensity for generous prescriptions of laudanum as a cure-all for every complaint of the physical or the spirit was off-putting. Simon preferred to follow good habits and avoid physicians when he could. He missed the doctor who had taken care of his brother Nicholas after his accident, but he had retired years ago and Isla had presented this medicating quack in his place. Needless to say, his family adored him because he kept them in a ready supply of alcohol and opium concoctions—Simon's warnings about the habit-forming nature of such fell on deaf ears.

White packed up his things and left, Simon watching him depart with a belligerent stare. "I do not know why you see him. Your health has not improved under his watch."

John coughed, clearing his throat before rising to ring a bell. "He has an excellent reputation, according to the ladies Isla takes tea with."

Simon ground his teeth, not wishing to start another quarrel, but it was clear the reason for the *excellent reputation* was that certain people of their set liked to receive their drugs without admonishment from a caring healer. His father had been such an individual. White was unlikely to criticize a patient over their use of medications.

"We need to speak about this heir," Simon stated, deciding to change the subject.

A knock on the door interrupted him, with Duncan entering after John called out to him.

"Milord?"

"Bring me my coffee, Duncan."

The footman's expression shifted to one beleaguered by great troubles. "The doctor, milord."

Simon rolled his eyes. White might be irresponsible dispensing the bottles of laudanum, but apparently he was adamant that John needed to forsake the bitter beverage for tea. A direction which Duncan attempted to remind his master of, but to no avail.

"Bring me my coffee!" John wheezed as he shouted his command again. Isla and John did not see eye to eye on this one subject. Simon, on the other hand, thought it was a ridiculous line to draw in the sand. If the laudanum flowed like wine, what harm could the coffee do?

After a few tense moments, Duncan relented and headed off to fetch the coffee.

"It is a dark day for the Blackwood title."

Simon lifted his gaze with a quizzical rise of his eyebrow, having lost the thread of the conversation.

John gesticulated a vague wave. "The heirs from Italy you are to speak of. It is a dark day for the Blackwood title. Good British blood has run through the veins of our ancestors for generations."

"Be that as it may, there are practical issues to discuss." Simon did not wish to hear about the venerated blood of Scotts, nor the downfall of their line by introducing Italian blood. He had tossed and turned all night, considering what it meant for the management of Blackwood estates, and the tenants and people that it affected. Then there was the immediate family to consider, a thousand trivial details which added up to a muddle of epic proportions.

"What of Nicholas?" Simon had concerns because John's health did not speak to his longevity. "Will the heir continue his allowance … when you are … no longer with us?"

John shook his head, his jowls flapping around to remind Simon just how much his older brother had declined. He had seemed a healthy man at the time he had inherited the title from their father, but within weeks, illness had set in, and just eighteen months later he was a man who looked like he might be a mere handful of years from the grave. It was a chilling reminder to eat well and keep up his routine at Gentleman Jackson's, expending his energies.

"This Italian upstart better not think of changing the arrangements in place!"

Sighing, Simon leaned back in his seat to relax his stance lest he display his irritation. This was not a time for prejudices or emotions. They needed to have a plan for their change in circumstances. "We know nothing about our nephew. When the title is his, he can make the changes he wishes to. My mother is well taken care of by her marriage contract and the entailments attached to her Scottish title, but both Nicholas and I are portioned a small allowance under that document. And what of me? I am to marry Olivia Boyle on the understanding that I was to be a baron with an income. What new arrangements would be needed so I might support my bride in the manner she is accustomed to?"

John coughed into his fist, squirming about in discomfort. "Where is that damn Duncan?"

"John?"

His brother huffed, resentment in his eyes when he cast a glance in Simon's direction. "The blood of the Boyles would have made a fine addition to the Blackwood line. We were seconds away from cementing everything Father wanted for this family."

Hearing the news yesterday had freed Simon of some of the restrictions of duty weighing him down. Fate had determined that he could follow his own path, but in a twist of macabre humor, it was to be with a wife not of his own choosing. Bloodlines had never been particularly interesting to Simon, and he was not quite sure how or why he had allowed himself to be convinced to pursue Olivia as a spouse. The gods were mirthful with glee at Simon for his blind adherence to tradition, which had led him to this outcome.

He had been trapped in a deep sleep and wakened to discover the entire world had shifted since he had gone to bed—more than ten years earlier!

This was neither here nor there. Simon needed to prepare for a changing of the guard, but John was not one to confront the troubles facing them. He preferred to put them off to another day, which never arrived. It would take persistence to reach an agreement about dealing with the rightful heir's insertion into their lives.

"Be that as it may, we must discuss the future."

If only I had not signed the marriage contract.

Simon pushed the thought away. *If only* was the journey into the depths of despair. He had signed the contract, and he must bear his responsibilities like a gentleman.

John lumbered to his feet, stalking over to the window to stare down upon the gardens. "I do not know how to say this, little brother, but this investigation of murder is not settled yet."

Straightening up, Simon cocked his head to peer over at his brother. "Do you believe I need to be concerned?"

"You have been accused of killing a peer, albeit unofficially. Once word gets out … At this moment, the unknown heir is not the most pressing issue."

Licking lips which had suddenly gone dry, Simon contemplated this announcement. He had been so preoccupied with ensuring his duties were attended to that he had not considered their contingent of visitors might be unconvinced by his alibi and, at this very moment, seeking to disprove Isla's assertions of their moonlit conversation on the night of the murder. "Should I find an alternative defense?"

John glanced back at him. "Where were you that night? You were not with Isla."

Embarrassed, Simon dropped his head down to examine his fingernails with studious intent. "I was … in the garden."

"With the chit next door?"

"With the young lady from next door."

His brother harrumphed in response. "You are protecting Miss Bigsby's reputation, but it is a matter of time until Isla's true whereabouts are discovered because she was out that night. If they find someone who puts her in a different location than the garden …"

John left the sentence hanging until Simon was compelled to complete it. "The men will be back to question me."

"It is all nonsense, of course. Filminster was an obnoxious little prat. One of his own servants probably clubbed him in a fit of pique. Or perhaps some riffraff who wished to rob his home. The duke and his relations have contrived a murder plot in their heads, but they presented no evidence. The temerity! Accusing a Scott of such a heinous act. Father would turn in his grave over such disrespect."

"This is not going to go away." It was not a question. Their visitors from yesterday were related to the deceased and would not let this rest. Simon had not thought about it much, knowing he was innocent of the crime, but if John was concerned … it cast a new light on the priorities he had set himself. He must be prepared to prove his innocence, and with a marriage contract in place with Olivia Boyle, he could not reveal he was alone with Madeline. If he had been free to wed her, perhaps. But, even then, the scandal would be intense for a woman in her situation.

Nay, Simon must resolve this debacle without dragging her into it.

* * *

MADELINE WAS RUSHING through her breakfast so she might leave for work on time, having tossed and turned the night before, worrying over Simon's predicament. It might not be her problem, but her worry for her friend's troubles was hard to put aside. Simon had worked so hard on behalf of his family since the night Nicholas had fallen from the window, and his distress might be contained deep within his soul, but she had seen the signs of his struggle during their conversation. Molly had done the right thing by fetching her to provide him with some encouragement. It was going to be a long road to discover his new life because Simon was not the sort to enjoy idling away on his allowance, with no purpose to his days.

She was just forking the last of her eggs when Henri entered.

"There you are!"

Madeline flinched in surprise at the shrillness of her sister's voice, impatience skittering through her mind. Based on the tone, Henri was to launch into some sort of lecture about Madeline's choices.

"Good morning. I was not aware you were here."

"I returned late last night from Uncle Reggie's. Have you heard the news about Simon Scott?"

Madeline stared down at her last bite, which was hovering between the plate and her mouth, her appetite deserting her.

She and her sister did not see eye to eye on the subject of the gentleman living next door. Henri disdained his abandonment of her twin, while Madeline did not like what had happened, but she had understood it.

Simon had battled with the heavy burden of guilt, blaming himself for the accident. It had taken weeks for Nicholas to return from his unconscious state, and Simon had suffered each second of his brother's coma. A fact she had learned when he had reappeared in the garden three months after the incident to inform her that his plans for the future had changed.

She suspected Simon had spent the entire twelve-week period anchored to his brother's side, willing him to return to the living. It was hard to imagine the strain he must have been under, his appearance haggard when she had seen him for the first time.

"There are heirs to the Blackwood title who have been found in Italy." Madeline put her fork down and prepared to rise.

"Well, yes, but I meant the other news."

Madeline paused, sinking back in her seat. One aspect of her sister's work for Uncle Reggie that Madeline did not like was the fountain of gossip. She would brush it off and walk away without hearing it, but if it was about Simon …

"Other news?"

"Home Office is looking into Lord Filminster's death. Word at Westminster is that Simon is considered the prime suspect in the murder."

"That is ridiculous! Simon would never kill a man." *Especially not for the Blackwood title, which is the bane of his existence.*

"I swear it is true. Uncle Reggie told me that there is some sort of evidence that points to him attempting to hide the late baron's knowledge of the heir from the Continent. It is a mystery how no one knew of the nephews, but people are saying that Simon must have known."

"Does that make any sense? Simon was a babe when his older brother died! How in heaven was he to hide such information when he was a child?"

Henri frowned, considering the question. "Perhaps there was no contact with the family. Perhaps Simon did not know until Lord Filminster visited London, and when he learned of it, he acted out of desperation."

Madeline appreciated that her sister enjoyed her work, but she disliked the rumor trough of Parliament. She found average politicians to be a herd of pompous boars who savored intrigue and *on-dits* as if snuffling for truffles in the woods, rooting into reputations for their delicious tidbits of gossip with a gluttonous obsession. It was a distraction from their own shortcomings to pontificate about issues they could not comprehend from their privileged points of view.

Madeline far preferred tradespeople who produced actual work for their living.

"We have known him since we were children. Do you think him capable of such villainy?"

Her sister shrugged. "He has changed. How would I know what he might do to hold on to his position?"

"Simon would not commit a crime."

Cocking her head, Henri contemplated Madeline with an expression of sympathy. "I hope so, Maddy. Just … prepare yourself. In case."

Madeline shook her head. It was true that Simon had changed, but not that much. Not enough to kill a man in cold blood. She knew his heart, and there was not a drop of scoundrel in his blood. Not one drop.

"When was the murder?"

"The night of the coronation."

"Well, then. It is simple—I was with him that night until well past midnight."

Her sister groaned, dropping into a seat across the table. "Madeline! Say it is not so! If word gets out, your reputation will be destroyed."

Madeline sank back into her chair in dismay. If Simon needed an alibi, she would not hesitate to provide it, but it was true it would ruin her and likely the manufactory, too. But, more than that, what of his betrothed? Coming forward would create a scandal for Simon and Miss Boyle. The general public would not understand their long-standing friendship. Not to mention, there was a possibility that her testimony as an unmarried tradeswoman could be rejected out of hand. The authorities might think she was a lovesick fool, fibbing on behalf of the object of her infatuation who was far out of her reach!

She nibbled on a fingernail to think. What sort of evidence did Home Office have in their possession?

* * *

"LORD BOYLE IS HERE to see you."

The rain roaring outside made it difficult to hear, but he could make out that MacNaby pronounced this news from the study door with the slightest hint of reproach. What had his prospective father-in-law done to shake the butler's poise?

He rose, coming around his desk. "Show him in."

Boyle entered, rake thin in a damask burgundy suit swimming with floral ornamentations, which made Simon blink rapidly lest he lose his balance.

"Lord Boyle."

"Dear boy, I am afraid I had to visit unannounced. Terrible circumstances. Just terrible!"

Simon gritted his teeth, wondering what fresh torment was to be revealed. Dante had been incorrect in his narrative poem. He had already visited the first seven circles of hell, and Boyle was certain to fling the gates open wide to reveal the eighth.

"What is terrible, my lord?"

Boyle stalked up and down, ignoring Simon's gesture toward a chair. Rubbing his hands together in agitation, Boyle continued to mumble about the horrors of some unnamed distress. Simon firmed his jaw and folded his arms to wait him out.

"You are a gentleman, Mr. Scott. I am certain you understand that my Olivia—she had her heart set on being a baroness."

Simon rolled his eyes as Boyle continued wearing a frenzied path into the expensive Aubusson rug beneath his buckled shoes. He spoke about acquiring the title as if it were shopping for a pair of gloves or slippers at a milliner's shop. Which, Simon supposed, it was of a sort what had occurred. Seconds later, realizing what Boyle had said, he narrowed his eyes to consider the viscount's mutterings. Was Boyle going to beg off their contract?

Please, God, let it be so!

"My lord, do you wish to inform me of something?"

Boyle paused mid-pacing, his back turned to Simon and his shoulders coming back with sudden tension.

"We learned of the heirs, my boy. Olivia is fond of you, but you must understand that she had her heart set on a title."

"Are you requesting that I allow your daughter out of the marriage contract?"

He could hear the viscount's audible inhalation. "Lord Clutterbuck informed us of the news from Westminster about these Italian heirs. What a disaster! He has made it clear that he is willing to wed Olivia if she so wishes."

"Does she?"

Silence followed Simon's question, and he waited for the answer without drawing air. His heart pounded so loud in his ears, he was worried he would not be able to hear Boyle reply. Simon had not prayed so hard for mercy since the night his brother had fallen from his third-floor window and he had set himself on this current descent into misery.

Boyle turned about, his eyes downcast while he licked his

thin lips and swallowed. "It is nothing personal, Mr. Scott. Olivia would consider it a benevolent boon if you were to agree to destroy the contract."

Simon was light-headed, but he cautioned himself to not appear too eager lest he insult the viscount at the moment of his release from the gaol he had signed himself into. Boyle was a temperamental coxcomb who could change his mind in a heartbeat if he took offense. Months of negotiations had taught Simon to be cautious. "I am … gravely disappointed."

Boyle gave a nervous twitch at this pronouncement. "It would be a selfless act, Mr. Scott. I beseech you to grant Olivia forbearance."

"Not so small, Lord Boyle." Simon's mouth was dry, as his thoughts raced to calculate the right amount of reluctance to display to achieve this unexpected outcome he desired with every iota of his being.

A flush spread up the viscount's neck. He raised his gaze to implore Simon, his washed-out blue eyes desperate. "It would be an act of grace and honor for which I would be eternally grateful, young man."

Simon considered him carefully, turning to walk to the cabinet behind his desk. Opening the doors, he pulled out a key to unlock the safe and retrieve the signed contract before turning back to Boyle. "How do you propose to do this?"

Boyle exhaled in a rush, his eyes fixing on the pages in Simon's grasp. Reaching inside his coat, he pulled out a thick wad of papers and approached Simon's desk. "We shall each tear it up and burn the pieces."

Simon gave a nod of assent. Grabbing his sheaf at the middle, he prepared to rip the documents in half while pausing to ensure Boyle did the same. Then, at the same time, they tore with a loud rending, walking over to the small fire banked in the hearth to toss the contract into the coals. They each watched intently as the pages curled and charred, dissolving into ashes while Simon breathed his first hint of true freedom in over ten years. Olivia was no longer his burden to bear, and the last remaining barrier left between him and a future of his choosing was the accusation of murder.

* * *

MADELINE FOUND her feet walking to the garden without a conscious approval from her brain. The sun was setting, and the evening air cool on her skin as she adjusted her shawl to prevent a chill. She hoped that, perhaps, Simon might appear. She had been thinking about the murder investigation, and musing about why he had not informed her of that detail. Was he aware? If he was not, it was of pressing concern to alert him to the Westminster gossip. He might need to take measures to protect himself or obtain legal representation.

When she reached the garden, it was in shadows, but her spirits soared to see him waiting for her. His legs were sprawled out, and he had his arms folded as he contemplated the firmament of shimmering stars above. Hearing her approach, he turned to grin in greeting. Madeline paused in surprise. He appeared ... happy?

"Simon," she greeted, moving to perch on the other end of the bench but noting that he was not sitting on the far edge as he had been wont to do this past decade.

"Miss Boyle found herself a title to take my place."

Madeline tensed in surprise. "You are ... free?"

He blew a happy sigh. "It would appear so. No longer the heir to a baron, and no longer betrothed. I do not know what I wish to do with my future, but it is mine to decide."

"That is wonderful news!" Madeline wondered what it meant. It had been years since they had had an understanding, but was it possible he might consider ... She squashed the thought, not wishing to put pressure on a person who had been constrained by obligations for a third of his life.

Simon glanced at her, then focused on one of the gods staring at them in the evening light. Hermes, with his winged sandals and blank expression, looked down as if he listened closely to collect news to impart to the Olympians.

"Are you …? Would you …?" Simon's voice faltered, his expression clouded. "It's too soon. My life is … still complicated."

Madeline knew what he wished to say, and it was a struggle to repress her hopes. Still, she reminded herself that he had his troubles to face before they could consider the future. The boy she had known was slowly reappearing, but Madeline understood that the journey back to his former vitality would require patience. He was shedding the rigid, unnatural formality of recent years—piece by piece—while contending with unprecedented pressures.

"Because of the baron who was killed?"

"You heard?"

"Henri is a veritable aqueduct to the salacious whisperings of Westminster."

He was silent for a few seconds. "Apparently Home Office is unofficially investigating whether I may have murdered a peer to hold on to the title." Simon laughed, the sound hollow as it echoed against the statuary. "I would have thanked Lord Filminster for bringing our nephews to light because I have been released from the drudgery of expectations and given the opportunity to discover what I want as a man. Who I am as a man. Without the blighted title tying me down, I can forge my own way in this world. Once these issues are resolved."

"I will come forward to clear your name."

He shot to his feet, spinning to face her. "You must not

attempt such a thing! The damage it would do to you ... to your family and the manufactory ... No!"

Madeline blinked, disconcerted by his abrupt shift of mood.

Simon stepped back, relaxing his stance with a contrite expression. "This is my problem to solve, Madeline. A misunderstanding. The baron was the unfortunate victim of a villainous scoundrel who wished to rob him, or he caught his steward diverting funds from his books. It will be sorted. Promise me you will not risk your reputation?"

She had no intention of ignoring his wishes, but she would not hesitate to raise the subject with him again if the investigation headed toward an arrest. "My offer stands, but I shall not take any action without your consent."

"Your offer is appreciated, but Isla told our visitors that she was with me here in the garden that night. If you stepped forward, it would complicate the situation."

Madeline blinked again in surprise. It was a generous gesture from the baroness whom Madeline had always struggled to read. She had not thought Isla Scott to be a doting parent, but perhaps that was just her own reaction to the older woman's lack of expressions, which had always put her on edge. Simon had few criticisms about his mother, but he had once explained to her that the lack of emotional manifestation was due to her vanity. Lady Blackwood was as beautiful as one of the stoic goddesses peering down at them, without a line to mar her angelic face.

CHAPTER 7

⚜

*"But the ants, moved by compassion for Psyche, came to her aid,
sorting the grains one by one."*

Lucius Apuleius, Metamorphoses

* * *

OCTOBER 3, 1821

*S*imon had wanted to sweep Madeline into his arms
and plant a kiss on her soft lips, but right at the
moment of truth, he had realized that he could not drag her
into a murder investigation until he knew how serious the
situation was. Which was why he had decided to seek
counsel from their solicitors. He should have done so already
to discuss the ramifications of the new heirs.

Thus, he now sat at his desk with his fingers wrapped
around a quill to compose a letter that would be delivered by
one of their footmen, but he found himself at a loss for what

to write. If Westminster was rife with gossip, it was possible their solicitors might have heard something by now. Nevertheless, Simon could not focus his thoughts. An unknown heir and spare? An accusation of murder?

Shaking his head, Simon dipped the quill in the inkstand and wrote out a request for an urgent appointment. Sprinkling it with pounce to dry the black pigment before reaching for the bell, he was interrupted by a knock on the study door.

Simon called out, and Duncan entered to announce that their contingent of lords had returned to request an audience with Lord Blackwood and himself. Simon suppressed a groan at the news before turning over the letter for delivery. Why had he not sent for legal representation after the first visit? He supposed he had been rather distracted by the news and what it meant for him.

Soon the same party of gentlemen were shown into the room, bowing stiffly in formal greeting. Simon gritted his teeth in irritation. Did they travel together like a pack of wolves? Could they not send two instead of five?

After greetings were finished, the men took up the same positions as they had before, although the windows were closed to keep out the autumn air which had turned chilly overnight. The duke and earl stood in silence with their beavers tucked beneath their arms, and holding their gloves, which must mean they had declined the footman's offer to stow them away. Lord Filminster and the elegant coxcomb, Lord Trafford, sat at attention on the plump leather armchairs facing the desk, their hats and gloves perched on their knees as if to announce their general state of discord, while the youth, Gideon, retreated into the corner to contemplate the wood flooring beneath his feet while they awaited John's arrival. The lad kept his beaver and gloves on, a repeat of his deplorable breach of etiquette that Simon could not make sense of. Perhaps the boy was not familiar with the behavior of the upper classes, despite his fine attire?

All present straightened up with tense alertness when John entered and crossed the room to take a seat behind the desk which Simon had vacated. He supposed he should have requested extra seating, but he was not in the mood to sit, and the two peers hovering at the window did not seem any more inclined to relax than they had two days earlier.

"Do you lot attend each other everywhere you visit ... Your Grace?" growled John with impatience, echoing Simon's earlier thought.

Simon observed the oddity of the duke glancing across the room toward Gideon in the corner, again seemingly hesitating for a cue to speak from the youth. Gideon's eyes were fixed on his brother, but he must have been aware of the duke's unspoken question because he, almost imperceptibly, bobbed his head.

Why would a peer of such high rank, second only to the Royal family, seek approval from a lad barely out of short breeches?

"There is a murderer afoot, Blackwood. We will not venture into your home alone, given the circumstances."

John snorted in disgust. "This again! Are you a quivering rabbit, cowering from your own shadow? Must you rely on your cronies to defend you against an old man?"

"Not you." The duke's gaze found Simon, who had to prevent himself from stepping back at the simmering intensity in its depth. John turned his head to follow his gaze before shaking his head in outrage.

"Simon did not kill Lord Filminster! Lady Blackwood confirmed as much when you were here on Sunday!"

"Which has been proven to be a lie. I appreciate that a mother might feel compelled to put forward a false alibi, but Lady Blackwood was at the Forsythe dinner across Town until almost midnight. The night watchmen who serve this street confirmed that they did not witness the return of any Blackwood carriages until well past midnight, nor did any of the grooms from your neighboring homes. We did learn of one carriage that returned at approximately one in the morning, and another shortly thereafter."

"So you have been questioning our neighbors or their servants. Are you officially accusing my brother of this crime?"

Simon folded his arms in agitation, awaiting the response. Again, the duke glanced to Gideon, whose eerie silver eyes were fixed on John. Something about the boy was decidedly odd, but Simon's thoughts were too occupied with the discussion to work out what it was. Did he know Gideon from somewhere?

"Not officially."

John rose to his feet, leaning on the desk for support with a flush of anger rising up his cheeks. "Unofficially?" he prompted.

Halmesbury stared at him for several seconds before responding. "There is more information than what we disclosed on our previous visit."

It was not an answer. Simon berated himself for not sending for the solicitor first thing on Monday morning. He had managed to convince himself that the situation would dissipate, and perhaps had been too bemused by the news of the heirs in Italy. His lack of foresight now caused him to be uncertain of how to react to this second visit. He could appreciate that the duke had his wife to comfort over her father's death, and that young Filminster might be feeling some resentment that he had been accused of his father's murder, but flinging about incriminations was ... uncivilized.

"You withheld information?" Simon's tone was critical.

The duke's gray eyes returned to stare at him across the room. "You allowed your mother to provide false alibi?"

Simon expelled his breath, blushing in unexpected shame at being called out about the lie. "I was ... with someone whom I cannot reveal."

The fop in the chair stirred at this announcement. "That is convenient," he muttered to no one in particular.

Lord Filminster, however, seemed unhappy at this news, raking his chestnut mane to announce his lack of composure. Simon recollected reading that Filminster had wed the daughter of a viscount after compromising her the night of the coronation. The alibi she had provided had proven he had not murdered his own father. It was the first signal that anyone in the party might be uncomfortable with accusing Simon of a crime he had no role in.

Simon flickered his gaze over to the strange Mr. Gideon, but, as before, the youth had his eyes fixed on John, paying no mind to the terse discussion taking place. A memory echoed in the recesses of his mind. He could swear he had been on the receiving end of that focused stare at some point in the past, but he could not place it.

"So ... what is it?" John's question broke the awkward silence.

Lord Trafford rose to his feet, his lean face stern as he shot a glance to Gideon behind him. The two made eye contact, a strange frisson passing between them until the boy flickered an assent. Trafford turned back to glare at Simon. "I sent a letter to flush out the killer."

Simon frowned, his eyes skittering over to the desk.

"I stated a time and place to meet."

With this, Simon recalled the missive Trafford spoke of. Striding over, he began searching through his things, but the strange letter he had received was not there. "I received a note about a baron last month."

Trafford rolled his eyes. "Let me guess what has happened. My letter has ..." He threw out his hands, pausing with dramatic effect. "… disappeared?" His tone was laden with sarcasm.

"Well … yes. What of it?"

"Someone followed me home when you failed to appear —and attempted to hasten me to an early grave with the tip of a sharp knife."

Simon shook his head, his thoughts spinning with the unreality of the moment. "You are saying … I tried to stab you?"

"Not you. One of your servants."

His head was reeling. Simon leaned his buttocks against the desk lest he fall over in shock at the bizarre denouncement. "Why … would one of my servants agree to kill you?"

Trafford shrugged with an insolent nonchalance belied by the fury in his brown eyes. Brown? Simon could have sworn the young dandy had green eyes when he had been here last in his sage attire. "Misplaced loyalty?"

John broke into a fit of coughing, the hacking wheeze of his lungs painful to hear, which pulled Simon's attention away from his problems as he waited for his brother to recover. After a couple of minutes, John drew a deep breath and rose to his feet to face Simon's accusers with a baleful glare.

"I think you overestimate the loyalty of our retainers, gentlemen. I can assure you Simon has informed me of whom he was with the evening of the coronation, and he has good reason to withhold the identity of his companion. In the interests of cooperation, I shall send for my butler, who can assist you with questioning our servants, for I can also assure you that there are no murderous fiends living under this roof. Then I expect you to drop this inquiry into my brother or I will pay a visit to the Home Secretary to complain about these heavy-handed antics. The Scotts have been valued members of the noble class for centuries, and we shall not tolerate any further sullying of our reputation."

Trafford opened his mouth to speak, before sinking back into his seat. "Halmesbury?"

The duke stepped forward. "Questioning your servants would do much to set our minds at ease. We thank you, Blackwood."

John nodded, waving to the bell. Simon walked over and rang for MacNaby to make arrangements. Perhaps they could settle this disagreement without further trouble.

* * *

MADELINE HEADED to the secluded garden as soon as dinner was over, stopping to pull on a shawl to cover her bared shoulders in her rush to reach the garden. She knew Simon would come, despite his infrequent visits these past years. His absence had never been about them. Rather it had been real life impinging on the romantic world they had created together in the quiet of the foliage and stone.

Henri had given her grief, and her mother had glanced at her frequently throughout the meal, a question in her eyes. She could tell Eleanor Bigsby was worried about the situation with Simon and how it might affect Madeline's plans to consider the matchmaker's recommendations, but Mama had steered the conversation toward forthcoming social events to quiet Henri's misgivings.

Taking up her place on the stone bench, Madeline twisted her fingers as she considered her position. Then she shifted six inches closer to where Simon would take his seat to close the distance between them. Anticipation fluttered like butterflies in her stomach as she observed the half-moon above, fat with portent. It was the past waning away to usher in a new cycle, and Madeline had some hopes, despite cautioning herself that she did not know Simon's desires for the future.

But he is seeking me out again. Surely that means ...

The crunch of boots upon the walkway interrupted her musings, and she lowered her gaze to watch Simon approach. She took in his lean form, the wide shoulders and slim hips, before noting he appeared to be crestfallen. Her anticipation rearranged itself into anxiety.

Simon dropped onto the bench without a word, his hip brushing against hers as he bent forward to lean his elbows on his long, muscular legs.

"What is it?"

"I am meeting with our solicitors in the morning. My mother's alibi has been disproven, so I need to explore my legal options in case ..."

"This might be a serious problem to contend with?"

Simon nodded, his face glum. "The family of the late baron is convinced I have something to do with his death. The Duke of Halmesbury and his kin. Apparently, Lord Trafford, who is linked to them, was attacked after he sent me a letter last month."

Madeline wrinkled her nose in confusion. "What was in the letter?"

"At the time, I did not know who sent it. It merely stated that the sender knew something about my relationship with a baron and asked me to meet. I thought it was some sort of mistake and forgot about it, but now I cannot locate it amongst my things. This Trafford fellow attended the meeting, and he claims someone followed him home and attempted to kill him. He was most put out when I stated I received the letter, but it has been misplaced somewhere amongst my things in the study."

She considered this information, realizing she needed more information than the scraps she had heard from Simon and Henri if she were to provide any input of use. "My understanding is Lord Filminster is presumed to have been killed because he knew of your nephews living in Italy, who would be the rightful heirs if their existence came to light?"

"That seems to be their hypothesis."

"And Lord Trafford attempted to provoke a response from you to confirm that you might be the killer by sending you an anonymous letter, and he now claims an attempt was made to silence him."

"Which is ridiculous! The silly fop was likely attacked by someone wishing to divest him of his valuables. It is obvious he is moneyed from his clothing."

"What if someone in your household was aware of the Italian nephews?"

Simon frowned, glancing over at her with confusion. "What do you mean?"

"I imagine that these lords have investigated the murder quite thoroughly. Lord Filminster was almost arrested for patricide according to the news sheets, and the baron was killed two months ago. They have had time to explore the different motives for the crime."

"None of my family is capable of murder, Madeline!" His tone was stringent.

Madeline shifted away to the end of the bench, so she might think without the distraction of the heat emanating from his body. Simon was obsessed with his duty to the Scotts, ever since the night of Nicholas's accident. His emotions were too close to the surface. In her view, he must ask some hard questions so he might defend himself appropriately. She decided that as his friend, she must speak the harsh truth, even if it upset him.

"I like John, but your brother is frail. Men who are ill can behave out of character, and he might be concerned with legacy as his mortality beckons. Nicholas overindulges in spirits, which tend to limit one's morality, and might be worried about a stranger inheriting. He has two doting brothers who enable him in his habits, but who knows what your nephews might do. And your mother—" Madeline faltered. She had not the faintest notion of what Lady Blackwood might think about the situation. According to Simon's past anecdotes, the countess often repeated the opinions of her late husband with no emotion to indicate whether she agreed with the sentiments expressed or not. "—might have … reasons … we are unaware of."

Simon shook his head, tensing into a position of umbrage as if he would leap to his feet, yet he remained perched on the bench's edge as if contemplating it but not quite decisive. "This is ridiculous! John is too unwell to go about bludgeoning men to death. As you pointed out, Nicholas is too soused to talk his way into a stranger's study at midnight. And my mother has her own money and resources, so the situation affects her not at all. These lords have got this into their heads when there is an obvious explanation. I heard one of Filminster's footmen was killed in August. Perhaps he did it because he was caught pilfering when the rusticating baron arrived and found things amiss at Ridley House."

Madeline was silent for several seconds, thinking about his arguments. "Be that as it may, I am merely pointing out that you should attempt to find out more about the evidence they possess."

"We allowed them to question our servants, so John hopes that will put an end to it."

"Why did they wish to question your servants?"

"I … do not know. Trafford seems to think one of the servants attacked him."

Turning over what she knew in her mind, Madeline reached a conclusion. Simon would not like it, but—

"You are a skilled negotiator, Simon. I believe you need to

learn more about their investigation so you might help them to resolve their problem. The duke has an excellent reputation and is attempting to do right by his family. Approach him without resentment, and offer to assist so you might end this."

* * *

SIMON ROSE, ambling over to gaze up at one of the gods in the moonlight. It was Athena, holding her spear in hand and with a helmet on her head. The goddess of wisdom.

Madeline had always been a good friend, listening to his troubles and offering quiet words. Too often he had not heeded her advice, and he did not wish to continue as he had.

He supposed he might call on Halmesbury, where the duke might feel more at ease in his own home, and Simon could offer his assistance. Months of contending with Lord Boyle's fickleness had taught him tolerance, which he could apply to his own troubles. Somehow it was easier to execute his duty when he put his own wishes aside, but since the liberty to pursue his own goals was at hand, he acted like a vacillating simpleton. Madeline was right. It was time to apply his talents to his defense. It was the final remaining obstacle to beginning a new life.

Simon reached a conclusion, Athena staring down at him in approval. "I shall speak with our solicitors and then approach Halmesbury to offer my assistance. It must be a terrible experience to have a family member so brutally murdered. To think of someone to whom I am so intimately tied dying alone, with only a foe to witness his untimely exit from the world—it is chilling."

Madeline smiled. "Excellent. The duke is logical. Once he notes your sincerity, it will cast doubt on their theory, then you can pursue your own plans."

"And what would those be?" Simon was startled to hear the suggestive tone of his voice. It was not subtle, but his thoughts had shifted to the woman he had admired these many years. They had been practically children when they were forced apart by circumstances beyond his control, but since the obstacles had been removed one by one, his mind was never far from the fact that they were children no longer.

Madeline's smile faded and her gaze fell to his lips as she swallowed hard in the pulsating quiet. Simon could hear the blood coursing through his veins as he watched her. She rose from the bench, and his eyes were drawn to the sweet curve of her bosom, which rose and fell as if she had been exerting herself.

She approached him, coming to a stop a mere foot away to raise her face and peer up at him. She was a silver beauty in the night, and Simon could feel heat stealing across the surface of his skin in response to the tension which hung suspended between them. Reaching up, he extended a finger to draw it down the curve of her cheek. Madeline inhaled in surprise, her eyes fixed on his as he traced a path down her throat and down to her *décolletage* with agonizing patience.

She tilted toward him, and Simon submitted to his long-buried desires to lean down and capture her soft lips with his. They remained frozen, their mouths pressed together in bliss. When he reached the limits of his tolerance, he brought his arms up to pull her into a tight embrace, groaning at the exquisite joy of her body against his.

His hands trembled with the desire to slide down and explore her womanly curves, his blood thickening at the thought that if he could resolve this fuss, he could finally claim his prize. And there could be no greater prize than a naked Madeline in his bed every night for the rest of their lives.

Desperate craving took hold, as their lips dueled for hungry domination. When her mouth parted for air, he stole his chance to lock his tongue with hers in an intricate dance of mating as the seconds stretched out and Simon gave himself over to his long-held desires to feel and taste his Psyche and to experience the joy of letting his inhibitions go. Discovering that she was far sweeter than he had imagined in the darkness of his bedchamber, panting as if they had run a mile together when they broke apart.

Honey and fruit lingered when he lifted his head to stare down at her in wonder. "You waited for me? All these years?"

There was a long silence, her eyes moistening with tears. "I … almost gave up. But you are my Eros. I would do anything to reunite with you."

Simon swallowed hard, overcome by the thought of how close he had come to losing her forever—how he could still lose her, even as they were inches from finally uniting. But he had hurt her enough. He must come to her as an unburdened man and not drag the productive Bigsby household into his chaos. It was imperative that he prove he had not committed this gruesome crime without damaging her reputation.

"I am so sorry for abandoning you. And that I have nothing to offer you."

"You are enough," she whispered back, into the still of the night.

"Yet I must ask you to continue your wait because I cannot make any promises until I put an end to this firestorm."

She reached up to caress his cheek, a brush of butterfly wings to quiet the despairing beast within. "I will be here."

"I do not deserve your patience."

Madeline pulled a face, tugging on his heart with the ironic humor reflected there. "Regardless, you have it."

* * *

PATIENCE BE DAMNED. I have been patient for far too long!

Why had she allowed more than ten years to pass without taking a bloody stand for herself? For Simon? For them!

Madeline stomped along the garden path after Simon's departure with a tempest in her chest.

He was emotionally compromised by this situation he was in. By his neurotic family, who swilled spirits and walked through their days in the haze of laudanum and self-absorption.

While he insisted that no one in his clan could be capable of the flare of passion that had led to the death of the Baron of Filminster, Madeline had no such compunctions. She had witnessed the Scotts take advantage of Simon's guilt over Nicholas's accident for these many years, and could well imagine one of them bringing down a sculpture onto the head of a so-called foe who stood between them and their selfish pursuits.

Especially one who threatened their imagined comforts.

Personally, she thought the Scotts were something of a miserable bunch, and that Simon was the only selfless member of the family, to a fault. How he had escaped the personality flaws of his brothers—who would put Narcissus himself to shame—his imperious father, and his passionless mother was a question for the great philosophers.

As much as she liked John, and even Nicholas when he was sober, Madeline did not trust that they were incapable of doing wrong, given the right motive. She could like them without trusting them, as Simon should do.

Fortunately, Simon had agreed to speak with the duke after he met with his solicitors, but in the meanwhile, she was vexed. Vexed that destiny had seen fit to almost bring them back together, yet he was still out of reach.

And since Isla had already provided a false alibi that had been disproved, it would be even more impossible for Madeline to come forward in Simon's defense. She would be met with disbelief and scandal. Simon's mother was a vacuous doll who had ruined the only genuine advantage Simon had possessed in the aftermath of this heinous murder.

She could not believe that Simon—a competent manager of the Blackwood estates—had been so stupid as to allow a false alibi that could be disproven so easily. It was likely he had gone along with it in a bid to protect Madeline, but it was stupid nevertheless.

What a dunderhead!

Patience had led to lost time, and far too many mistakes to count. While Simon met with his legal firm, Madeline was determined to speak with Molly in the morning. There must be more that she could do than *be patient!*

Madeline had two problems to overcome. To protect Simon against the accusation, she needed to know if anyone in his household had perpetrated the crime. And, of higher concern, if one of Simon's mad relations had killed a person two months earlier, he could be in danger.

Molly was the one person she could think of to speak to. She seemed to have a good head on her shoulders, an intimate knowledge of the eccentric Scott household, and no agenda other than to set things right.

If Madeline attempted to discuss these complications with her mother, Eleanor would be far too concerned that Madeline could be hurt, or about losing her agreement to work with a matchmaker.

Talking with Henri would be useless—she was far too concerned with what the denizens of Parliament might have to say about this affair rather than Madeline's personal desires or her integrity as a woman to support the man she loved.

Simon was waking from an intoxicated slumber, and she was going to be here to assist him back to his personal quest to find his place in the world. Their place in the world. Together. As soon as she could overcome the last remaining obstacle to their happiness.

She entered through the library, shutting the terrace doors and turning to cross the room when she came face to face with her mother. Madeline shrieked in surprise, clapping a hand over her racing heart.

"Mama?"

"You have taken to visiting the garden after dinner again."

It was not a question. Eleanor towered over Madeline, six feet of worried mother staring down at her with palpable disappointment. Her handsome face was composed in the light of the oil lamps that the servants had yet to extinguish, but her eyes contained a swirling mixture of emotions in their amber depths.

Madeline was disoriented by the sudden mental shift. She knew this conversation was inevitable, but she had not expected it this night while she was contemplating bloodshed and lifelong dreams almost within reach. "I have."

"Why?"

She considered the events of the past few days. There was much that had happened, but Eleanor did not need all the gruesome details. Her mother wished to know what her plans were.

"Simon … is free from his obligations."

"Henri says he is a suspect in a murder?"

"Simon is not capable of unwarranted violence."

Eleanor stared down at her, bemused as she folded her arms. Madeline's stomach tightened as she awaited her response until her mother finally sighed. "No. He is not."

Relief surged through her in a wave. Her mother's opinion was important to Madeline. They had worked together at the manufactory since her youth, with Mama apprenticing her in varying facets of their stone empire with patience and detail. There were few people on this earth who Madeline respected more than the exceptional woman who forged her way in the world of business with daring and confidence.

Eleanor had developed artificial stone that held up to the elements, developed a client list that included the King himself. Uncle Reginald had opened doors for Eleanor as a young widow, but her mother had done the work to bring her kingdom into fruition. A vote of confidence from her was priceless.

"Simon is no longer tied down by his duty to the Blackwood title. When this accusation is settled, he will court me."

Her mother dropped her gaze to the rug beneath their feet as if lost in thought. "I hope he sees it through to the end. He has cost you much time."

Madeline was no longer the girl who had let her beau go in her youth, helpless as he slipped away due to his perceived culpability in Nicholas's injuries. Since that time, she had taken her place in the Bigsbys' business, negotiated orders and payments with their clients. Managed men. She knew what she wanted. Life was not going to rip her hopes and dreams away a second time.

Madeline drew herself up to her full height, still several inches shorter than her intimidating mother, but she had found her fire and she was confident in what she wanted.

"I learned my lesson. I will not make the same mistakes again. This time, *I* will be the one who sees it through to the end."

Madeline was proud of the firmness in her voice. Eleanor raised her head, a gleam of approval lighting her eyes as her lips curled into a wide smile. "A woman must fight for what she wants in this world."

"Precisely."

"Then when the time comes to hand over the reins of Bigsby's, I shall be proud to do so, daughter."

Madeline warmed at these words. It was high praise, indeed, coming from Eleanor Bigsby.

CHAPTER 8

"Next, Venus ordered Psyche to gather golden wool from dangerous wild sheep, whose very touch could kill her."

Lucius Apuleius, Metamorphoses

* * *

OCTOBER 4, 1821

*H*e was in their garden, a full moon casting a silver glow on Madeline, who was dressed in a silk gown that flowed in the slight breeze. Trees stood silent watch over them, rustling like the roar of waves pounding a moonlit beach to create a bubble of time and space far removed from the ordinary world.

She was turned away, smiling over her shoulder at him, mischief painted upon her delicate features. Accepting her invitation, Simon reached out to unbutton her bodice, desire twisting and coiling through his veins as the gown slipped to reveal a creamy shoulder.

Lowering his head, he licked at a constellation of delightful freckles revealed in the moonlight. His pulse quickened as he tasted her sweet skin, thudding in his ears as he pressed forward to slide his hands around and cup the bountiful breasts that had haunted his dreams these many years.

Madeline moaned softly, her head falling back against his chest as he leaned down to inhale the scent of fruit and woman. His staff hardened as he caressed her, his thumb strumming over the stiffened tips to draw an exalted gasp from the delectable goddess in his arms. She arched into his hands, begging for his touch with sweet abandon, while her rounded buttocks gyrated against his loins, which throbbed in violent approval—

Simon woke up with a groan, his body on fire and his chest heaving from his ragged breath, to realize with great disappointment that morning had arrived. He tried rolling over to recapture the intoxicating dream, but it was no use, despite the insistent pulsing between his legs.

He had found respite from his legal problems in his slumber, but now they clamored for his attention, shoving the illusion of Madeline out of reach. If he wished to bed his elusive Psyche, he would have to clear his name so he could claim her as his wife.

* * *

MADELINE STIFLED A YAWN, entering the breakfast room to find her sister with a news sheet in one hand and a forkful of eggs in the other.

"Where is Mama?"

"She was summoned earlier for a meeting. Now that the coronation is done, the King has turned his attentions to building a palace worthy of his magnificence."

"Ah. The one that has Parliament fearful over his grand tastes."

"If grand means expensive, yes. They are still choking from the coronation bills."

Madeline collected her plate of food, taking a seat at the table. After tossing and turning all night with worry over Simon, she was looking forward to speaking with Molly. She needed to eat and remove herself to the garden in short order.

She cut her fruit and raised a piece to her mouth when she realized Henri was staring at her with an apprehensive expression. "What is it?"

"The news sheets." Her sister reached over to drop the folded page in front of her.

Madeline peered down, pulling a face as she read the report. "I thought Home Office was keeping it unofficial."

"It appears someone spoke out of turn. There is no mention of an official declaration from Home Office."

Madeline laid her fork down and leaned back to think. "He did not do it."

"So you have said."

"Mama agrees with me."

Her sister twisted her lips in displeasure, capitulating. "But if Simon's reputation is destroyed by this, he could drag you—us—down with him. You must acknowledge the need to be careful."

Madeline sprang to her feet, vibrating with outrage. "Are you suggesting that I desert an old friend because of what people might say? Do you believe me so fickle?"

Henri leaned back in her spindly chair to think. "I suppose that would not be in character. It is just that … Oh, Madeline. I am your sister, and I do not wish to see you hurt again."

Madeline dropped back down. "I appreciate that, but he is my closest friend. Simon has had a difficult time since his brother's accident, but this is almost as terrible as that night. I cannot be selfish when he needs me."

"He has not reciprocated such loyalty."

"To be fair, I have a wonderful mother and sister who never cause any drama, while Simon …" Madeline sought the right words. "He lives in a household of idle aristocrats who suffocate him with endless bother, so we cannot say what he would do if I was in a muddle."

Henri's foul mood lifted in an instant when she burst out laughing. "I am not one of your clients, Maddy! Do not attempt to bury me in flattery."

Madeline responded with an unrepentant grin. "My flattery is always sincere. It does not work otherwise. It is true you are an excellent sister to seek me out about my welfare, and I appreciate it. We might not always see eye to eye, but I know you have my best interests at heart."

"I do, you know. This situation with Simon has been on my mind. And Uncle Reggie has not said much, but I can tell he is worried."

"What is the news at Westminster?"

Her sister picked up her fork to toy with her eggs, a reticent expression settling over her face. To Madeline, it was like peering into a mirror, because it was the same expression she had seen while she was dressing. They might have disparate personalities, but their current concerns matched as closely as their features.

"It is not good news, I am afraid. Simon might be in hot water. What with the heirs that have been discovered in Italy, and the fact that his alibi has been disproven … he needs to find a defense, Maddy. This is not going to simply fade away."

Madeline moistened her lips, agitated at this pronouncement. It was as she had feared. If Simon was not the brother of a baron, the coroner might have already arrested him.

"Why is Home Office holding back from announcing an investigation?"

Henri shook her head. "From what I can tell, Simon is fortunate that the new Lord Filminster was unjustly accused of the crime. They are afraid to accuse another member of the nobility without sufficient evidence after such an embarrassing error."

"Which means that, ironically, the men accusing Simon of the crime are also the reason for the reluctance to investigate him officially?"

Her sister bobbed her head in agreement. "Home Office are loath to misstep after the coroner's egregious mistakes in the days after the baron was killed. That is why they are allowing the duke to take the lead. From all accounts, it was what Halmesbury wants, probably because His Grace desires discretion." She pointed at the news sheet. "Unfortunately, that report brings it to the broader public's attention."

Madeline stared down at the cut strawberry on her plate that she had abandoned, her stomach knotted with anxiety as she considered the peril Simon was in. It was incredible to think of him being arrested for a crime he had not committed.

She considered her options as she had done throughout the night until the first threads of dawn had stolen into her room to inform her sleep was a futile pursuit. If coming forward to testify that Simon had been with her that night was the last remaining option, she would do it. But first, there was more to learn. Lady Blackwood's impulse to help her son had made his predicament worse. Nay, Madeline was determined to apply logic to untangling the web that ensnared Simon.

It was not dissimilar to acquiring an important new client. One collected information about them, and employed strategy to guide them into working with Bigsby's.

"There is still time for Simon to dissuade their attentions."

"Agreed. He needs to prepare."

* * *

SIMON WATCHED his solicitor exit the front door with a heavy cloud of foreboding glowering above his head. The regal old retainer had not heard the news about the unknown heirs, but had confirmed that once their parentage was verified, he and Nicholas would fall down the list of potential heirs.

He was mildly regretful to hear the news. The past ten years had been dedicated to learning about the Blackwood estates and caring for the needs of their tenants and households. It had been a point of personal pride to be competent and take care of everyone under his sphere of influence, so it was difficult to imagine a stranger taking up the reins as he stepped out of the way.

On the other hand, it opened the door to him going into trade. Simon had always been fascinated by the world of industry, especially by Mrs. Bigsby, who had made a success of her business despite the deck being stacked against her as a woman. He, too, wanted to build something enterprising. The life of landowners and peerage was dull compared to what Eleanor Bigsby had done to construct her empire.

Simon was at a loss about what to do with the rest of his morning without direction about the murder. Their legal firm was to send a barrister to discuss the ramifications of the investigation. The solicitor, specializing in estate law, had been unwilling to proffer any advice on the accusation without consulting with his colleagues, so Simon expected to receive a note later that day to inform him of the details of the meeting.

Nicholas came traipsing down the stairs while Simon was

still lost in thought, his gangly form showing signs of wear from his slumped shoulders to his haggard countenance. He was aging faster than Simon was.

"Nicholas!"

His little brother flinched, glancing over the balustrade to find Simon peering up with a stern expression. God help him, he was going to force Nicholas to have a conversation this morning.

"Simon."

"Where have you been? I have not seen you since …" Simon raked through the past few days. "Since the family met over the news about the heirs."

"Drowning my sorrows."

"Deuce it, Nick, must you be so melodramatic?"

"How can you be so calm? I was counting on you being the heir! These new fellows might cast me out. How am I meant to get by on the pittance from our parents' marriage contract?"

Simon could not help it. He snorted. "It is far more than most people earn making a living."

Nicholas straightened up to his full height, his ire obvious in every inch of his body. There was no sign of the sarcastic twit Simon had spoken with just days ago. "I am not of the working class. I do not know how to get by on a reduced allowance. You may yearn to work in the trenches of industry but I … I am meant to be a son of the privileged classes."

"Considering we do not know what the future holds, you will have to think how you wish to participate in the real world. Carousing with your cronies is not going to reveal the riches that existence offers."

Simon caught a glimpse of Duncan, but the tall footman with the square face and dark blond hair obviously realized a family squabble was under way and hastily retraced his steps to avoid interrupting.

"Thunder an' Turf, Simon! You are an obnoxious, self-righteous prick!"

"And you are a lazy, over-imbibing lout who could benefit from honest work." Simon winced. They were harsh words, but recent events had him under the pressure of a steam engine about to blow. As the time approached to welcome the new heirs into their household, and with a murder accusation hanging over—around?—Simon clasped his neck as he contemplated the possibility of the hangman's noose.

He had not the patience to mince words any longer. Nicholas was on a terrible path, and they must engage in mutual cooperation. John's health was of grave concern, a transfer in title therefore a pressing possibility, and his younger brother's days of idle pleasures must end. Simon had to chart a path out of his current situation, and Nicholas was his responsibility to see to.

His brother was seething, his usual supercilious mask long forgotten, as he glared down at Simon. "You are a bacon-brained cur to speak to me so. My head is pounding or I would take you to task with my fists."

Simon burst out laughing. "You could not plant a facer to a fly, Nick. You have not the strength!"

Struggling down the stairs with a pronounced limp, his brother came down the hall with his full umbrage on display. "Do not tempt me to prove that I have more than enough strength to fell a grown man!"

Stepping back in surprise, Simon paused to look Nicholas up and down before responding. His brother's eyes were bloodshot and bracketed by black circles, causing Simon's heart to tweak in sympathy. He hated that the boy he had known had vanished the night he had fallen three stories from Simon's window. "I apologize. I was thrilling at solic-iting a genuine emotion from you and got carried away."

It was true. These past few years, Nicholas had seemed a lost cause. It was almost invigorating to be engaging in an argument—it was more truthful than their recent superficial discussions.

Nicholas relaxed, placated by the apology. "What will we do?"

"We are hardly indigent, Nicholas. You have an allowance, and Mother has her endowment along with her titled entail-ments. And I will help you if our purposes do not align with the arriving gentlemen."

His brother shook his head in dismay. "Is there nothing we can do? You were to be Lord Blackwood. We have nothing in common with these men from Italy."

"We can break bread with our nephews and form a connection with them. There is no need to anticipate an eradication of your situation. They may be more than amenable to continue as John and Father have done."

"That seems unlikely. We know nothing of their thoughts, and I ... should ... have ..." Nicholas trailed off with an anguished expression, hanging his head in supplication.

"Put more thought into what you wanted from your life?"

Nicholas gave a glum nod. "It is true I abuse the spirits, but these damn injuries cause me such pain."

Simon's breath froze in his lungs. Lawks! His younger brother had never revealed such intimate information. "They trouble you?"

"They do."

"Would you ..." Simon was almost afraid to ask the ques-tion lest his brother retreat back under his glib facade. "If we found a physician who could provide you with real help ..."

"It might be time. I am frightened by what comes next. My whole life, I knew I had you and John to take care of things, and the prospect of a changing of the guards is terrifying."

Simon thought that Nicolas might have more on his mind, but he did not wish to ruin their shared moment by pushing for more disclosures. He suspected the best course of action was to accept that Nicholas was willing to consult with a new physician. Someone other than the laudanum-peddling Dr. White who treated the entire Scott household. Except for himself—Simon was never ill.

"I have a physician who might be able to help. May I … arrange a meeting?"

His brother inhaled deeply, thinking about Simon's proposal with tension in his face. Simon perceived that his brother was considering a startling change in behavior, and remained silent to allow Nicholas to think it through lest he interrupted prematurely.

"Yes, that is acceptable."

Simon realized he had been holding his breath while he waited, expelling air in a rush with heady disbelief but careful not to exhibit his elation. Finally! He had been trying to convince his brother for years! Simon was not going to question him about what had changed, or why Nicholas was willing to take that first step. Nay, the safest course of action was to seize the opportunity to help him, which would set things right between them.

"I believe this is a good decision."

Nicholas gave a half chuckle, shrugging it off. "Do not grow maudlin on me, stinker."

Simon laughed. The urge to embrace his brother was overpowering, but he knew it would be too much, so he kept his arms fixed to his sides and enjoyed the first win he had experienced in days. Nicholas had agreed to see a doctor other than that medicating fraud, Dr. White. This was a splendid day despite his numerous botherations.

* * *

MADELINE SPED along the garden path as swiftly as her skirts permitted, her slippers crunching loudly as she almost ran. Her conversation with Henri had delayed her from meeting with Molly, and it was imperative she speak with her.

She hoped her friend had waited for her, but it was not a formal arrangement that they meet after breakfast. More of a happenstance of their morning routines converging. Given what her sister had revealed, Madeline was even more determined to learn what she could about the goings-on of the Scott household.

Bursting through the archway, she was elated to find Molly reading a book in the morning light. As she approached, she realized Molly was not reading, but staring at the cover as if she had forgotten what she was about and never opened the book.

"Molly?"

She flinched, raising her head. "Madeline. I am sorry. I was woolgathering."

Madeline sank onto the bench, worried about her friend because she knew she had been making noise equivalent to a stampeding herd of elephants. It would take a smothering of worry to render Molly so deaf. "Is something wrong?"

Molly's face was bemused. "I do not know. I have been thinking about this situation with Simon and … I suppose I feel rather helpless. He is an honorable man, and it is not right that he is in this situation. And …"

A cloud passed over her features, and Madeline had an intuition about what she did not wish to state out loud.

"You are wondering if there is a reason why the evidence points to Simon?"

Molly did not respond for several seconds, her voice

weak when she finally answered. "Is someone in my household responsible for the baron's death?"

Although it was causing Molly such anguish, Madeline found herself giddy to hear the sentiment voiced. Despite the horrific nature of their speculation, it eased Madeline's guilt to hear her own thoughts echoed back to her from another source. "I confess, sleep eluded me as I turned that very fear over in my mind."

Molly turned to her with an expression of profound relief. "Truly?"

"I believe that it is not only possible, but that someone must look into it." Madeline steeled her nerve to say what she had come to say. "*We* must look into it."

Her companion's eyes rounded in alarm. "Could we not just convey our worries to Simon?"

"I attempted it just yesterday, but Simon is compromised when it comes to the Scotts. He will not admit the possibility that one of his relations may be a cold-blooded killer, and along with all the other issues he is dealing with—"

Molly interrupted, intense with earnest interest. "We should. We should look into it without adding to Simon's burdens. I so want to assist, and what can it hurt for us to do so? It would be better to uncover any disreputable secrets without external intervention." She sounded emphatic, reaching a decision from only a gentle prod. It was as Madeline had hoped when her mind had plagued her with the worst outcomes all night.

"Just so. There is scandal brewing, so I do not wish to add to it, which is why I think we are uniquely positioned to investigate. A little. To be sure."

"So what do we do?"

Madeline grimaced. This was the part that made her feel queasy. It would be such a horrible violation of privacy, and they would need to forget anything they found that did not pertain to the murder or an attempt to hide knowledge of the heirs.

"We search their desks and papers to see if there is any evidence pointing to contact with the late Lord Filminster or his relations, knowledge of the heirs in Italy, or …"

"Or what?"

Madeline pouted in thought. "I do not know. I have never investigated anything before. Perhaps the letter Lord Trafford sent? The one that has gone missing? If Trafford is correct, that letter was used to seek him out to attack him. Simon cannot find it, which means the killer may have it."

An audible groan followed that statement. "I hope not. It would be a wonderful thing to confirm there is no hint of foul play, and the killer does not live in my home."

Madeline chuckled despite their macabre topic. "I will certainly sleep better if I know you and Simon are not in the proximity of a deranged villain."

"That is true." Setting her book aside, Molly clapped in assent. "It is something. Better than nothing. Let's do it!"

"Where do we begin?"

Tapping her fingers over her mouth in deep thought, Molly mulled the question over with care. "John has a desk in his rooms that he keeps locked, but I know how to unlatch it because he sent me to collect his journal for him when I first arrived because he was not feeling well."

Madeline arched a brow. "That seems secure."

Her friend rolled her eyes in response. "It is human nature, I am afraid. My mother was oblivious to the fact that there were servants who could access her private papers. I was constantly putting them away for her."

"Then we must think of how to get you into John's rooms. Does he leave them for dinner?"

"He does, and Duncan serves at the dinner table, so he will not be there. And the valet is abed again with his maladies. It is my belief he gets soused, but Simon cannot fire him because John likes the little arse."

"Molly!"

"What? You are not my mother, Madeline Bigsby. I shall say the words which fit, not the words which are fitting."

Despite her dire worries, Madeline burst out laughing. "I have not witnessed this side of you?"

"I am simply growing more relaxed in your company, which is a blessing. It has been exhausting being proper all the time, but the Scotts are so unpredictable in their moods, it has been my strategy to not draw any attention to myself."

"Well, feel free to air your words as much as you need." Madeline paused to recall what they had been discussing before Molly's shocking departure from her usual deportment. "What of Nicholas? I hear he is quite plaintive about how the new heirs affect him."

"He is. I can access his room once he departs for the evening. Perhaps when I go to bed, I can sneak down the hall."

"Do you consider Lady Blackwood a suspect? Should we try to get into her rooms?"

Molly shrugged. "I have no notions of what Isla Scott is thinking, but it cannot hurt to see what is in her rooms. It will be interesting to see where the china doll sleeps because she has never invited me in."

"Or bestowed you with a hint of expression?"

"Truly! I sometimes wonder if she is human or some fey creature from the otherworld. Can you conceive of never smiling, nor frowning? I never know what to say in her presence, so I hold my tongue." Molly motioned to her lips for emphasis.

"I suppose the best time to access the baroness's rooms would be dinner?"

"Yes. Her lady's maid frequents the kitchens during

dinner to indulge in household tattle. Miss Dubois, though pretty of features, is acrimonious by nature, and takes great pleasure in recounting salacious *on-dits* whenever she has the opportunity. I suspect she extravagantly embellishes most of her stories for dramatic effect."

Madeline giggled. "I think I like this more irreverent side of you!"

"Then you would have loved my mother. She did not tolerate fools, and wielded a cutting wit with rapier sharpness." Molly's face went glum. "I miss her so much."

"I am sorry."

"There is no need. These morning visits with you have lifted my spirits. You are a good friend."

Madeline was touched by the compliment, reaching out an arm for a quick embrace. "I enjoy this, too. You helped me forget some of my troubles."

They sat in comfortable silence, the sound of leaves rustling in the breeze as birds twittered from undisclosed locations, and sweet solace stole through Madeline. "I shall come to dinner to ensure everyone remains downstairs while you search. My presence will cause such consternation, they will forget all about you."

The thought of entering the Scott home was daunting, but she had no time for reservations, so she would be audacious to achieve their aims.

Molly cleared her throat. "There is one more place we should search."

Madeline tried to think. "Where?"

"Simon's study."

Madeline could feel her cheeks heating, embarrassed to speak of intimate issues. Molly and she had talked about varied subjects, but never broached personal topics until these past few days. However, if they were to be co-conspirators in deceitful deeds, she must act in good faith and trust her new friend with confidential information. "Simon could not have done it. He was with me that night."

Her friend was silent as she digested this. "Were you ..."

"As friends. Simon was reluctant to wed Miss Boyle, so he spent some final hours reminiscing about better days here in the garden before he signed the contract."

"Well, I am happy to hear that. I like Simon, but I did not wish my affinity to cloud my thoughts when there might be a dangerous criminal in the house."

"I understand. We have one down, three to go."

"I would still like to access the study. To be sure that the letter from Lord Trafford was not simply misplaced? Lying under the desk or something. It would serve as confirmation or disprove that there is something afoot within." Molly gestured toward the Scotts' house.

"Fair point. We will include the study."

A shiver traversed down Madeline's spine. It would be strange to search Simon's things without his permission, and she hoped she would not learn anything she did not wish to know.

CHAPTER 9

"*A gentle reed whispered to Psyche, 'Wait until the sheep are resting in the shade, and then collect the wool caught on the branches of the trees.*"

Lucius Apuleius, Metamorphoses

* * *

"You should wed Olivia Boyle."

John's declaration was met by the loud ticking of the mahogany clock on the shelf. Tick, tick, tick, it said while Simon considered how best to respond to his older brother's absurd recommendation.

Simon pondered the possibility that he was still abed, dreaming this bizarre conversation in the comfort of his sheets. He would much rather dream about Madeline, tucking her soft body to his as they slipped into slumber together. But perhaps the lamb from dinner the night before had been tainted to bring on such odd proclamations. He tapped the arm of his chair with drumming fingertips just to confirm it was daytime, and he had indeed dressed with the help of his valet just an hour earlier. The leather-clad padding was solid enough to the touch. He must be awake, then.

"Why on earth would I do that?" It was a serious question. Simon could not think of a solitary reason he would want to do such a thing. "Her father is making arrangements for her to marry Lord Clutterbuck."

"It would elevate the Blackwood legacy to align with such an ancient family, and Clutterbuck is old enough to be her grandfather. You would be doing the featherbrained chit a service."

Simon did not often drink, and when he did, it made his head feel muddled. Not unlike how he was feeling at this very moment. Did John have a legitimate reason to suggest such folly, or was this more of the legacy foolishness that had held Simon fast all these years while his real life slipped away?

"I do not wish to wed Miss Boyle. She is a ridiculous flibbertigibbet who would eventually drive me stark, raving mad. She and Lord Clutterbuck are suited in every aspect other than age."

One of the privileges of not being the heir to the Blackwood title was that Simon was no longer beholden to his father or his older brother. He could do what he wished, and as soon as he worked out what that was, he would begin. First, however, he needed to find some method of proving he had not murdered a peer, which he would be doing if John had not sidled in to take a seat at Simon's desk. After Simon had quickly vacated his seat to make way for his brother.

Simon wondered if he should look into moving into one of his clubs. The minor irritations of playing second to first his father, and now his brother, were growing into significant annoyances with the news that he was to seek his own fortune. Not least of those aggravations was, despite all the work he had done these past years to oversee the Blackwood holdings, he still had to spring to his feet like a private secretary each time the baron visited the study.

He did not mind paying his respects, but it was he who did all the work, while John signed documents with barely a glance. Simon hoped that the new heir, Marco Scott, would be as fastidious to details as he had been because the baron was in too much physical discomfort to worry about details such as their tenants' leases, or advising them about managing their crops for maximum profits. John did not pay attention to representing his district at Lords, relying on Simon to determine the votes he cast to protect the combined interests of the people of Blackwood.

The thought of all he needed to teach the incoming heir gave him a headache.

I hope Marco allows me to orient him to this role.

"You must consider the bloodlines, Simon. These ... curst Italians ... will sully centuries of Blackwood's legacy if their claim turns out to be legitimate."

Simon suppressed the impulse to grimace. "The people of Italy have bestowed upon us architecture, art, and sculptures so exquisite that they inspire faith itself at their divine perfection. I am certain that Marco, being half-English, will bring a fresh perspective to the Blackwood title, one that shall only strengthen all you hold dear. Furthermore, Italian culture is renowned for its devotion to kin, so he will undoubtedly honor those that come before him."

"Word is that this Marco is a bear leader. Were you aware of that?"

"He tutors young Englishmen on their Grand Tour?"

"That is correct. What have you to say to that? How can such an individual be qualified to be the next baron?" John's tone was plaintive and challenging, a combination which grated on Simon's nerves. Did his brother not recall that Simon was under suspicion for a violent crime? Perhaps there was a better time to discuss the inanity of Marco Scott's prior occupation, but John must have been obsessing over his mortality this morning.

"So he is familiar with our English ways, an accomplished academic, and a gentleman who appreciates the importance of preservation."

"You make it sound an asset."

"It is. How did he come to be in such a role?" Simon acknowledged to himself with some shame that he had not displayed any interest in the relations who would arrive from the Continent, but his thoughts had been otherwise occupied.

"Apparently he is from an important family in Florence. *Merchants!*"

The last was hissed in disgust. Simon suppressed a smile at this. John would be most displeased when he learned Simon planned to enter into industry. He would deem it worse than the merchant class. It had always been Simon's plan, ever since he had learned Eleanor Bigsby's story as a young lad and been fascinated that someone he knew had created such success in the span of years. What it must be like to build wealth and employ people with the sweat of one's brow rather than being born into it.

Granted, she had some coin to purchase the business when she arrived in London, but she had multiplied that initial investment many times over since then.

"Faith! The merchant background means he likely has a head for the business of managing property. Along with his interest in the grandeur of the past, he possesses the perfect skills for a future baron."

"Blast it, Simon! You almost seem pleased at this unfortunate turn of events."

131

I am. If I can settle this murder investigation, I will be able to court Madeline.

He was not going to inform John of that. He would fight that battle at the appropriate time, which was not while he awaited the arrival of Marco, nor while he needed to persuade the Duke of Halmesbury that he had not brutally clubbed the nobleman's father-in-law to death. How grisly to consider the late baron bleeding out on the floor of his own study!

Simon glanced over to the open area, which was adorned by a rich rug of navy, gold, and ivory, with a shiver of repulsion at the imagined bloodshed. Recalling his promise to speak with Halmesbury, Simon shook his head to clear his thoughts. It would have to wait until he met with their legal firm, but he wished he could call on the duke to clear the air and offer his cooperation.

"I am merely pointing out it might not be so terrible to invite them into our lives."

"Personally, I wish we had never learned of their existence and could have continued in ignorant bliss."

John rarely spoke of Peter. Simon glanced at his oldest brother, for just a second wondering if he might have done something to keep their nephews from being uncovered, but dismissed it as disloyal. John was not a bad person, even if recent illness had made him more inconsiderate this past year. It must be difficult for him as the baron, that he had never been able to produce heirs, only to discover his late brother had had two healthy boys. It was odd to consider that Simon himself had had a brother he had never met, to his knowledge, considering how much he liked the two he had grown up with.

Perhaps a change of subject was in order. "What of the questioning of the servants?"

"From what I gather from MacNaby, three of the servants

cannot confirm their whereabouts at the time of Lord Trafford's attack. Do you think his letter had something to do
with it, or did some ruffian follow him home to relieve the
fop of his valuables?"

Simon growled in disappointment at this news. "Which
three?"

"MacNaby, Duncan, and Roderick. MacNaby said he
went to the market after a botched delivery left Cook
without ingredients for breakfast—she apparently has
arthritis in her knees and did not trust the kitchen maids to
make purchases on her behalf. Duncan said he was in the
attic to stow away furniture from the guest bedroom, which
is being refurbished, but no one saw him for those hours,
while Roderick was sent by your mother to Covent Garden
to purchase violets."

"Bloody hell! All the way to Covent Garden?"

John shrugged at the vagaries of women. "She favors a
specific flower seller there that sells the best blooms, and she
had an urgent need to make violet water to freshen her
handkerchiefs."

"Do you think any of the three are involved?"

John straightened in horror, staring at Simon from across
the desk with his mouth agape. "What are you asking? You
wish to know if one of us—a Scott—instructed a servant to
run off and kill this Trafford fellow while they were running
errands? Have you lost your mind?"

Simon rose, walking over to the window that faced the
garden. "I do not know. It is possible that someone in our
household killed the baron? These lords seem so utterly
convinced I am guilty, which does give one pause, does it
not?"

"Who, then? You think I went to dinner and decided to
kill Filminster on the drive home because he irritated me at
the ceremony? Or perhaps it was Nicholas who somehow

learned of this baron he has never met and pretended to go out carousing, so he might stop over and murder Filminster for upsetting his older brother. No! It must be your mother, because Filminster is an obnoxious old goat, and she thought it would be aesthetically pleasing to rid the world of his ugly mug."

Simon decided it was not the most opportune time to point out that John had revealed the murder victim had been accusatory at the ceremony of him hiding heirs—a fact which he had shared with the entire family before they all departed for their evening arrangements on the night of the coronation. It was the reason Simon even knew who Filminster was before the news of his murder. Yet ... what was he suggesting? That one of his brothers or his own mother was a cold-blooded killer?

These accusations had him on edge, seeking shadows within shadows. He did not envy Filminster's family for what they must be feeling under such trying circumstances. It was astounding to consider that a violent brute had attacked a peer, ushering him to meet his maker decades before he was ready.

"Calm yourself, brother. It was a fair question, but I take your point. I do not think anyone in this household committed a brutal murder, but it is unfortunate that MacNaby, Duncan, and Roderick cannot be accounted for when Trafford was accosted."

John settled back, placated by Simon's words. "It would be the men who have worked for us the longest. MacNaby has been our butler for three decades, while Duncan and Roderick have each been here for more than a decade. Why could the three in question not have been retainers we hired in the past few months, to soundly disprove the theory that we have a member of our staff so loyal they would kill a peer for one of us?"

Simon stroked his beard, appalled at what John had pointed out. "Blast! I never even thought of that. Deuce it, John, they grow even more convinced I am guilty. We need to find them another suspect because they are not going to let this rest!"

"Nay, brother. I see no sign of them backing down."

* * *

MADELINE ACCOMPANIED MOLLY INTO THE SCOTTS' home. She had instructed her coachman that she would be leaving for the manufactory later than usual, having no pressing appointments this morning and the need to learn the truth compelling her to begin their search. Molly and she had worked out the details, and the hope was that by the end of the evening, they would have searched through the things of all four Scotts.

It was daunting, daring, and reprehensible, but Madeline had been frozen by inaction after Nicholas had had his accident, and she would not repeat the same mistake. She would do whatever it took to prove that the Scotts were blameless, or to uncover the fiend who attracted this cloud of trouble to the man she loved. Molly and she both had reservations about what they planned to do, but deemed it a necessary evil if there was a dangerous assailant lurking in the house. Murder was not a trivial subject.

Molly knocked on the study door, both women glancing at each other in apprehension. They were both in disbelief that they were going to proceed.

Simon called out for them to enter, rising in surprise when he caught sight of Madeline in the doorway. "Madel— Miss Bigsby!" He caught himself at the last second, flickering his gaze to Molly before returning to find her. It was good to see him, even if she felt rather guilty about the subterfuge they had planned.

Madeline approached his desk, spreading her skirts to take a seat on the facing chair, while Molly came to stand by her side.

"I have invited Madeline to dinner." Molly sounded breathless as she stated what they had rehearsed in the garden. Madeline suppressed a wince. She did not think either of them were accomplished at pretending, but they were going to do their best in Simon's best interests. Madeline had reached the same conclusion as Molly—there was no reason to burden Simon with suspicions about his family, but, nevertheless, someone had to pursue it to a proper end.

Simon squinted, evidently perplexed as to why he was being informed in this manner or why Madeline needed to attend this briefing with Molly. "Ah ... I ... yes, of course. You are a member of the family, so I suppose you are at liberty to invite guests to break bread with us."

He shot a questioning look to Madeline, who made as if she did not see it, fidgeting with her skirts. It was not a sophisticated plan, but neither she nor Molly had a knack for lying, so it was the best they could do on such short notice.

"Could I have a word in private, Simon?"

Simon peered back and forth between them with a perplexed expression. "Do you mean without Miss Bigsby present?"

"Yes, if we could speak about a disrelated topic. I do not want to bother Miss Bigsby with ... household matters."

He stood frozen in bewilderment, clearly at a loss about what a strange interaction he was caught in and not sure what Molly was asking him to do. "Yes, that is acceptable."

"In the library."

"Uh ... yes." Simon gave a short bow of respect to Madeline, following his cousin from the room and pausing to close the study door behind them. Left to herself in the room, she rose and rushed over to the other side of the desk. She needed to search for the letter with lightning speed, so she dropped to her knees to start with checking the floor. Sometimes pages from her desk at work would vex her by falling into tight crevices or flittering away with annoying speed to land under a piece of furniture. Bringing her cheek down against the flooring, she peered under the shelving but saw no pages there, although she could confirm the servants cleaned thoroughly by the lack of accumulated dust. She stood back up to search a pile of correspondence on the desk but found nothing but letters from the various Blackwood estates.

Her gut tightened with suspense, knowing that Molly would keep Simon from the room for a few minutes at most. The hope was that they would find the blackmail letter from Trafford to disprove that someone in the house had taken it from his things, but so far …

Madeline sucked in a rush of air for courage and began to open Simon's drawers. The first held quill, nibs, extra inkstands, sealing wax along with a seal, and blank pages. Shutting it, she reached for the second drawer. This one held correspondence, which she leafed through but noted nothing but neatly organized notes from the stewards at the respective estates. She fanned the pages, which were tied together with string, but no loose pages fell from the stacks.

Realizing she was running out of time, Madeline shoved the drawer shut and tried another. This one was mostly empty with only a leather journal, which she opened to fan the pages again, careful not to read any of the sentences inked upon them because she did not wish to violate his privacy.

The other drawers were similar. Madeline straightened up and spun around to face the shelving behind the desk.

Hastily grabbing the account books one at a time, she fanned those too, but no letter had been accidentally caught amongst their pages. Checking about her, but out of ideas, she raced back to take up her seat before Molly and Simon returned.

Attempting to calm herself, the disappointment was cloying at her stomach. She had so hoped to find it, the first step to confirming that the Scott family was innocent of any wrongdoing.

She supposed it was possible that Simon had already attempted to find the letter—he kept a neat work space—and it would be much simpler to ask him if he had done so. But he had been disturbed at the idea of suspecting one of his relations, and if Madeline raised the issue of the letter, it would lead back into a discussion about the murder. She was not sure she could hold her tongue when she was so anxious for his freedom and his safety, so this was the best she could do at such short notice. Perhaps Molly would find something this evening while the family was at dinner.

* * *

SIMON STOOD IN THE LIBRARY, struggling to articulate his thoughts to the young woman who had been living with them these past months. He wished his step-cousin to feel at home in … her new residence—Simon scoffed at his inability to order his reasoning—but it was a grievous breach of etiquette to have an unmarried young lady attend dinner, especially given the marked differences in their stations.

"Molly, you and I both appreciate Miss Bigsby, but …" Simon rubbed his beard, hoping that the second time he opened his mouth, eloquent words would pour out. "You do understand … it is unusual?"

This was true. Madeline had never dined in the Scott household, despite their close connection. He would hate to inflict his family's aristocratic disdain on the lady he had admired so ardently.

"As long as she has a chaperone, it should be acceptable. If anyone witnesses her arrival, there is nothing untoward to infer because both I and your mother are in residence, so she could be invited to dinner by one of us."

Deuce it! What on earth was Molly thinking? She had shown a nuanced understanding of what was *de rigueur* in polite society up until now.

"That … is true."

"So it is acceptable? As long as she has a chaperone?"

It was not, but Molly had lost her mother this year, and they were family. If not by blood, at least by marriage. He did not wish to embarrass her when she had made so few requests for herself since joining their household.

"I … suppose that is acceptable, but I think it would be wise to inform my mother. She may not approve, so it is best to give her warning to avoid any display of displeasure." Simon paused, tilting his head as he reflected on the woman in question. Isla Scott would hardly make a display. He continued, choosing his words with care. "I mean, *voice* her displeasure. Both Lord and Lady Blackwood might have remarks about … Miss Bigsby's … rank within their cloistered world if they are not given sufficient time to prepare for such an event."

Molly pursed her lips, appearing to think about his suggestion. "Hmm … it might be an awkward dinner."

"Just so." He did not wish to subject Madeline to the more temperamental behavior his family was capable of. They were all rather on edge about the strangers who would arrive from Italy, so the probability of them saying something rude was vastly increased.

"Can you inform them of the dinner arrangements?"

"I would rather not." It came out instantly, as a reaction.

Simon had a lot on his mind, and coaxing his brother and Isla into behaving themselves, or attempting to answer their inevitable questions about why Madeline was coming to dinner would be subdued if Molly was the one to present it. They were still mostly on their best behavior because none of them knew her all that well, while with Simon, their full displeasure would be expressed.

"I would appreciate it. You see, I cannot be at dinner this evening."

What the living hell?

Simon almost cursed out loud. Up until now, Molly had appeared pragmatic, a trait that Simon had appreciated when compared to the characters living under this roof. It was clearly a facade. She was as eccentric as any member of the Scott household!

"I am sorry. You are saying you invited Madel—Miss Bigsby to dinner, but you shall not be attending?"

"That is correct."

Simon gave up on proper behavior. If she was to make such odd demands, proper behavior be damned. He would be direct.

"Why?"

"I … am not feeling well. I have a tickle in my throat, and I think I should rest until it passes."

"Then why, for the love of heaven, have you invited Madeline to dinner?" Simon could hear that he sounded irate, but this conversation made him feel like he was on a visit to Bedlam to speak with the lunatics. Molly, whom he had believed to be a sensible person, was proving to be an egregious disappointment as a pragmatist.

Molly turned her gaze to a gilt-framed painting over the fireplace, licking her lips. Simon had the impression she was seeking a reply, which made him narrow his eyes. Was she up to something? Why was Madeline involved?

"At the time I invited her … I was feeling well, but am no longer. I do not wish to retract the invitation, so perhaps she can come as your guest?"

Simon raked his hair and wondered if it was possible he was dreaming this entire conversation. "My guest?"

Molly gave a firm nod at this, but Simon sensed she was feigning bravado.

"Are you attempting to matchmake us?"

She blinked, her expression confused until settling into a hopeful smile. "Yes?"

"Are you asking me a question or answering mine?"

She squared her shoulders into a more confident stance. "Answering you. I think that … you and Madeline would make quite a pair."

"Why is Madeline going along with this?"

"I … told her … that … I needed the company … so … she does not know I am attempting to matchmake?"

"Is that a statement or a question?"

His cousin bit her lip, hesitating for a fraction of a second. "A statement!"

"So you are requesting that I have an unwed woman over for dinner, and that I inform my brother and mother of it while you take a tray in your bedroom?" It sounded so absurd he could scarcely believe he had uttered such a sentence.

"I would appreciate it greatly."

Simon repressed a groan. He wished he knew Molly better so he could make sense of why she was doing this to him. Snubbing Madeline by retracting the invitation was too dreadful to consider, particularly after all she had done for him the past few days, despite his years of neglect.

"What of the chaperone?"

"What chaperone?"

His nostrils flared with irritation. Was Molly woolgathering? She did seem distracted. "The one she needs to appease etiquette? If you are not to be at dinner? My mother will not be pleased as it is. I cannot deceive her into thinking Madeline is here at her request, and she is not the sort to volunteer for such a scheme. Announcing this will be complicated enough without explaining her lack of companion and, if I am to pretend I invited her, there must be a chaperone."

"Oh. I suppose she might bring her mother or her sister."

Sweet heaven! Eleanor Bigsby setting foot in Lord Blackwood's home? He supposed he should be thankful his father lay in his grave or this dinner would have sent him there.

CHAPTER 10

❧

"For her third task, Psyche was sent to fetch water from the River Styx, where no human could reach its treacherous source."

Lucius Apuleius, Metamorphoses

* * *

*M*adeline could feel the blush of shame rising up her neck and over the shells of her ears when Molly and Simon returned. She hoped it was not evident on her face, but her cheeks were regrettably warm. She wanted to blurt out how she had violated Simon's inner sanctum, but she was determined to stick to the plan she and Molly had devised.

I am doing it to help him. When all this trouble is a distant memory, I will confess what I have done.

The reassurance did little to settle her discomfort.

"Molly will not be able to attend dinner, so you shall be my guest."

It took a second for Madeline to register that Simon was

addressing her, but once the words filtered through the recesses of her mind, she felt a quiver of pleasure. It might all be contrived, but she had never been invited to dinner in the baron's home before. She wondered what Molly had said to explain her absence. Their initial attempts to think of an explanation had led to frustration until Molly had concluded it would be easier to think of an explanation on the spot than continue to anticipate it.

"That would be lovely," she responded. It would. At some point in the future, this murder would be resolved and they would be able to court. Tonight would be a hint of what was to come, and she would enjoy meeting him in public for the first time. Even if that just meant a family dinner.

"However, we must organize a chaperone."

Molly nodded. "Simon has pointed out that he cannot declare you as his guest without a proper companion to protect your reputation. Do you suppose Mrs. Bigsby or your sister can attend?"

Madeline clenched her teeth, her stomach growing agitated. How would she explain that? Mama was going to have outspoken reservations to entering this building with her. Madeline was still pinching herself that she had visited not once, but twice.

This is but a step on the path to happiness.

Pursuing one's dreams was never easy. Her mother could attest to that, so perhaps Eleanor Bigsby would be more amenable than Madeline presumed. Steeling her nerve, Madeline announced her reply with only a hint of shrillness to belie her confident tone.

"My mother would be the most appropriate. I suppose I must be on my way so I can join her at work, where I might make the arrangements."

"Of course." Simon stepped forward to offer his hand. Madeline accepted, a frisson of pleasure at his touch thrumming over the surface of her skin. She rose, peering up at him with a yearning in her heart as his blue eyes gazed down at her to reflect the affinity she knew she must be exhibiting.

She and Molly must conduct their searches as quickly as possible because her future beckoned her. This chapter of death must be closed to proceed.

"Do you ... have plans for the day?" Madeline hesitated in letting go of him after she rose to her feet, wanting to prolong contact for just a second more. She had waited a lifetime to join her Eros. Now that they were approaching that day, her impatience knew no bounds.

He nodded his head toward the desk. "I must respond to our stewards. These past few days I have fallen behind ... due to distractions."

Such as being accused of murder.

He did not say it aloud, but Madeline could sense the words quivering in the air between them. Simon's gaze never left hers, and he was clearly longing for some time alone with her. Perhaps he was thinking of their kiss? The first proper one they had shared?

As if to confirm this theory, his gaze dipped to her mouth for a second before he stepped back to release her. Madeline felt a rush of despair at the broken contact, wishing they could begin anew without the blasted Home Office threatening their destined union.

* * *

"You are quite aware of who they are, so I shall not formally introduce them." Simon's voice was firm. Mrs. Bigsby was accompanying her daughter to dinner this evening. They had been neighbors for decades, nodded to each other in the street when boarding their respective carriages, and his late father had feuded with Mrs. Bigsby through their solicitors before eventually giving up on obtaining sole ownership over the garden linking their properties.

His mother sniffed. "I fail to comprehend this attitude. It is how we conduct ourselves in polite society."

"You will condescend by taking full advantage of your rank to lord it over them, and I will not allow it. We shall greet each other as longtime acquaintances and proceed to dinner."

"Why are you so adamant about this?"

Because Madeline will be my wife if I can prove my innocence. And, Mrs. Bigsby will be my mother-in-law.

That would prompt an entirely different argument which Simon was not willing to begin at this late hour. Madeline and her mother would be arriving soon, so it was imperative he obtain agreement from his mother without provoking a war as they walked through the front door. "I value my friendship with the Bigsbys, and I do not wish to make them feel inferior."

John coughed into his fist, his face pale in the light of the oil lamps. "I concur with Simon. We shall greet them as longtime friends. Father took it too far with Mrs. Bigsby in the past, talking nonsense about her at his clubs in an attempt to get her dismissed from projects throughout the peerage. It was not his finest hour, and being amicable is the least we can do to extend an olive branch."

Simon shot his older brother a look of gratitude. It was a flash of the man John had been before his health had begun to suffer, and he could not be more grateful for John's timing in revealing his true character. He had become so belligerent of late, which Simon assumed was due to his declining health.

"Your father would be most displeased," Isla retorted.

Simon's brother gave a dry laugh. "To be fair, Isla, Father spent a great deal of his time being displeased."

"It was his primary calling in this life," announced Nicholas with a sour tone.

Simon shot a fierce glance at his little brother, who was in an apathetic sprawl on the settee near the window. "Please assure me you are not here this evening to stoke tensions in a bid to amuse yourself?"

Nicholas shook his head, his expression foul. "I am here because we agreed I should be. I cannot help it if refraining from drink is making my head thrum like a toneless harp."

"Quiet it, then. I need you to display courtesy and respect for our guests."

Nicholas rolled his eyes before shutting them with an agonized expression. "Aye."

"Mother, we have lived next door to the Bigsbys for thirty years. We have greeted them in the street, and I have grown up alongside Madeline and Henrietta in the garden. I insist we treat them as old acquaintances."

Isla exhaled with a slight parting of the lips, the only sign she was appeased. "Very well. I suppose we can do away with the formalities in lieu of the time you spent together as children. But what if they are confused by the lack of introductions? Eleanor Bigsby knows well that we have never been formally introduced."

Simon had considered this, but he planned to welcome them as old friends. "MacNaby will announce dinner within minutes of their arrival, and then we shall engage in delightful conversation to make it clear what our attitude is."

That was the flaw in his plan. Isla tended to pick at her food while barely speaking and, of late, John grew grumpier as his bedtime drew closer. Nicholas had grown dour since they had learned of their nephews who were to inherit in

Simon's stead, and ever more sullen since embarking on sobriety in the past day or so.

That his family had not known about their guests did not help, or John might have slept in this morning to improve his stamina. This dinner was so unexpected. Nevertheless, Simon was invested in its success. Once he settled this quarrel with the duke and his relations, it would be time to pursue his own path, and Madeline was the companion he wished to have at his side when that day arrived, so Mrs. Bigsby must be treated as an honored guest. He would carry the entire conversation himself, if he must.

MacNaby spoke from behind, interrupting his thoughts. "Mrs. and Miss Bigsby."

Simon spun on his heels, rushing forward to bow over the hand of Mrs. Bigsby and then Madeline's. "Welcome to our home. We are, indeed, honored to have you."

Rising back up, Simon sought his composure as Madeline winked at him with mischief in her eyes. "Thank you for having us, Mr. Scott. We have long wished to enjoy the company within your home."

Mrs. Bigsby smiled politely in agreement, her amber eyes wary as she turned her gaze to the other occupants of the drawing room.

Simon flashed a grin, composing his face to turn back to his family. "Lord Blackwood, Lady Blackwood, Mr. Scott, are we not honored to host Mrs. Bigsby and her daughter?"

John had risen from his armchair, appearing heavy as he lumbered forward. "Welcome, Mrs. Bigsby. It is our honor to host you this evening."

"My lord." Mrs. Bigsby sank into a curtsy, displaying an unexpected grace for a woman of her stature. Being nearly the same height as Simon, it was one of the qualities that had fascinated him as a boy; he had imagined her as a warrior from an epic tale, striding into battle to strike fear in the hearts of her competitors. "It is a pleasure to visit your home. The art is splendid, and I notice several works by Thomas Lawrence—a true privilege to behold."

She pointed to the opposite wall where several large portraits of Scott ancestors stared at the inhabitants of the room.

"You know Lawrence's work?"

"Of course. We study all renowned artists in our quest for inspiration. Our manufactory takes pride in producing the finest works that will withstand the test of time."

Simon's tension eased as John and Madeline's mother moved to view the paintings. Dinner might prove a success despite his reservations.

* * *

MADELINE TOOK her seat at the elegant dining table, an original Chippendale if she were to guess, with tapered legs and intricate carving. It was bedecked with fine crystal, shiny silver, and exquisite china. Hothouse blooms were artfully arranged in porcelain pots, beeswax candles flickered from silver candelabras, and gilt-framed mirrors around the room strategically reflected the light to chase the shadows from the room. Footmen in fine livery were lined behind their chairs to attend them.

It was precisely what she had expected it to look like, and she was ecstatic to be invited, albeit under spurious circumstances.

"Where is Miss Carter?" Lady Blackwood sat at the end of the table, opposite to the baron. Her emotionless eyes cast about, evidently noting for the first time that Molly was not present. Madeline bit her lip, anxiety coiling in her stomach.

"Miss Carter is not well this evening, so she is taking a dinner tray in her bedchamber," replied Simon from near the head of the table where he was seated diagonal to the baron.

"I should see to her." Lady Blackwood made to rise, sending Madeline into panic. If Isla Scott returned to the family wing, it would be a disaster. It was Madeline's role to ensure such a thing did not happen.

I must stop her!

"Oh, Lady Blackwood! I am so disappointed! I have so anticipated speaking with you tonight." Mama narrowed her eyes from across the table, dubious at Madeline's words as she struggled to find an excuse to keep Lady Blackwood from leaving the dining room. "You are the envy of the entire neighborhood. I was hoping to convince you to reveal the identity of your modiste!"

Creases appeared between Mama's brows as her questions mounted. Her mother's disbelief was palpable as all gazes rested upon Madeline. It was true that Lady Blackwood was always attired in exquisite gowns, but the idea that Madeline would want such garments would be difficult to comprehend. The Bigsbys favored attractive but practical dresses, which allowed them to go about their work. In their world, expensive silk was only worn for formal dinners such as this.

Lady Blackwood settled back into her seat with her usual lack of expression, but Madeline sensed she was pleased to have her vanity pandered to. Perhaps she would forget Molly's absence if Madeline could distract her for sufficient time. The dowager baroness might be difficult to read, but her choice to never display emotions upon her face revealed at least one character trait for a businesswoman such as herself to utilize to her advantage—vanity.

"I confess, I am reticent on the subject. Nothing ruins a

good modiste more than being overwhelmed with more orders than she can manage."

Madeline blinked at the selfishness of the statement, though she supposed she should not be surprised by such arrogance from a prig of the privileged class.

Simon interjected from down the table. "Would you not want to elevate the proprietress in question? Bring her new clientele as a sign of appreciation for work well done?"

"Do not be naïve, dear boy. Your father always maintained that the lower classes are constantly seeking an opportunity to take advantage of their betters, and it is one's role to uphold the separation of the peerage from the common folk."

Nicholas sputtered out soup in startled mirth, dropping the spoon onto the table as he struggled to keep a straight face. Simon's jaw firmed in anger, Madeline able to perceive the hardening of his expression even from afar, and she wished to reassure him they were not offended. He opened his mouth to speak—

Lord Blackwood burst out laughing, ending on a cough into a lace-edged handkerchief that the footman, Duncan, raced forward to place in his hand. "Please forgive Lady Blackwood, Miss Bigsby. Her wit can be rather biting at times. My father certainly had specific ideas about classes, but we are more enlightened than he, or we would not be enjoying dinner with such admirable company."

It was obvious that the baron's interruption was intended to deflect any affront Isla Scott had inadvertently caused. Madeline noted Simon relax, and she guessed he was grateful that John had interceded. Not for the first time, she wondered if Lady Blackwood was a bit of an idiot. It would account for her vacuous expression and lack of original thoughts, along with the repetition of the late baron's abrasive philosophies.

Duncan stepped forward to wipe the tablecloth beside Nicholas's plate, placing a clean soup spoon and retreating back to his position.

Simon shot Madeline a glance of apology, introducing a discussion on a recent opera, and soon the topic was being discussed with enthusiasm, Nicholas returning to moping into his soup bowl. While Isla complained about the shabby costumes of the performers, Madeline's thoughts wandered to the young woman upstairs who was searching the rooms in the family wing while they dined two floors beneath her feet. She hoped that by the end of the night, Molly and she would have answered the question as to whether a murderer resided in this home.

No further incidents occurred, other than a strange moment when Isla knocked into a wineglass, but a footman shot forward to catch it before even a drop was spilled. The baroness's eyes flickered in gratitude to the servant. Roderick, if memory served Madeline correctly.

The baroness gifted a rare smile to the table in general. "How terribly clumsy of me! I suppose tensions have been a little high these past days with the news sheets casting such dreadful allegations against the family."

Madeline experienced a twinge of sympathy, realizing it must be difficult for the baroness to have her oldest son accused of violent crimes. "It is terrible how irresponsible journalists can be. They have no compunctions about questioning a gentleman's reputation despite the lack of evidence."

"Thank you, Miss Bigsby. Few understand the troubles associated with being in the public eye."

A couple hours later, Madeline and her mother departed with an unspecific promise to return for another lovely evening, and Madeline thanked her mother for her patience as they walked home through the garden.

Eleanor Bigsby chuckled without humor. "You refer to Lady Blackwood's remark about classes? Or how young Nicholas behaves like a spoilt little arse? Simon is a gentleman, so I shall prevail through occasional dinners with the dimwitted Lady Blackwood and arrogant lordling, if I must."

CHAPTER 11

"Psyche, armed only with her courage, descended into the underworld, passing through the gates of Hades with no promise of return."

Lucius Apuleius, Metamorphoses

* * *

OCTOBER 5, 1821

"The baron's desk held nothing of interest. Old journals, poetry from his youth, correspondence with friends. I found naught to suggest he knew about his nephews."

"What of Nicholas?"

Molly made a face. "I think his life consists of carousing. There were little personal items, at all. Just a few notebooks from his time at Oxford, no correspondence, a few novels, and old textbooks from his education."

"And the baroness?"

"Her room is as immaculate as her icy countenance. I was terrified I would leave evidence of my search, so it took the longest to search. There was a writing desk with four actual locks. I tried to find keys, but there was no sign of them anywhere. I even searched the vases and jewelry boxes, under her mattress … Perhaps she keeps them on her person."

"Hmm … That piques my interest, considering how much it costs to include the locks. She must be fastidious about her privacy." Madeline had not slept a wink all night, impatient to learn what Molly had found. It was a beautiful morning, the sky a crisp blue and the garden resplendent with foliage and twittering birds, but she had no time to pay it mind when such important events were afoot.

"I agree about the locks. They seem to have been added rather than part of the original design. But what motive could she have? Do you think the baroness is capable of hoisting a sculpture to beat a peer over the head?"

"We do not know what the workings of her mind are, and she could have had a servant do it. The duke and his friends have stated that a manservant is involved, so we must not discount it."

"Faugh, Madeline! Must I fear the servants, too?"

"I do not know, but we cannot declare our investigation complete unless we have viewed the contents of her desk. What could the baroness have locked inside that requires it? We must confirm the contents to lay our anxieties to rest."

Molly slumped back against the stone bench, her bonnet obscuring much of her features except for a pensive pout of the lips. "I must claim to be unwell a second time?"

Madeline hated the notion of another night of insomnia while she obsessed about the contents of a mysterious desk. "Perhaps I can visit to distract her. I will tell Mama I will not be going to the manufactory today so I can call on the baroness to thank her for hosting us last night. Might that get you into her rooms a second time?"

"I can try. There is no method to predict when the room will be empty, but I could keep watch and hope for the best. But what will it change if I do not have the keys?"

Madeline growled in frustration, before recalling an incident a few years earlier when the key to the door from the mews to the alley had broken in the lock. She had watched in fascination as her coachman had extracted the pieces out, then picked the lock open so he could replace it with a newer one. Johnson had worked in construction at one time, he had informed her.

It had not seemed too difficult as someone accustomed to carving stone. Perhaps he could show her how to do it. In turn, she could tutor Molly. She hoped the other woman was as handy as she was and that there was some method of relocking it when they were done.

If the contents proved to be benign, she and Molly could stop invading the Scotts' privacy and, at the appropriate time, she could confess to Simon what they had done. Her stomach protested that inevitable moment, but she was determined to proceed.

* * *

THEIR SOLICITORS HAD SENT word that a renowned barrister would be calling in the afternoon to discuss the investigation into the late Lord Filminster's death. The news had been a relief to receive, Simon impatient to call on the duke and offer his assistance so he might do something—anything—to begin making plans for his new life. Everything was stalled until he could settle this thing.

MacNaby's announcement from the door that their visitors had returned was met with a feeling of dread spreading through the pit of his stomach. He wondered if he could send them away until after his meeting with the barrister.

"Have you informed his lordship?"

"Yes, sir. Duncan has gone upstairs to collect him."

With an air of resignation—best to know what fresh and damning information had come to light—he bade the butler to show them in. Recalling Madeline's advice to utilize his skills in communication, he requested that coffee be brought in to combat the brisk chill of autumn.

The five gentlemen entered with their usual somber air. Halmesbury, Saunton, Filminster, the coxcomb Trafford, along with the odd youth Gideon, filed into the room to take up their usual positions.

Simon bowed to each in turn, attempting to conduct himself with the usual etiquette of meeting with such men, but the tension was palpable. Silence fell, Simon struggling for anything to say when outnumbered by five hostile opponents and not coming up with anything. It might have been different if they would speak so he could respond, but this was an unprecedented situation.

Minutes ticked by, the coffee tray brought in by Roderick, who informed him that his mother had requested that John drink his tea that the doctor had recommended, which was in a separate pot. Simon nodded without registering what he had said, as he considered the possibility that he might be arrested for a crime he had not committed.

Could he hang, despite his innocence?

Now that he could wed Madeline, should he allow her to step forward as his alibi? Would them taking vows mitigate the scandal?

And would Mrs. Bigsby testify that Madeline did visit with him in the garden on a regular basis? Even Henri, perhaps, if he was betrothed to Madeline?

The notion of putting Madeline or her family's business

at risk was not something he wished to contemplate. Surely there was another resolution to be found?

He was caught in a nightmare. So close to the life he had always dreamed of, only to be thwarted at the final hour. Had he done something to anger their creator so that he would be the butt of some cosmic jest?

The barrister cannot arrive soon enough!

John entered, his appearance bleary and his posture stooped as he walked over to take a seat in Simon's chair. Simon offered coffee around, but the men refused, so he prepared a cup of tea for his brother and passed it to John, who twisted his face when he saw what it was, but accepted it to take a sip.

Halmesbury cleared his throat, straightening from the window. "We regret to inform you that the movements of two of the servants could not be confirmed."

Simon bit his retort back, remaining silent so John could take the lead as the senior man on their side of this dispute.

John coughed into his handkerchief before responding. "Which two?"

The duke glanced to Gideon standing in the corner with his hat and gloves still on, before addressing the baron. "Duncan Campbell and Roderick MacGregor. As you know, Duncan was upstairs, but no one saw him the entire morning. We traced the route to Covent Garden and spoke with the flower seller who could not recollect whether he sold violets to the footman, Roderick, that morning. We also calculated the time, and it should not have taken him more than one to two hours to make the purchase, but he was absent for a minimum of three to four hours."

"What are you saying? That Roderick tried to kill Lord Trafford? That our second footman is willing to commit murder on behalf of Simon?" John sounded weak, taking another sip of tea, and Simon realized his brother was attempting to fortify himself. Shame washed over him to somehow have caused this blight on the Scott household while his brother was ill. Was it not enough that his brother must face the fact that people he did not know were to inherit the family title, while dealing with questions of his own mortality? A surge of anger that these men be so callous of his brother's health followed, as he clenched his fists to glare at the duke.

"Runners have been employed to observe your home and servants. We deem this necessary for the safety of our families. They will be stationed in the street outside. The Home Office has been apprised of the information we have gathered, and a new coroner is being appointed to the case. It is expected that an inquest will be called, and Simon shall be named a suspect. We felt it proper to inform you directly, as a courtesy."

Silence followed, John placing his teacup down on the saucer with a clink while Simon attempted to digest the news that he was to be publicly accused of murder. Seconds later, he noticed that their visitors had riveted their attention to his brother with varying degrees of alarm, and turning about, he found John was panting with a hand to his chest— *over his heart!*

In a panic, Simon burst forward to catch his brother as he tumbled from the chair, when a band of steel wrapped around his own abdomen to hold him back. The towering duke of nearly seven feet had caught him in an uncompromising embrace while the youth, Gideon, raced forward to kneel by John's side.

"What is this?" His shout broke the eerie silence of the study, but the duke held him back still, despite his struggle to break free. The man was a monster! Simon was a large man himself, but no one could fight off such a giant!

The fop followed Gideon over, standing aside as the

youth began to examine the baron. "Calm yourself, Scott. Gideon is a skilled physician. We brought him in the event of a medical incident."

Relief swept over him as Gideon undid John's cravat to pull it loose, before unfastening the buttons of his waistcoat to pull it open. It was hard to believe that such a young lad could be a doctor, but he relaxed, the duke slowly releasing him until he was standing free.

"I need assistance lifting him." The sound of a woman's voice had Simon tensing up again, racing forward to kneel at John's side as, before his eyes, Gideon pulled off his gloves and tossed his hat aside. Time slowed down as Simon watched a heavy coil of plaited blonde hair unravel down his —*her*—back!

"What the living hell?"

Trafford cleared his throat. "I may have misspoken. I mean to say ... Lady Trafford is a skilled physician."

"This is ... your wife?"

"No time for this. I need to lift him." The pragmatic tone of the viscountess brought Simon's reeling senses back to the present priority. John was an alarming shade of gray mottled with red that spoke to the urgency of the moment as he wheezed in pained hysteria. Simon slid an arm under his brother's back to lift him to a half-sitting position. Lady Trafford quickly pulled the coat and waistcoat off in sections with Simon adjusting his hold. Finally, she grabbed hold of John's linen shirt and lifted it off in two stages as Simon moved his arm.

"Lower him."

Simon complied, following her gaze to see she was noting large purple and dark brown splotches that marred John's torso. He frowned at the discolorations, which appeared to be chronic. "What is it?"

The viscountess failed to respond, leaning down to sniff

at John's skin. "Lord Blackwood, it is rather early in the day. Did you consume garlic at breakfast?"

John's eyes displayed his terror as he continued to wheeze, but he shook his head.

She turned her silver gaze to Simon. "Was dinner heavily seasoned with garlic?"

"No. John does not much care for it, so Cook only applies light quantities to our meals. What is it?"

She leaned down to peer into John's eyes. "My lord, what medicines do you take?"

"Some … laudanum … Nothing …else."

"Any skin creams?"

John shook his head, his confusion evident. Lady Trafford pulled back to address Simon.

"And, Mr. Scott, to your knowledge, does anyone else in your home suffer from the symptoms of his lordship? Chest pains, coughing, shortness of breath, the odor of garlic, changes in skin pigmentation on the front, back, limbs, soles, or palms?"

Simon shook his head. He was still in shock to see the state of John's skin beneath his clothes and frantic that his brother had not informed him of how poor his health was.

"Pins and needles, abdominal pain, swelling or reddening of the skin, or white spots?"

"No ill health, to my knowledge. My younger brother has issues from old injuries, but nothing else."

"And Lord Blackwood has a physician?"

Considering the emergency, Simon thought it would not be the time to mince words. "White is an ancient, drug-peddling quack. I doubt he can diagnose an illness which requires any judgment." It was true—the evidence was bared. Dr. White was useless if his brother was in this condition, and the physician had never asked such specific questions.

Lady Trafford cocked her head, staring down at the

discoloration. "I am afraid we need to empty his lordship's stomach with some urgency. It will not be … pleasant."

John reached up to grab her wrist, staring up with terror in his eyes. "Wh … why?" he croaked out.

"You have been poisoned, Lord Blackwood. Gradually and for some time, by my estimation."

Simon's jaw dropped open as he leaned back on his heels to rake his hair in anguish. "What?"

"Lord Blackwood has consumed arsenic for some time. See how some of the discolorations appear older than others? If you lean down, you can smell the odor of garlic seeping from his pores. If no one else in the household has any of these symptoms, it would suggest that Lord Blackwood consumes something that the rest of the family does not. We will take him to his rooms, and he must drink large quantities of tepid water with egg white, sugar, and magnesia, which will cause him to … empty his stomach. Who can prepare it while I attend him?"

Simon shook his head in confusion. "One of the servants. I shall call for them."

Lady Trafford stayed him from rising. "Nay, Mr. Scott."

Trafford dropped down on his knees beside his wife. "You wish it to be someone who has not been in residence too long?"

Lady Trafford nodded.

"How long, Audrey?" Trafford asked.

"Less than six months."

Simon threw up his hands in question. It was as if an entire conversation had been conducted and he had missed the discussion. "What are you talking about?"

Across the room, the Earl of Saunton stood observing. "Mr. Scott, someone needs to assist your brother, who cannot be the one guilty of poisoning him. Someone who has been in your household for less than six months."

The implications filtered in, and Simon realized the truth. "I—we—have a poisoner living under our roof? Someone is trying to kill my brother?"

"It would appear so, Mr. Scott. Someone has been trying to kill your brother off. Lady Trafford will treat him, but someone needs to help. Someone we can trust. Someone who has been here no more than six months. You do not meet these criteria."

Simon raked his hair again as his spinning thoughts swirled with the ramifications of John's poor health. He recalled Nicholas's lament over their change in circumstances just the day before. His little brother would not attempt to clear a path to Simon inheriting, would he? It seemed too terrible to consider, but perhaps his guilt over Nicholas's injuries had blinded him to his brother's true character? "His issues began more than a year ago, not six months." Simon knew there would be a time when he needed to make sense of all this, but right now, with his brother wheezing with panic on the floor, he must answer the immediate question. "I do not know the specifics of the maids in the kitchen, but Molly Carter joined our household less than six months ago. Four or five at most."

"Then Miss Carter must be summoned. We need her help to brew the water and ingredients. And we need a sheet so we can help you carry Lord Blackwood to his bedchamber."

Simon nodded, springing to his feet to ring the bell. John needed treatment as the first priority. Questions would have to wait.

* * *

MADELINE WAITED IN THE GARDEN, but Molly did not return at the agreed time. Checking her timepiece did nothing to speed up the passage of time, each second ticking at the pace of a snail crossing over a leaf.

It was quite unlike her friend, and Madeline knew something was wrong. Perhaps Molly was caught in a conversation from which she could not escape? Or, perhaps, some fresh hell had broken loose in the Scott household and her friend could not get away to inform Madeline of the latest development.

All she knew was, the more minutes that passed at a terrible and painful pace, the more butterflies settled in her stomach to make her queasy with worry. She suffered a dreadful feeling of unrelenting doom until she could no longer stand it. She wanted to squeal at the sheer, insistent frustration that was building up to consume her. Somehow, despite her patience this past decade, she no longer possessed an iota of forbearance. There must be some method of resolving this mess.

She wished she had signaled Simon the night before to meet in the garden after dinner, but her guilt over searching his study was sure to spill from her lips if she was not careful, so she had remained at home after the meal.

A full hour later than the time she and Molly had agreed to, Madeline stood up to return inside. Paying a call on Lady Blackwood would at least reveal if the Scotts were amid a worsening crisis. She might even steal a minute conversation with Simon to ensure he was well.

* * *

SIMON and the men stood in the hall, the sound of retching from John's bedchamber producing a somber air as they waited. Lady Trafford, her husband, and Molly were inside assisting his brother to empty his stomach after the mixture and a tub had been brought up, along with clothing from

Trafford's carriage so his wife could change. Evidently, they did not wish the servants to observe that Lady Trafford had been dressed as a gentleman.

He winced in sympathy when he heard John cast up his accounts yet again. The young baron, Filminster, gazed at the closed door with a pained expression, while the duke had walked away to gaze out the window at the end of the corridor.

The Earl of Saunton, however, stood leaning against a wall with a nonchalance that seemed oddly out of place. As the sound of vomiting receded, Simon frowned at the earl, irate at the nobleman's composure while he tried to come to terms with the knowledge that someone had been attempting to murder his brother for a year or more.

Horror and impatience merged, and he could no longer withhold a rebuke. "You seem unnaturally calm under the circumstances."

"I have some experience with the ill, and I have recently dealt with death, Mr. Scott. I am more prepared than most for such a moment."

Simon gritted his teeth. "Fair enough."

The earl studied him with emerald-green eyes that glowed in the half light shining in from the window. "You understand that this will result in further investigation?"

Simon cursed, dropping his chin despite the crisp edges of his collar digging in. Did they suspect him of this, too? It was damning that the man who held the title that Simon was suspected of killing the Baron of Filminster for was now proven to be the victim of foul play, too.

From down the hall, the duke's baritone interrupted his torment. "Your anguish for Lord Blackwood appears sincere, Scott. I had to use all my strength to hold you back when you panicked at his collapse."

Simon let out a dry, humorless chuckle. "Huzza! You do

wonders for my self-esteem with such a declaration. I was naught but a feeble milksop, struggling to fend you off."

"Not at all. I had the advantage of gripping you from behind. My apologies, but I did not know your intentions, and Lady Trafford needed freedom to act."

"And now? Do you think me capable of engaging in violent crime?"

The duke turned to gaze at him with a solemn expression, filling the window with his large form. "Your distress for his health appears genuine, but it does result in questions given the cause of his illness."

"Who would want to poison John, you mean?"

"Indeed. It also implies that we were correct in our theory that my father-in-law was murdered by someone in this household. If not you, then who?"

"Poisoning is an act of premeditation. Your father-in-law was killed in an act of passion. Would that point to two different perpetrators?"

"Nay, Mr. Scott. You describe the problem from the wrong angle. Poison is the weapon of patience, while clubbing someone to death in a fit of rage suggests that the killer had run out of time. The late baron was persistent ... and annoying. If the killer believed he had to act in haste, he might choose a vastly different method than his nature dictates."

Simon shook his head in disbelief. "I cannot say who may have done it. There has been no indication of violence from members of this household. Perhaps Lady Trafford is incorrect about the cause?"

"Perhaps, but Lady Trafford searched through your brother's things while she was waiting to begin the treatment. She could not find anything that contained arsenic to explain his symptoms. You should think about how he could have received it ... and who might have given it to him."

Memories of Nicholas and Duncan flashed through his mind. Duncan spent a significant amount of his time committed to John's well-being, but the head footman had also assisted with Nicholas after his accident. They had become friendly, as close to friends as a servant and child of the nobility might become under such circumstances. But the servant had always seemed intelligent and practical to Simon. The thought that Duncan might be coerced into murder by his younger brother seemed incongruent with his affable character.

Simon shook his head. "I cannot believe anyone in this household could be a cold-blooded killer."

The duke shrugged. "Unfortunately, your belief, or lack thereof, does not signify. If not you, then who?"

It was a rhetorical question, the duke shifting his gaze back to the window as Simon's thoughts scattered in every direction as leaves in a strong wind.

CHAPTER 12

"The voice warned her: 'Do not open the box, no matter what you desire, for it contains only peril.'"

Lucius Apuleius, Metamorphoses

* * *

*A*fter retching his guts out, John was drowsy and falling asleep in his bed. His color was slightly improved since his collapse in the study, and his breathing had eased. Footmen had removed the evidence of his emptied stomach, and the windows had been thrown open to air out the room.

Lady Trafford had requested lavender water to dispel the noxious odor of illness, and was now instructing Molly on the baron's care.

"You are to keep the door closed at all times. No one must have access to the baron until an investigation has been conducted. I will have meals delivered from our own kitchens, but he is not to eat or drink anything from this house."

Molly nodded, her face pale and earnest while Simon listened on with gratitude that Lady Trafford was a woman committed to the art of healing, and practical about the security of the situation. He had already been informed that he would not have access to John, which he had agreed to. The duke was more than willing to remove John to his own townhouse if there was any balking at Lady Trafford's instructions, but John wished to remain in his own rooms, so he had directed Simon to cooperate fully. Simon concurred, noting that his brother was weak and did not need the undue stress of being moved after such prolonged and violent vomiting.

"A guard from our home will be arriving soon to stand in the hall, so if you do need to rest or leave the room, he will ensure no one else enters while you are otherwise occupied. My husband will introduce you directly, so there is no question that he is the guard we summoned and he, in turn, will introduce you to his replacement for the evening shift."

Simon's cousin bobbed her head in acknowledgment, leaning in to whisper as she glanced over to his brother, "Will he be all right?" John was frail and helpless within the embrace of the canopied bed.

Lady Trafford paused, lowering her voice so that the patient would not overhear. "It will be a long and painful recovery. Arsenic corrodes the organs, but I believe the doses have been minute, likely to persuade a coroner that he suffered from a long illness. I think Lord Blackwood's health will improve without those doses."

Simon realized he had been holding his breath in an effort to overhear the viscountess answer from several feet away. Exhaling heavily, he stroked his beard with a trembling hand. Anger and confusion warred for domination. Who was there to be angry at, without knowing who was behind this? Well … There was one person with whom he was livid—the incompetent Dr. White!

Was the old fool a fellow conspirator to whomever was trying to kill John?

Nay, it seemed more likely White had missed the signs. Nevertheless, Simon was going to demand some answers by sending for the doctor.

* * *

MADELINE LIFTED the heavy brass knocker and brought it down on the door, rapping as hard as she could for several seconds. Still there was no response, causing her growing queasiness to increase. Something was wrong—she could feel it in the pit of her stomach.

Why were the servants not answering?

She tried one more time, then gave up to head home. After striding through her home, she exited through the library terrace and hurried down to the shared garden to access the Scotts' property. Making her way up to their terrace, she approached Simon's study to see if he was in.

Peering in the window, while being careful to use the wall as a shield, Madeline experienced the first flush of relief when she caught sight of him at his desk, scribbling with a quill upon a page. Reaching out, she rapped her knuckles on the window. The sound was muted by her glove, but Simon straightened to look over to where she was hiding. Catching sight of her, he rose from his seat to stride across the room and open the terrace door.

"Madeline?" He stood aside, ushering her in with a wave of his hand as he peered about to ensure no one witnessed her entry.

She entered, pausing to glance up at him, noting the tell-tale signs of strain. The accusations against him were wearing him down—she could see it in the shadows across his face and the rigid set of his shoulders. How she wished she could do more than merely ease his burdens.

"You should not be here." His voice was gruff, but his blue eyes ran over her with appreciation. "You look lovely."

Madeline hesitated, reaching up to check her bonnet and tucking in an errant lock of hair. "Do you know where Molly is? She was to meet me more than an hour ago?"

Simon's face hardened. "Molly is with John. He ... has taken a turn for the worse ... and ..." It seemed as if he wished to say more. "I will have to explain later. Tonight, perhaps? In the garden? I must send for his physician and inform the family to ... I ... Can we meet after dinner?"

She nodded, blinking in surprise at his vacillating sentences which were uncharacteristic of him. "I shall wait for you."

Simon reached out to take her hand up in his, lowering his head to press a kiss to her knuckles. "I must speak with my mother and Nicholas about John with some urgency. Can you let yourself out?"

"Of course."

He smiled briefly, crossing the room to fold the page he had been writing on and head out the door. Madeline stood watching as he shut the door behind him and tried to think what to do. She was supposed to show Molly how to pick locks, and despite her agreement to leave, Madeline was still obsessing over the mystery of the writing desk in Isla's bedchamber.

She stared at the door and considered climbing the stairs to the third floor to find Isla's rooms. The floor plan of the Scotts' home was the same as theirs, just reversed. Isla was in the back rooms facing the gardens, which was the equivalent of Madeline's own at the head of the back staircase. She knew this because Simon had mentioned how the family had moved about after his father had died a little less than two years earlier. If he was calling the Scotts together to discuss his brother's health, Isla would not be there, or would be summoned away shortly. It would be so easy to exit the study, find the entrance to the servants' staircase, and race up to the third floor.

Madeline bounced on her toes, impatience brimming through her as she rose and fell with a nervous energy that pressed her to move forward. She reached up to remove her bonnet to aid in her peripheral vision, still debating what she would do.

What if I am caught?

There is so much at stake! I cannot just stand by.

It is a horrible invasion of privacy.

It was. If Isla had nothing of import within the locked drawers, Madeline would feel awful about what she had done.

Then a chilling thought struck her as a slap across the face. Simon had said John's health had taken a turn for the worse. What if he was too ill to defend Simon from the Home Office investigation? She lost her calm as she followed this train of thought.

What if John dies?

There would be no one to shield Simon from an accusation of murder if the baron was gone, and the heir was not yet arrived. A nephew who was a stranger to Simon and who might believe the allegation over Simon's word.

That settled it. Proprieties be damned. If she was caught, she would have to face it. Perhaps she could say she was looking for the necessary. Someone needed to ensure that Simon did not take the blame for this terrible crime.

If one of the Scotts had done it, if he was arrested, and she had stood by and done nothing … Madeline leaned her head back to stare at the ceiling above, panting with anxiety, then fixed her gaze on the door. Right across from the study would be the entrance to the servants' staircase, and all she had to do was cross the room, open the door carefully to ensure no one was about, and dash across the hall. A tingle of nervous anticipation raced through her veins, and she lifted her foot to take a step. And another. And soon she had reached the door and was on her way to Isla Scott's private rooms.

There were no servants upon the stairs, and she could hear clanging from the kitchens below, but no one was about as she quickly began her ascent. She was grateful to be wearing her slippers, making barely any sound at all as she raced up the steps with her skirts in hand. Scarcely believing her good fortune, she reached the third level and placed her ear to the door. Cracking it open, she peered through the crack but saw no movements. If the baron was ill, the servants might be occupied on the second floor where his bedchamber was. Licking lips that had gone dry, Madeline entered the hall and crossed to the baroness's bedchamber door, placing her ear against it to listen for the sounds of occupation. She prayed that Miss Dubois, the attractive but sour French lady's maid, was occupied elsewhere in the grand house.

After waiting a minute, her pulse racing with fear that a servant or Isla would appear, Madeline cracked the door open to reveal an unoccupied room.

She exhaled in relief, entering to shut herself in and look about. It was a boudoir, as elegant as the baroness herself, with blue silk wallpaper, gilt-framed landscapes of lochs and forests, and an intricate rug woven with blues and greens covering the polished floorboards. Positioned near the window was an elegant chaise lounge adorned with blue and green tartan pillows. Somehow, the room managed to be both beautiful and austere, not unlike its inhabitant.

But that was neither here nor there. She had but minutes to contend with the narrow davenport writing desk, with a sloped surface covered in rich leather. Madeline approached, finding the four drawers on the side of the desk that each boasted a keyhole. Molly was right. It appeared the brass locks had been added at a different time.

Crouching down onto her knees, Madeline pulled the desk forward on the casters, wincing at the creaking. She reached into her reticule to pull out the pins that her coachman had fashioned for such a purpose. Resting her face against the wood of the desk, she began to work the first lock while listening for the click.

It turned out to be rather simple, and soon she had the top drawer ajar and was rifling through the contents. There were some writing supplies, quill nibs, pencils, and blank pages, but at the back was a stack of folded letters tied with a ribbon. Madeline reached deep to grab hold of them, pulling them out to read the address written on the outer folds.

Her fingers were shaking as she leafed through them, terrified a servant might walk in at any moment. Struggling to focus on the writing, she gasped in surprise, forgetting about the risk of being caught as she comprehended what she was holding. When Molly and she had discussed their plan, it had been the move of a desperate woman willing to do anything to help the man she loved. She could not attest that she had expected to find something, but what she now beheld was the most damning of evidence.

The top letter was addressed to Lord Blackwood in faded ink, so likely the father and not the current baron lying ill on the floor below. The return address was noted as Bianca Scott of Firenze.

Madeline leafed through the stack, which was about an

inch thick, the pages yellowed with age. The letters at the bottom were from the same address but from Peter Scott. These had been written nearly three decades earlier, before he had died in Italy!

It was what she had been looking for, but not expecting to find. Had the late baron Blackwood received these and given them to his wife? Or had Isla somehow intercepted them and hidden them away all these years? Either led back to the fact that the baroness had been well aware of Peter Scott's nuptials, and therefore the children born from that marriage.

I must make haste to read these letters in the safety of my own home!

Madeline pushed the drawer shut, fiddling with the long brass pins to lock the drawer while her fingers trembled something fierce. It was horrifying to contemplate the significance of what she had found. Stuffing the letters into her reticule, she scrambled to her feet, pushed the desk back into place, and made for the door.

Listening carefully, she heard no sound, so departed to cross the hall and enter the back stairs just as the door swung open to reveal one of the footmen. Roderick, she thought was his name, froze in surprise, then glanced over her shoulder to the door of Isla's rooms.

* * *

IT WAS A BIG HOUSE, with countless rooms, so Simon did not know if Nicholas or his mother had heard about the incident with John. He was aware the servants must be in an uproar, Duncan having brought the bedsheet that the lords had used to carry his brother up to his rooms on the second floor. MacNaby had arrived, only to be turned away by the duke and his friends, with an instruction that the servants were not to access the hall to John's rooms. The butler's amiable demeanor had splintered, as he had dashed away to inform those belowstairs.

Simon was sure the kitchen was agog to have Molly and Lord Trafford invading the recesses of the basement to prepare the magnesia mixture that had been fed to John.

Their visitors were still upstairs awaiting the guards, but when John had slipped into sleep, Simon had decided it was the time for answers.

After inking the note to summon Dr. White, Simon had left Madeline in his study. He wished he could tell her what had transpired, but the words had not come. It was not something to blurt out as he raced away, so he thought that by this evening, he could gather his wits to explain what had happened. How his brother was being—he choked at the thought—*poisoned* into his declining health of the past eighteen months. Barking out such incredible information while he was in a hurry seemed ill-advised.

Then, too, he wished to break the news to Nicholas himself posthaste. His younger brother was the most likely culprit. He stood the most to gain after Simon, and to discover if he were involved, Simon would disclose the events so he could gauge Nicholas's reaction.

Climbing the main staircase to the third floor, Simon headed to the front bedroom, which faced the street, and knocked on the door. Two wings of the house were accessed down long corridors leading away from either side of the landing, and he supposed after he had spoken with his brother, Simon might check to see if his mother was in her bedchamber.

"Who is it?" The tone was both belligerent and morose. Nicholas had not had a drink for two days, and his mood was both sour and miserable. Simon paused, wondering if his younger brother's change of heart could have been brought on by a bout of guilt. Had Nicholas bludgeoned the Baron of Filminster to death in a drunken rage? Was that the reason he was reconsidering his abuse of the liquor?

Simon gave a quick shake of his head to clear his thoughts before reaching to open the door.

* * *

MADELINE PERCHED on the edge of the settee, too embarrassed to look the baroness directly in the eyes as she fidgeted about. Her shame was made worse by the knowledge that her reticule was stuffed full of correspondence she had stolen from the baroness.

"Roderick, bring us a tray of the ... Ceylon tea."

Madeline glanced up at the strange pause to find Isla staring at her, her face expressionless in the midday light shining through the windows of the family drawing room.

The footman hesitated, before responding in a halting voice, "The ... *Ceylon* ... tea?"

Lady Blackwood's eyelids fluttered as if she were mildly irritated. "That is correct. Hurry it along."

"The same tea as Lord Blackwood drinks?"

"That is correct. And, Roderick, make it strong. Miss Bigsby has the appearance of a young lady who enjoys a strong cup of tea."

Madeline flushed, mortified that the servant had escorted her to the baroness to explain he had found her in the hall by her bedchamber. Ever since that announcement, Madeline had been waiting for a rain of questions, but Lady Blackwood had simply ordered tea. Lifting her shaking hands, Madeline wrung them together until she noticed the baroness flicker her eyes down to the agitated movement. Not wanting to draw attention to her overstuffed reticule,

Madeline laid her hands on her lap and commanded them to remain still.

"My mother always said a cup of tea could grease any social interactions. It makes all parties feel at home." Isla Scott's tone was as modulated as her expression, giving nothing of her thoughts away as it clawed through Madeline's belly and set her heart hammering. She had not thought her pulse could race any faster than it had been when she had had the temerity to invade the baroness's chambers, but there was a hitherto unknown speed it could accelerate to. Madeline could barely contain the flight of panic, but did through sheer force of will. The noblewoman sitting before her might be a cold-blooded killer, and Madeline must maintain her composure until she could speak with Simon. She suspected she would unravel when that moment arrived, babbling out what she had done and what she had discovered as a consequence. How angry would Simon be when she revealed her sneaking about to find the letters for him?

"Tea is a most hospitable offering," mumbled Madeline, her thoughts scattered into the wind as she attempted to pull herself back together.

"What were you doing on the third floor?"

"I was looking for Molly. I realize it was most improper to enter your home, but I was worried about her. She was to meet me this morning. When no one answered my knock at the front door, I ... thought ... I ... um ... would try to find her."

The baroness narrowed her eyes just a fraction. They were a deep and fascinating blue in the afternoon light. Madeline could not make out the black of her pupils, which were mere pinpoints to disrupt the expanse of vivid color. Perhaps Isla Scott was sensitive to the bright light?

"You are friends with Miss Carter?"

"We chat after breakfast."

"I see."

The conversation came to a halt, and Madeline waited in frustration until she realized that Lady Blackwood was awaiting the tea. Perhaps she needed it to *grease* their interaction. Madeline waited in silence, drowning in a swirl of emotions, while she commanded her eyes to remain fixed on the room.

Do not draw attention to the reticule!

The silence drew on for several minutes, the only sound the ticking of a clock on the mantel and the sound of Madeline's heart thumping loud enough to wake the dead.

"I wanted …" Madeline attempted to recollect what she had been about to say. "Thank you for a lovely dinner. You run a gracious household, Lady Blackwood."

The baroness stared back at her without comment, ratcheting Madeline's nerves until she was dizzy with distress.

"Do you … have plans for this evening?"

Lady Blackwood continued to regard her without speaking. Madeline was enthralled by the incandescent blueness of her gaze, feeling the tug of hidden riptides pulling her beneath the surface of the endless ocean reflected in their depths. With a surge of relief, Madeline heard the door open, and Roderick entered with a tea tray.

Soon the tray was settled on the table between them, and the baroness had poured two cups, offering one to Madeline. The baroness held the saucer and cup on her lap but did not take a drink.

"Try it, Miss Bigsby. It is an exceptional blend from the shores of Ceylon."

Madeline looked down into her cup, trying to think what to say. "I thought they grew coffee in Ceylon?"

"They do, but I discovered these delightful tea leaves from the region. I blend it with premium Indian leaves. Please try it and tell me what you think?" The baroness bobbed her head in encouragement, her expression remaining stoic.

Madeline tentatively took a sip. It had a pleasant flavor with a rich aroma. The fragrance of exotic lands along with just a hint of … She frowned, trying to place it—garlic?

"It is delightful."

Lady Blackwood bestowed her with a hint of a smile. "The taste matures. Drink it up and you will see."

Madeline politely sipped more, putting the cup back on the saucer when the cup was half empty. Her heart rate had picked up again after having calmed to a more sedate pace, and she was too warm. Perhaps the day was too hot for such a hot beverage.

The baroness leaned forward to peer into Madeline's cup, settling back with a satisfied air. Perhaps Simon's mother took inordinate pride in her tea blend?

"Miss Bigsby, you must forgive my impudence, but are you hoping to make a match with my son?"

Madeline's throat closed up in frantic reaction. She did not know how to respond, her heart pounding so loud she could not hear her own thoughts. "I … My mother has hired a matchmaker to seek a suitable gentleman."

"Someone appropriate to run your little stone business?"

Madeline picked up her tea to drink some more, attempting to calm the anxiety racing through her body. Her breath was coming in alarming pants. She was accustomed to dealing with difficult conversations but, for some reason, she was struggling to maintain her calm as her body reacted with alarming oversensitivity.

Finish this conversation and leave!

She could feel a flush stealing across the surface of her face, and Madeline tried to think what the shortest path to departing would be.

"I … Yes." Madeline could no longer disguise her panic as

she wheezed to draw air. Her throat was closing up and spots were appearing before her eyes. Desperate to maintain the appearance of calm, she grabbed the cup to drink again, hoping the hot liquid might provide solace to her raging anxiety.

"I do not think so. I think you have plotted to raise your station in this world by attempting to trap my boy into a wedding. Is that not why you were sneaking through the house? You wish to force his hand, perhaps, by causing a scandal so you might join the nobility?"

Madeline frowned, dropping the cup with a clatter onto the floor as she gripped her stomach. Searing pain had her doubling over. The baroness ignored all of it, continuing to speak as if nothing were out of place.

"My son was meant for greater things. He has a destiny to fulfill, and I shall not permit you to interfere. I thought I had rid us of you once, but here you are again, like a pernicious weed determined to ruin his life. It took considerable persuasion, but my husband finally heeded my warnings to keep Simon from meeting you. That night … it was as if destiny itself intervened, pushing Nicholas from the window and driving the two of you apart. A dreadful time, having my youngest son so near death, but I admit to a certain euphoria that Simon eventually came to understand his duty. He shall be the first of my line to ascend to an English title."

Madeline could not follow the rambling threads, crumpling onto the floor as she struggled to focus on the room. Black shadows were filling her vision as she gasped for air, and with growing horror, she realized it was not her emotions causing such high-strung reactions—she had been poisoned!

Isla Scott rose to her feet and crossed the room, gazing down at Madeline from her imposing height. She stood, poised like a murderous china doll, her contempt radiating in waves of malice. "This will end soon, Miss Bigsby. You ought to have known your place. You are but a lowly trade rat, while Simon ... Simon is a god, descended from a noble Scottish clan. He shall be the greatest Baron of Blackwood ever to grace this earth. It is his destiny. And yours ... is to be cast out with the refuse."

With that, the baroness stepped over Madeline's writhing body and left the room, closing the door behind her. Madeline could feel a darkness reaching up to pull her into the abyss, pain racking through her abdomen as she tried to claw her way to the door for help. Her reticule was a cannonball roped around her wrist, but she was determined that the letters be found. She had loved Simon for so long, and she refused to allow death to claim her when they were so close to uniting. He was her Eros. They were destined to live for an eternity in their celestial garden, united by mutual love and respect. It could not end this way.

The door might as well have been seven miles away, each inch of progress a battle of will against her perishing body as she heaved and moaned. Then the door began to swing open, and fate itself intervened with a miracle as Simon appeared.

"Dy ... ing," she panted, clutching her stomach to quell the pain.

CHAPTER 13

"Upon opening the box, Psyche fell into a deathlike sleep, for inside was not beauty, but a sleep that belonged to the underworld."

Lucius Apuleius, Metamorphoses

* * *

Simon had thought this day could not get any worse, but opening the door of the family drawing room in search of his mother had revealed a nightmare beyond the tolerance of any man. His love crumpled on the floor.

"Dy ... ing," Madeline moaned, curling into a ball.

It was as if time slowed down. Running forward, he dropped to his knees beside her to assess what the hell was wrong with her. Scooping her up, he brushed the hair from her face and noted her skin was red and swollen. There was an odor of orange blossoms, tea, and ... He choked in shock. *Garlic!*

Recalling the symptoms Lady Trafford had called out earlier when attending to his brother, Simon realized Madeline had remained in his home after he left her in the study. Someone must have persuaded her to drink the tea on the table as an opportunity to trick her into consuming arsenic. There was only one person whom it could be, because he had just left Nicholas in his bedchamber. He wished he knew why, but this was not the time to contemplate such things. Madeline needed his help.

"Madeline, it will be fine." Holding her in a tight embrace, he hauled to his feet, fear humming through his veins to weaken his grip on sanity at the very thought of a world without his Psyche. "I am taking you to a doctor. Just breathe, my love. Just breathe."

Simon prayed the Traffords were still here. Last he had seen of their visitors, they had requested their carriages be brought to the front after their guards had arrived to protect John. Hitching Madeline high, while she whimpered in pain, Simon hastened toward the front hall.

With a light-headed relief, he saw Lady and Lord Trafford exiting the front door and shouted out to stay them. The couple spun around at the yelling, Lady Trafford's eyes riveting to the figure in his arms as she raced forward without hesitation.

"Who is this?" she asked, examining Madeline in his arms.

"My heart," was the response Simon could croak out in anguish. "Is it arsenic?"

Lady Trafford tilted her head as she peered down at the moaning slip squirming in his arms. "Current circumstances would suggest it, but a much higher quantity." Lady Trafford turned to her husband, who was hovering a few feet away with an expression of alarm. "Julius, do we still have some of the magnesia mixture left?"

Trafford nodded. "Unless the kitchen staff have thrown it out. We made much more than we used, but it will need to be reheated."

Lady Trafford turned her silver gaze back to Simon. "I suggest we go to the kitchens. Your ... heart ... needs more urgent care than your brother did, so we should see to her right there."

Simon nodded, spinning on his heel to head toward the servants' staircase. "Madeline is strong. One of the strongest people I know. She will be well. She ... must be well."

Despite his assertion, Simon's soul was in turmoil. This was his fault—he should have informed Madeline of what had happened with John. She had not known about the poison, or she would not have drunk the tea he had seen laid out on the table. Tea, which pointed to the culprit more than any other clue to date. She had not possessed the facts to protect herself.

Damn it, why did I not take the time to tell her what was happening?

If she died ... God forbid, he could not even think about such an outcome. She had to live, or he would follow her to the afterlife in his despair.

* * *

MADELINE PROTESTED when Simon placed her down on a hard surface, reluctant to be parted as she fought against the gathering shadows. She reached to cling to him, not willing to let him go.

The soft press of lips brushed over her forehead. "Lady Trafford is going to make you better, Madeline."

"Who ..."

"She is a physician who helped John this morning."

He released her, and a figure stepped forward to help Madeline into a seated position as a cup was brought to her mouth. "Drink, Miss Bigsby. I know you are struggling to breathe, but you must drink."

Madeline was confused at the presence of an unknown woman instructing her, gulping down the tepid mixture and spewing much of it when she attempted to draw air in her lungs. Half the contents must be pooled on the floor, not to mention her bodice was soaked through, but before she could fall back to the table, she was presented with a second cup.

"Again, Miss Bigsby."

After the second cup, the gagging began, and a bucket was thrust beneath her chin as she began to cast up her accounts, which was an odd combination of shame, agony, and sweet, sweet relief.

* * *

SIMON AND LORD TRAFFORD stood aside, averting their eyes as Madeline suffered the indignity of vomiting. He had ushered the servants out of the kitchen to allow her some modesty but, truthfully, it had given him something to do as he stood about helpless.

"This is the young lady you were with the night of the coronation?"

He swallowed hard, but considering the circumstances, he must pray for Trafford's discretion. In for a penny, in for a pound.

"Yes."

"Who is she?"

"The daughter of our next-door neighbor. It was an innocent encounter—that night. Miss Bigsby and I did not ... engage in anything untoward. We merely conversed."

Trafford mused over this, taking many seconds to respond. "You ... love her?"

Simon's throat thickened. "More than myself. Miss Bigsby is more than I deserve."

Trafford made a snorting sound in commiseration. "As is Lady Trafford, old chap. She has tolerated much botheration from me."

Hearing this somehow helped, and the two men glanced at each other. Simon realized that they had reached a truce, Trafford evidently making a judgment to reconsider his assumption of guilt.

The gentleman cleared his throat. "So ... who might have ... done this?" He waved a hand toward the table where Lady Trafford was assisting Madeline, the sound of retching making Simon's stomach clench in sympathy. She should not be suffering such torture.

Simon stroked his beard. There was nothing that either he or Trafford could do, so this was as good a time as any to unpack the contents of his mind. "My ... mother."

"Lady Blackwood? What reason would she have?"

It was an excellent question, and one he had to contemplate with great attention. His mother had always seemed something of an empty vessel. She never displayed much emotion, and her statements were usually repetitions of his father's thoughts about the topic at hand. There was only one character trait he knew for certain ... "Vanity."

Trafford cocked his head. "I do not understand—"

"I know not the details, but I can assure you that whatever her motive is, it can be summed up in one word as some form of vanity."

"Well, perhaps ... I should have my footmen come in to help the ladies while you and I go have a little word with Lady Blackwood?"

Considering how far his mother had taken things, she had to be considered a danger. The time had arrived to confront her before she could wreak more havoc.

"If Lady Trafford believes Miss Bigsby will be all right without us?"

The viscountess was helping Madeline to drink down a fresh cup of the magnesia mixture when they approached the table. She listened to their plan.

"Miss Bigsby has informed me that she received the arsenic minutes before Mr. Scott discovered her, which means we began treatment in good time. Our men can assist me so you can put an end to the danger." Lady Trafford pressed her lips together, frowning as if weighing the gravity of the situation. "A lunatic did this, and their freedoms must be curtailed before another person is harmed. Instruct the kitchen staff to discard all food and drink in the house. It is better to err on the side of caution."

Simon placed a hand on Madeline's shoulder. "Would it be all right if I left you? I promise to return soon."

Madeline's face was pale when she glanced up, her amber eyes red-rimmed and her skin blotchy but less swollen than he had initially found her. She raised a hand to brush it over his, nodding in agreement. "Put ... an ... end ... to this."

He released her to step back, but she shot out a hand to stop him. "My reti ... cule."

Simon looked down to find a fat, embroidered reticule dangling from her wrist. He gently unlooped it to set it aside.

"Nay ... open it."

Simon tugged it open to find a number of letters jammed inside the bulging fabric. He pulled them out, raising his head in question. Madeline was drinking, but she bobbed her head toward the letters. He looked down, not understanding until he caught sight of the return address inked on the outer fold.

"Bianca Scott? Peter's wife?"

Madeline paused her drinking. "Found ... them ... mother's ... desk."

Simon raked a hand through his hair, staring down at the damning letters. "She did it! She killed Lord Filminster!"

Trafford reached out to grab the stack, leafing through with dexterity. "There are letters from your brother Peter here. You have not seen these before?"

Simon shook his head. "Certainly not."

"I believe we know why no one knew about your nephews. She must have hidden any correspondence that mentioned them. We need to confront your mother, and then find the servant who has been assisting her. There is more than one killer in this house."

"Sodding hell!" He clapped a hand over his mouth, mortified to curse in front of the ladies, but he had forgotten all about the attack on Trafford. Dealing with his mother was indeed an urgent matter. She would have needed a servant to help her intercept incoming mail, which proved there was a manservant involved.

Madeline finished her cup of magnesia, pulling her bucket close to her torso as she began to heave. "Rod … rick … made … tea."

"Roderick!" Simon's mind flashed to various incidents over the years as he pieced together the past. "He has always been rather solicitous to my mother. Perhaps he is infatuated?"

"Perhaps they are engaged in an affair."

Trafford's remark was tossed out in an off-hand tone, but the sentiment had all eyes in the room rivet to him in dismay. He shrugged. "It is not unheard of for a noblewoman to take up with one of the servants. If Roderick is a footman—" Trafford paused to throw Simon a questioning glance. He nodded in acknowledgment. "—they are hired for their height and handsome appearance. Not just noblewomen are drawn to them, but gentlem—" Trafford stopped abruptly, his eyes darting over to his wife and the heaving Madeline who, despite the fact that she had resumed retching into the bucket, was peering at him with wide eyes. "Never mind," he mumbled, evidently remembering at the last second that the ladies present might not be aware of the sort of thing he had been about to mention.

Simon suppressed a shudder. Now that Trafford mentioned it, it was conceivable that his mother and Roderick might be engaged in carnal relations. There were numerous opportunities in a household such as theirs, and the day's revelations had proved he did not understand the inner workings of Isla Scott's mind.

Trafford thankfully interrupted his musings, which were repulsive to consider. "Scott, you summon my men from the mews for me, and I shall stand guard until they arrive."

Simon nodded, striding to the kitchen exit that would take him up a short flight of stairs to the garden. Despite the unexpected *camaraderie* they were forming, he understood that Trafford did not yet trust him sufficiently to leave him alone with the women. Given the miasma of death permeating his home, Simon could not blame the viscount for his prudence.

The kitchen staff were milling in the garden as he crossed, at a loss about what they were meant to do since they had been chased from their posts, as they chattered in nervous groups. Beckoning them over, Simon informed them that Madeline and the baron had consumed tainted food. He wished he could inform them of the truth, but it was best they remain ignorant until his mother and her manservant had been confronted and ... arrested ... he supposed?

Deuce it! This will prove to be the biggest scandal of the century!

Simon issued orders to the housekeeper to immediately empty the kitchen and wine cellar of all food and liquids. Lady Trafford wanted all the floors to be cleared. Even their liquor in the study and first-floor rooms would need to be destroyed, but he did not wish to send anyone beyond the servants' level, which would be secure with Trafford's men to stand guard.

"Even the tea and coffee, Mr. Scott?" The matron was aghast at such extravagant wastefulness.

"Especially the tea and coffee. All of it is to be discarded. I shall provide you with additional funds to replace what we throw out. We cannot risk anyone's health."

It was true. There was no telling what Roderick and his mother might have done with the arsenic. Lady Trafford had impressed upon him that the poison was tasteless and odorless. It sometimes emitted a mild garlic odor when heated, such as in the tea Madeline had drunk, but this could not be relied upon as an indication of its presence.

Cook was thoroughly discomposed, fretting over how to prepare dinner and feed the staff. Sensing her distress and forcing down his own impatience, Simon drew out a purse and instructed her to arrange for pies to be brought in, sparing her the need to prepare anything for the evening. He suggested she send her most trusted maids to the grocer for fresh breakfast supplies. The kitchen staff bustled back inside, caught in a disordered flurry to carry out their tasks. Simon considered cautioning them against gossip, but in the current state of things, it would only serve to fan the flames.

Simon hurried back with Trafford's footman and coachman who took up stations close by Lady Trafford and Madeline. Yet, he found himself hesitant to leave Madeline's side. His inaction had nearly resulted in her losing her life, and now he was to abandon her again?

She was laid out on the kitchen table, panting from her exertions, and Simon was tortured by her suffering. It should be him, not her, but his mother must be prevented from causing any further injury. "Lady Trafford, you will send for me if you need me. Madeline is my first priority."

The noblewoman looked up, her expression reflecting sympathy for his anguish. "Do not worry, Mr. Scott. We have this well in hand."

Simon walked over to lean down and press a kiss to Madeline's clammy forehead. "I will return soon."

Amber eyes found his, and she blinked hard in acknowledgment, too weak to speak. He and Trafford departed, running up the servants' staircase two steps at a time, with Simon leading the way to his mother's rooms. Surely she must have returned there after leaving Madeline to expire on the floor? He hoped he had the strength not to choke her for what she had done to his fair Psyche, or his older brother on the second floor. The sheer malevolence was incomprehensible to him.

Bursting into his mother's private drawing room without so much as a knock, they found no one there, but Simon noted that the desk Madeline had mentioned was pulled out from the wall and all four drawers were opened in a disarray. It was out of character for his mother to tolerate untidiness, but perhaps she had been angered to find her stolen letters missing. He briefly wondered where Miss Dubois, his mother's French maid, was when he was distracted by a stack of leather-bound notebooks—journals, perhaps—laid out on the chaise lounge.

Hurrying over, he lifted one up to confirm they were filled with his mother's scrawling lettering. He dropped it down, turning to notice the bedroom door was ajar. Striding over, with Trafford shadowing him, they entered to discover Isla Scott sitting against a bank of pillows on her bed. The drapes were drawn despite the early hour. His mother's eyes fluttered open to reveal a deep blue, her pupils almost invisible despite the dim light within the room.

"Simon?"

Her voice was weak and her breathing shallow. He

approached with a feeling of dread, noting the empty bottles of laudanum next to the bed with the caps strewn on the floor and her hair which had been loosened to frame her face in a becoming manner. Simon stroked his beard in agitation as he considered the presented nature of the scene.

"Mother?"

"She broke into my desk … the little tart."

Trafford came to stand beside him, flickering his eyes from the bottles and back to Simon with a raised brown eyebrow.

"We have … both … paid the price …"

Simon's suspicions were correct. His mother had taken an overdose, believing Madeline was lying dead two floors below. He stepped forward, thinking to lift her and race her down to the kitchen for help, but Trafford put out a hand to stay him.

Leaning in, his companion lowered his voice. "She will be arrested. Face public trial and be hanged at the Tower. Perhaps this is … humane? A painless departure?"

Simon swallowed hard, tears springing into his eyes as he considered the devastation his mother had created in so many lives, while facing the fact that his only remaining parent was expiring in front of him.

She had attempted to kill Madeline. He wished he understood why.

"My journals are … my confession … to clear your name."

Simon approached the bed, still trying to decide what was the right thing to do. "Why, Mother?"

"You will be baron … the greatest Campbell … Papa would … be so proud."

Simon frowned, attempting to unravel the words. "You mean my father?"

His mother's face creased into a euphoric smile. "Lord

Campbell … My papa … I disappointed him so … but … not anymore. My son … will be Baron … of Blackwood."

"Mother, there are other heirs."

Her eyes drifted closed. "I … have … taken care of …" With that, his mother slipped into unconsciousness. Rushing forward, Simon attempted to rouse her, but to no avail. Lifting her up in his arms to discover she weighed barely anything at all, he strode toward the door to take her to the kitchen so that Lady Trafford might … He did not know. His mother was hardly breathing, a curtain of rich brown hair cascading over his arm, and he knew she might quit long before he reached that destination. Trafford might be right about allowing her to pass, but his integrity required he at least attempt to wake her.

They descended three flights of stairs, but by the time they reached the servants' level, Simon knew it was too late. Isla Scott was no more, and he thought she might be pleased if she had known she had never looked more beautiful than she did in mortal repose.

Halting, Trafford understood without him stating it. The lord removed his glove to feel for a pulse, glancing up at Simon with a shake of his head. It was at that moment that Simon noticed the odd detail that his companion's moss-green eyes were marred by large brown spots, musing that it was strange how tragedy such as this could focus one's attention on insignificant minutia.

"I should … take her back upstairs?"

"Agreed. There is no reason to upset the ladies with a corpse while your Miss Bigsby is so ill."

"What did she mean … do you think? At the end? Did she imply she had taken steps to get rid of the heir from Italy?"

"I could not tell if she knew what she was saying, but we do have Roderick to find."

Simon groaned. This day was turning out to be far worse than he had ever experienced.

"I suppose it is a mercy she is gone."

Trafford licked his lips. "I know it sounds cruel, old chap, but I believe it is for the best. The duke and his family can rest assured that justice has been done, and your household can avoid much of the upheaval this would have caused so that your brother can recover his health in peace. Lady Blackwood's final act is a kindness to all concerned."

Simon turned around and began to climb the steps back to his mother's rooms. "How bad will it be?"

"I think the duke can convince the authorities to settle Lord Filminster's death without an inquest. Rumors may fly, but I see no cause to involve the public in something that is settled. Home Office might be amenable to allowing the matter to fade away. Perhaps we can have this declared … an accidental overdose?"

It would indeed be a boon to the Scotts if the duke would assist them to quiet the scandal sure to be unleashed. They continued their climb in silence, ascending much slower than their hasty descent as a sign of respect to the dead. He was not sure if his mother deserved it, but he was grateful that nothing more was said until they reached her drawing room to lay her out on the chaise lounge after Trafford had removed the journals. Simon took the time to pose her as she had been in the bedchamber, guessing she had taken pains to look her best for when her body was discovered.

Stepping back, he studied her for several moments with a numb sort of sadness before collecting a blanket from her room to cover her up. He would need to make arrangements, but first—first they must find the footman who had assisted her in her deadly mission to secure the title on Simon's behalf.

It made him ill to think about it. They had not known

each other very well. Isla Scott had risked everything, murdered a man, tried to murder his brother and Madeline, to ensure Simon inherited, while he had long wished for another life without duty to a title and entailments to take care of. He would choose Madeline over inheritance under any circumstances, and it was his dearest hope that she would be all right, his fears for her health persisting despite Lady Trafford's assurances. She had consumed a considerable quantity of arsenic.

"So where would a crazed, infatuated footman hide after he has poisoned an innocent woman?"

Trafford pointed. "Well … should that window be open?"

CHAPTER 14

"*Venus sought to test not only Psyche but her own son, forcing them both to endure the consequences of disobedience.*"

Lucius Apuleius, Metamorphoses

* * *

Isla's drawing room was on the corner of the house, with a bank of windows facing the garden where the servants had gathered earlier and two more windows on the side of the house. The same direction as Simon's bedchamber faced, which meant there was a trellis of creeping ivy. Considering the coolness of the day, and the stiff draught blowing in, there was no logical reason for the window to have been opened. He believed it had been open when they had first entered in search of his mother, but he had not paid it any mind at the time.

Simon crossed over, leaning through to look about. It took a moment, but when he swung his head to the right, he found Roderick clinging to the trellis like a man caught in a terrible storm. The footman was trembling something fierce, and his face was as white as a sheet against his brown hair.

Peering down, Simon surmised his mother had ordered the footman to climb down to John's bedroom below to end his life. So she must have known about John's collapse in the study, but had not come to discover his condition, which was rather telling that she had been expecting it. He was still having trouble reconciling that his mother had been trying to kill his older brother to force a path to Simon inheriting the title. Was she disregarding the heir and spare who would be arriving from Italy?

Considering she had proved herself to be a madwoman, perhaps in her macabre fantasy of grand legacy, she had elected to forget their existence.

Staring into the chasm of lunacy, Simon was disturbed by the knowledge his own mother had been conspiring death and mayhem these past two years. And intercepting mail between his father and Peter for almost as long as she had been married, to prevent reconciliation.

Fortunately for John and Molly in the rooms below, Isla must have been unaware that Roderick was deathly afraid of heights.

"Do you need assistance to come back inside?" It was not the time to interrogate the petrified manservant, despite the horrifying revelations of the past couple of hours.

Roderick shook his head with vehemence, his grip so tight around the bars of the trellis that his knuckles shone white even through the pallor of his skin.

Simon cocked his head, struggling to decide his next move. They were at a stalemate, Roderick frozen just a few feet away, their gazes locked in an uncomfortable challenge.

The footman finally spoke in a tremulous voice. "Where's Isla?"

Trafford chose that moment to lean out beside Simon,

jostling him in his impatience to see what was going on. "You seem the right height and size. Are you the one who stabbed me outside my home?"

Roderick grimaced without responding. Trafford took it as an assent.

"What about Miss Bigsby? Did you poison her tea earlier?"

Still no response.

"What of Lord Blackwood? Have you been administering poison to the baron?"

Trafford paused, but no reply was forthcoming.

"Did you, perchance, help Lady Blackwood to kill Lord Filminster?"

Shutting his eyes tight, Roderick's mouth moved as if he were praying.

"Damnation, you scoundrel! Give me an answer! What about hastening Mr. Scott's father to an early grave?"

Roderick's eyes flew open in shock as he exclaimed loudly, "That was an accident!"

Simon's stomach dropped, his breath catching as he whipped around to stare at Trafford, aghast. The lord simply shrugged, his expression nonplussed. "I was only guessing, old chap. With the creeping shroud of death haunting this house ... I thought I'd toss it out there. I fully expected him to deny it, I swear."

When Simon turned back, Roderick had crumpled again into a shivering terror. "Where ... where is Isla?"

Trafford snarled, his voice dripping with contempt. "Lady Blackwood is dining with the devil in the depths of hell, answering for her sins. If you hurry, you might just catch her there."

Simon sputtered, turning to meet Trafford's strange green-brown eyes again.

His companion shrugged once more without a hint of

remorse. "What? It is this or a public hanging for the murders of not one but two barons. And three more counts of attempted murder. Not so, Roderick?"

The footman declined to address the question, instead concentrating on the one thing he seemed to care about.

"Isla is dead?"

"She is."

Roderick swallowed hard, turning his head to gaze down at the ground three stories below. He scrambled up the trellis, and Simon, realizing his intention, made to climb out onto the window ledge to grab him.

Trafford clasped hold of him in a tight embrace. "You will not risk your life for a cold-blooded killer, Simon Scott! Ye gods, if he fights you off, you could fall with him, and for what he has done, the sentence is death. If not today, then soon."

"Dammit, Trafford!"

They struggled against the frame until an unearthly howl caused both of them to pause in their scuffle and spin back to watch as Roderick, having climbed up to the attic level, had released his hold to plummet to the ground. A loud thud from below introduced a deep silence. Both men gazed down at the broken body lying at the foot of the house for long minutes until Simon roused himself.

"Is it over?"

Trafford raked a hand through the mass of wheat curls at the crown of his head, blowing out a shaky puff. "I believe it is. Is it not horrifying to witness a man, a valued retainer of many years, trip and fall out of a third-story window before your very eyes? Discovering the baroness's dead body must have addled his brain with grief to make him so clumsy."

Simon frowned, his thoughts as thick as a heavy downpour as he tried to follow what Trafford had said. "What?"

"Your footman. It was a tragic accident that he stumbled

and fell when he discovered Lady Blackwood had expired from an opium overdose."

Thinking he might have imagined the past few minutes, Simon stepped away from the window to fall against the wall, sliding down until his buttocks hit the floor.

"Is that what happened?"

Trafford joined him, sprawling his legs out. "I know Lord Filminster and his bride would enjoy some peace after all they have been through these past weeks. A lengthy inquest which links these deaths to that of his father would be quite a public spectacle to entertain the masses for the months to come. I suggest you take those journals"—Trafford indicated the notebooks that his mother had referred to—"to your study so you might learn what all of this was about, and we summon the coroner to report the dreadful mistake in medication and the terrible accident it instigated."

"Will that work?"

"With the duke's support, it should. Home Office has proven themselves indiscreet, so I would leave it to Halmesbury to explain these tragic accidents away. It will allow your family to heal in private, and Lord Blackwood will need peace to recover his health."

Simon contemplated months of scandal and found that the alternative was far more appealing. The villains had been uncovered and were now dead. There was no specific reason to endure further suffering. "Thank you."

Trafford chuckled, shaking his head in dismay. "I cannot believe this muddle has been laid to rest. Will you inform me of the details? Once you have read the journals?"

Simon nodded. "If the others wish to return, I can brief all of you on the contents in a few days. It is reasonable that you are informed of the details. I … appreciate your willingness to be discreet. With John's health and the potential scandal for Madeline … Thank you."

"Not at all, Lord Campbell."

He blinked. "What did you call me?"

Trafford quirked an eyebrow as he turned his head in query. "Are you not the heir to your mother's titles? Viscount of Campbell, Baron of Lochinver? I confess I do not recall the rest, but it is another reason to not reveal Lady Blackwood's nefarious activities. They might get in the way, and you have people who need you up north."

Simon groaned, dropping his face into his hands as the truth struck him like a clap of thunder. "Stuff!"

His companion burst into gales of laughter, doubling up with tearful mirth. "You and me both, Campbell. Welcome to the peerage."

* * *

MADELINE WAS LYING in a huddle on the kitchen table, her throat raw from casting up her accounts more times than she could count. There was nothing left to hurl from her digestive system. Not one drop of tea, nor any of her breakfast. Certainly not dinner from the night before.

She lay shivering while Lady Trafford had the servants clean away the last vestiges of illness. All except her soaked gown. She vaguely considered bathing, but she had not the strength for such an endeavor. Falling asleep was inevitable in her weakened state, but she was afraid that she might not awaken, so she kept rousing herself.

Her lids were as heavy as chain mail, but Madeline was resolute in keeping them open a slit to ensure she was still in the land of the living. What if she closed them to never awaken?

She forced them open to find a pair of polished riding boots had come to a stop beside the table she was laid out on.

"Do you wish to go home? To your bed?" Despite her

drowsy state, Madeline's heart pounded with joy at Simon's presence.

"If you ... stay ... with me," she mumbled, her tongue thick in her mouth.

"I shall never allow us to part again, fair Psyche." He gathered her up in his arms, pressing a kiss to her forehead as he lifted her up.

"I ... must be ... a fright."

"You are always beautiful to me."

"What ... about ... Lady Trafford?"

"She is following us to settle you in. I have sent word to Mrs. Bigsby to come home."

Madeline's lids drifted closed, despite her resolve. If she were to never wake up, then her last seconds were the happiest she had ever been within Simon's powerful embrace.

* * *

MADELINE SCARCELY STIRRED while her lady's maid undressed and washed her in her bed. At least, that is what Lady Trafford informed Simon of when she reopened the door to the bedchamber.

"Will she recover?"

"It is difficult to say given the quantity of arsenic she consumed, but I believe so."

"Will her health suffer as a result?"

"Miss Bigsby is young and healthy." Lady Trafford failed to elaborate past that, and Mrs. Bigsby chose that moment to appear in the doorway.

"What happened?"

Simon held up a hand, shooing the lady's maid from the room and shutting the door behind her. "We have informed the servants that your daughter ate tainted food. Madeline has been too ill to inform us precisely what transpired, but she drank tea with the baroness who dosed it with arsenic. Lady Trafford is a trained healer who helped relieve her of the contents of her stomach. Now she is resting."

Mrs. Bigsby firmed her jaw, walking over to the bed to examine Madeline herself for several seconds, leaning over to brush the hair back from her face before straightening with a mixture of grief and anger upon her features. "I have questions, but let me begin with, where is Lady Blackwood now?"

Simon swallowed. "She has suffered an overdose of laudanum. The coroner has been summoned to examine the body."

"Good."

The simple acknowledgment made Simon wince, and he supposed his mother's decision to depart this world had been circumspect. Mrs. Bigsby had the appearance of a vengeful angel, and he could picture her tearing the much smaller Isla apart limb by limb with her large hands if she had had the opportunity to do so.

Over the next half an hour, Simon and Mrs. Bigsby discussed what had happened, Simon revealing the details that he knew until the moment arrived for him to express his tremendous regret.

"I beg your forgiveness, Mrs. Bigsby."

"What for?"

"This ... for what my mother did."

Madeline's mother rose from her seat, walking over to the window to gaze out over the garden as if she were lost in thought. Simon waited for her reply, the drumming of his fingertips belying any attempt at composure.

"You are not your father—the one who tried to ruin my business. You took steps to rectify that when you gained control of the purse strings." It was true. When his father's declining health had forced him to hand over the financial reins, Simon had discreetly placed several large orders with Bigsby's for the Blackwood estates. It was his way of making amends for any harm his father had caused, which John had concurred was the right thing to do.

"It was the least I could do after he campaigned against your business," Simon replied quietly.

Mrs. Bigsby nodded. "The gesture was unnecessary, but it was appreciated. And you are not your mother, who … did this." Her eyes drifted to her pale daughter, lying still on the bed. She shook her head, as though to banish the dark thoughts. Then, turning her gaze back to Simon, she continued, "You are you. I hold you accountable for your own actions. The sins of your parents belong to them alone."

"That is generous."

"It is how I would wish to be treated. We all have our own mistakes to answer for, so I cannot hold you responsible for the actions of others; otherwise, we would never find peace. Thank you for acting so swiftly to ensure Madeline received help. Lady Trafford tells me that the timing was crucial."

"I was fortunate to catch her when she was leaving."

"And what would you have done if she had already left?"

Simon paused, considering the events of the day, grateful to Mrs. Bigsby for her generosity despite his cloying sense of shame. "I would have repeated what was done with John. Assisted her to evacuate her stomach while sending someone to summon the viscountess back."

"So it was not luck. Lady Trafford's presence is a comfort, but I believe you would have done the same after witnessing what happened with your brother earlier in the day. What has happened to Madeline, and to your brother, is unspeakably evil, but you took decisive action when you were needed. For this, I thank you."

Simon exhaled deeply, profoundly relieved that Eleanor

Bigsby had always been a just person who had treated him without prejudice as a boy, despite his father's blackguard behavior during his childhood.

"However—"

Simon straightened up in alarm.

"—expect Henrietta to be rather more excitable than I. I believe she will arrive home soon."

The perceptive mother was proven right. Henri arrived within minutes of her announcement, bursting into the bedchamber with a shriek. "What is this?"

Mrs. Bigsby quickly drew Henri out of the room to inform her of the day's events out in the hall. Simon could hear the emotional replies from Henri, interspersed with Mrs. Bigsby's low murmurs, for several minutes until Henri grew quieter. When they reentered, Henri scowled at him with an accusatory glare and took up the seat next to Madeline's bed. She stared down at her twin in anguish, brushing Madeline's hair aside as if to confirm with her own fingertips that she yet lived.

Simon watched in silence, the guilt that had dissipated during his conversation with Mrs. Bigsby returning to claw at his gut.

Henri exhaled sharply. "Will she be well?"

"It would seem so," Mrs. Bigsby responded from the window. "Lady Trafford thinks Madeline is in good health and will make a full recovery."

"Lady Trafford? The doctor's daughter who married the Earl of Stirling's heir?"

Mrs. Bigsby nodded. "She apprenticed at her father's side. It was she who treated Madeline when she collapsed."

Henri rubbed her face. "There are rumors she treated Lord Trafford, too. After some sort of attack that he suffered. Then he married her to abate the scandal."

Simon raised his brows, but remained silent. He had seen

how Trafford admired his wife, and he did not believe that deterring her ruin was the sole reason the buck had wed the intriguing healer who had saved both Simon's brother and Madeline this day.

After a while, Henri left, shooting him another scathing glare as she departed the room with her mother which left Simon to resume his seat at Madeline's bedside and wonder how much Eleanor Bigsby had revealed to Henri out in the corridor.

A couple hours later, Madeline stirred from her fitful sleep. "Thirsty."

Simon held her head up to assist her to drink the broth that had been brought up on a tray, Lady Trafford having left instructions to have her consume as much fluid as possible to replenish what she had lost. Madeline drank down two cups before falling asleep again, Simon noting she was more peaceful than before.

Mrs. Bigsby came to relieve him at dinner time, and he rushed home to complete the arrangements for the bodies and to check on John. The guards were still standing in the hall, but John's rooms were no longer locked and Duncan was assisting Molly when he entered.

After Duncan left to collect broth from the kitchen, John beckoned for Simon to sit beside his bed as he struggled into a sitting position.

"Molly tells me the mystery has been solved."

"My mother."

"Do we know why?"

"To clear the way for me to inherit."

His brother blinked profusely as he considered this. "Was Isla ... mad?"

Simon huffed a humorless laugh. "My mother refused to allow an emotion to cross her face. I think it is safe to assume that she was addled in the head. I shall read her journals to learn more, but I suppose we should have known something was amiss."

John shook his head, and Simon was pleased to note his pallor had improved somewhat since his collapse that morning. "It will not help to mull on that. When you interact with someone on a daily basis ... it would be difficult to notice a descent into gradual madness over a period of time. Not to mention, Isla being so undemonstrative."

Simon stroked his beard, thinking about the horrors of the day. There was much to discuss with John, but for today, his brother must be allowed to rest. "I am so sorry."

His brother frowned. "For what?"

"For bringing this on our household."

"Do not be ridiculous. You are my brother. Isla's actions are her own. How were you to know she was a potential Bedlamite?"

"I do not know ... but I should have."

"While Father was a terrible bigot. He harassed Mrs. Bigsby to an extent which was far beyond the pale. Am I to be blamed for that?"

"I do not think his dreadful behavior had anything to do with you. And Mrs. Bigsby does not seem to hold it against us."

John lifted a hand, palm up. "There it is. In the best of all worlds, you or I would have noticed something was wrong. But she was your mother, and I do not think it a good idea to dissect your conscience over it. Learn from it, but move on. You are a good man, and I regret that I have not shown more appreciation for the work you have done in my stead. I suppose you are a Scottish viscount now?"

Simon raised his eyebrows in disbelief. "Can you believe it? I thought my mother would live a hundred years. She could have been mistaken for my sister. It never struck me that I would become Lord Campbell. I never wished for a title, but now I possess four or five. I still have to find our Debrett's to see which ones. The irony is, I have never been to Scotland."

John chuckled, before coughing into a handkerchief. "What will you do?"

"I do not know. I do not wish the titles to define me. I wish to follow my own path, but this has become complicated. Again."

"I can attest that a close brush with death has made me rethink my priorities. Even more so when I discovered my ill health has been part of a vindictive plan. See to the people and responsibilities attached to the titles and, then, perhaps you can find a way forward that allows you some liberties."

"I hope so."

Next, Simon visited Nicholas in his bedchamber, his brother still contending with the physical miseries of casting aside drink, to inform him of what had transpired since they had spoken earlier. His younger brother was morose, having heard the news that their mother was dead.

"I am not sure how to feel about it," Nicholas admitted in a dull voice. "We were not close, and I did not know her well. I think she did not have much time for me as the youngest."

"That might be the case, but I do not think Mother was close to anyone. John and I have just spoken about how we each had a poor sense of who she was. She, in the most literal sense, wore a mask to hide not just her emotions but her thoughts."

"I suppose we are safer without her."

It was a sad truth that they were.

Simon departed soon after to return to Madeline's side, with the infamous journals tucked under his arm. He had promised Madeline they would remain together, and he planned to do just that as long as he could.

CHAPTER 15

"Mother, your cruelty knows no bounds, for I love her more than life itself!"

Lucius Apuleius, Metamorphoses

* * *

OCTOBER 6, 1821

*M*adeline awoke midmorning. She had done naught but sleep, drink cold broth, and use the chamber pot with the help of her mother since being put in her bed. Taking stock of her body, she discovered there were aches and twinging pains in her limbs. Her belly hurt, and her throat was raw. There was a definite weakness in her muscles, and a general fatigue that spoke to her troubles of yesterday.

But…

Turning her head, she found Simon watching her with a pleased expression.

"I feel better."

"You appear better. Your color has improved considerably."

"What did Lady Trafford say?"

"She assures me you are young and healthy. She will be here soon to check on you."

"What about my work?"

Simon grinned, lifting a hand to caress her cheek and producing a single red rose from behind his back. Madeline reached for it, sniffing deeply of its fragrant petals before clasping it to the coverlet covering her figure. "Your mother will take care of it. She is sleeping in after helping me take care of you all night, but I think your manufactory is large and productive enough to do without the two of you for a few days."

Madeline wrinkled her nose, reaching up to check her hair. "This is not my most attractive aspect," she declared.

"Every aspect of you is attractive. I have no complaints."

She smiled, pleased at the compliment. "What comes next?"

He chuckled. "You recover."

"And then?"

"You recover some more. Would you like me to bring you some reading?"

She pouted at his evasiveness. "What about us?"

"Hmm ... what about us?"

Madeline huffed in frustration. He was obfuscating, but she was too weak to insist on a proper answer. She assumed Mama would not allow a gentleman to encamp in her bedchamber unless an understanding was to be reached, but she supposed they would discuss it when the time was right.

With all that had happened, she yearned for the future they had discussed in their youth. One where she worked with the artists of the manufactory while Simon worked alongside her mother to handle the business dealings. But she did not wish to require this from him or take advantage of his guilt over what had been done to her. Madeline wished that Simon would offer her their long-discussed imaginings of partnership of his own volition. After all they had endured, all the ups and downs of yesteryear, it seemed meaningless unless Simon raised the issue from his own desire to wed her, and not from some misguided sense of obligation because his mother had attempted to murder her.

She supposed that what she desired was for Simon to demonstrate his commitment to them.

"Is there more broth?"

* * *

SIMON HAD BEEN READING his mother's journals for several hours, continuing to pore over the pages of her spider scrawl while Madeline was being assisted to bathe in the next room.

There was much to answer, including the inadvertent revelation from Roderick about his father's death. The more he read, the more disturbed he became, but it was his burden to bear. He needed to absorb the contents so he might brief the people affected by her actions.

This afternoon he would need to go home to figure out what the current state of his entailments were in Scotland. He had no notion if his mother had been a good peeress who took care of her duties, but considering the madness inked on the pages, he assumed that there were tenants up north who sorely needed some attention from a responsible care-taker. It would all depend on the stewards who oversaw the respective estates.

Too many of the nobility treated their titles as a right, but Simon was well aware it was a privilege with accountability. Thus he must ascertain the situation for the people under his leadership, and take steps to confirm the stewardships were in expert hands, or replace them as necessary. Simon hoped he would find some method to pursue his own goals. If the past few weeks had taught him anything, it was that his duty had superseded his own dreams to leave him a lifeless husk. Since learning he was not to be Baron of Blackwood, his vitality and interest had begun to return. He did not wish to live a lifetime of unhappiness, which would put the past dreary decade of misery to shame.

Soon he returned to sit by Madeline, who fell into a deep sleep after the exertions of being up to bathe and change her nightclothes. The sound of her rhythmic breathing as he read on was the most beautiful symphony he could imagine. Lady Trafford had pronounced that Madeline was on the mend during her visit at midday.

When the sun was low in the sky, Simon set aside the most recent journal and looked up to find Madeline had awakened, her amber eyes watching him as he read.

"Do you have your answers?"

"Mostly. The journals begin when she came out, and then there are a few years missing. Around the time she wed up until I was about two or three years of age. Then there is a meticulous record up until a few days ago."

"Is it horrifying? To read your mother's private thoughts?"

"Very."

"What did you learn?"

"I learned that my grandfather was enraged that a daughter was to inherit the title. He had his heart set on a son, but after four daughters, he was forced to admit defeat.

It would seem he made Isla aware of his feelings throughout her youth."

"Your poor mother!"

Simon shook his head. "Nay, fair Psyche, each one of us has our crosses to bear, and her father has been dead longer than I have been alive, so her past does not justify the present. You and I know about burdens better than most, denying our own happiness these past years. Most do not consider their personal troubles as a license to embark on a tyranny of murder. Three men are dead. Trafford, John, and yourself could have been killed. Yet all of you are innocent of doing her any harm."

Madeline chewed on her lip as she thought over it. "You are correct. I sympathize with her circumstances but not her solution. But … who is the third man who is dead?"

He dropped his chin in anguish, still reeling at the words inked upon the page. "My father. Mother and Roderick had taken to slipping him opium, unbeknownst to him, which was perilous considering Dr. White had him on laudanum. They fumbled the dosages one night, each dosing him without being aware the other had already done so, thus causing an overdose, so it appeared he had suffered an apoplexy in the night."

"Faith! Why did they do it?"

"They were engaged in an affair. Opium ensured my father would sleep through the night so Roderick could visit her bedchamber without fear of being caught. Father's accidental death seems to have accelerated her descent into madness, and these extensive journals were some sort of outlet for her repressed emotions. All the things she never said. And I think she had the affair with Roderick to manipulate him into doing her bidding, but I imagine the guilt over killing my father further addled her head."

Madeline emitted a low snuffle of disgust. "It is all so … abhorrent."

"It is. And a slippery slope. When John came home from the coronation to complain about Lord Filminster, she was horrified to hear that the baron might be aware of Peter's sons. They were acquainted, so she visited him after dinner at the Forsythes' to learn what he knew. When he mentioned he had reached a decision and just completed writing a letter to Home Office to inform them of my nephews, she struck him with a statuette so she might search his study. The laudanum she took must have dulled her humanity because there is no remorse when she writes about him bleeding out on the floor. She makes it sound as if it were terribly inconsiderate of him because drops of his blood ruined her favorite slippers, and Roderick had to destroy them on her behalf."

"And the footman who was killed in Filminster's household?"

"She paid him to search for the letter to Home Office when she could not find it."

Madeline sat up, trembling with fatigue but shooing Simon when he tried to help. "I must push myself a little. Lying about too much will weaken me further." She twisted around to rearrange her pillows, then leaned back in a half-seated position.

"What of John's wife? Did she have anything to do with that?"

"No and yes. My mother guessed from Susan's symptoms that she might have been suffering from arsenic poisoning from her skin creams, but remained silent. It inspired her plot to poison John."

"Lady Blackwood did it all? She killed your father, Filminster? Tried to kill John, Trafford, and myself? It was all her?"

Simon was still struggling to come to grips with the extent of her villainy. "It was. Her and Roderick."

"I hate to be cruel, but it is a mercy they are dead."

"I agree. Picking up the pieces will be difficult enough without adding a scandalous public trial."

"And what of Dr. White? Do you know why he did not notice the symptoms of arsenic poisoning during John's long illness?"

"Dr. White has disappeared. Called away on urgent business, his household is telling us. He could be involved in the murder plots, or perhaps he is afraid to answer for his incompetence."

Madeline emitted a guttural sound of frustration, staring up at the ceiling for long seconds until turning her gaze back to him. "What happens now?"

"You take care of your health while I see to the inquest for their deaths. Then …"

Madeline's face lit up, her expression hopeful. "Then?"

Simon hated to disappoint her, but he had things to take care of. "Then … I must leave for Scotland, I am afraid."

Her face fell, her jaw falling open in protest. "What? Why?"

"I must inspect the estates I am now responsible for. See to my responsibilities as the new lord."

"Lord?"

Simon nodded. "My mother held titles of her own. I am to be confirmed as the Viscount of Campbell, Baron of Lochinver, and … a couple of minor ones which I do not know how to pronounce. Once I am confirmed, I must see to the estates. I do not know what their condition is, who the stewards are, and what measures need to be taken to care for the tenants and staff."

"How long will you be gone?" Madeline's tone was forlorn, and Simon wished he could speak to their future, but he could not even speak to his own until he had gathered more information. After all he had put Madeline through, he needed to put his affairs in order without burdening her with his problems. Until he had done that, he did not wish to create false hopes.

CHAPTER 16

"With his golden bow and quiver of arrows slung across his back, Eros flew down from Olympus, his heart guiding him to his beloved Psyche."

Lucius Apuleius, Metamorphoses

* * *

NOVEMBER 26, 1821

*T*he weeks had passed at a slow pace, with Madeline recovering her strength one day at a time. A month earlier she had returned to work, but just in the afternoons. Lady Trafford wanted her to take the time to convalesce, so even after so much time, Madeline was still attending to her duties at Bigsby's on a reduced schedule.

She would have protested, but the aches and weakness of her muscles in general attested that the noblewoman was

218

correct to curtail her activities. Her health was returning, but her body needed the time to heal.

Madeline had spent the extra time with Molly, and visiting John to read to him as he made his own slow recovery. Nicholas was filling out, putting on muscle due to eating regular meals and forgoing spirits.

And Simon wrote to her every day. It was strange to correspond with him. Her letters frequently did not arrive with him because he was traveling from estate to estate to inspect their conditions, so the conversation was rather disjointed. He would recount what he had found at the estate he was visiting, and describe the beauty of the mountains and lochs he viewed on his morning rides, and write of how he wished she could one day accompany him to experience the grandeur of the Scottish countryside. Of the seven estates entailed to his titles, Simon had been pleased to discover competent stewards managing estate affairs at four, apparently retainers hired in his grandfather's time. A fifth steward he had deemed uninspired but acceptable. Another, he had decided, would need to be replaced, and she had not heard from him about the seventh yet.

Madeline was hopeful that he would be returning soon, since he had now reached the final stop in his journey, but Simon had not indicated if that was the case. She missed him, wishing she could work longer hours to occupy her mind because, having lost her last iota of patience, she had written a most immodest missive this morning, demanding to know his intentions.

The rules of courtship be damned.

And as soon as she found the courage to post it, she would.

It was a difficult position she was in. On the one hand, she was a successful woman of industry, and on the other, she was a gently-bred woman who followed the rules of polite society. Attempting to reconcile the two required balancing two worlds in opposition.

It did not help that Simon was an important man, now a peer in his own right, and Madeline did not have a clear concept of how they would manage their divergent lives into a single partnership given the unexpected change in his circumstances. All details that, in their past, in a time of childish optimism, they had never discussed. Unifying such complexities would take a great amount of thoughtful planning, adding to her frustration at his prolonged absence which prevented genuine discourse. She yearned for his return so they might frankly discuss a shared future.

"It is cold this evening," remarked her mother as they ate dinner. "You should put on a pelisse if you plan to visit the garden tonight."

Madeline scooped up white soup with her silver spoon. "I do not wish to visit tonight."

Mama raised her face. "Why?"

"Is there a point to doing so? Simon is not here. There is no possibility of an encounter."

Her mother's lips quirked into a smile. "I do not know about that. He seemed to be looking forward to visiting with you when we met this afternoon."

Madeline dropped the spoon, splashing soup so that Henri protested in dismay, "Hey! Watch it, Maddy!"

"Simon is back?"

"He must be. We signed contracts this afternoon."

"Contracts?"

"Indeed. We have been corresponding over terms these past weeks. He was here to sign off on his purchase of stake in Bigsby's."

"Bigsby's! You sold him shares?" Madeline was astounded. Mama had always eschewed investors in her business, preferring to remain independent. She had once had an unpleasant experience with a minor partner who had attempted to oust her from her own business, and had to fight it out in the courts before buying the opportunist out.

"I did. The contracts include clauses to protect your and Henrietta's rights of ownership. I hired the same firm of solicitors that wrote the contracts for Lady Jersey. She retained her ownership in the family bank when she wed."

"Why did you sell him shares?"

Mama shrugged. "It seemed reasonable if he is to join our family. He mentioned you might be interested in managing the artisans if he is to work with me in running the manufactory. We will hold not just a Royal Warrant, but claim nobility within the family, which will be excellent for business."

Madeline jumped to her feet, elation coursing through her veins. "Yes! Yes! I must find him!"

"I am here, fair Psyche." Simon's deep voice interrupted from behind.

Madeline whirled around to find him leaning casually against the doorframe. He looked tall and elegant in a gold brocade waistcoat and black coat, the crisp white linen bright against his sun-kissed skin, his beard freshly trimmed.

"Do you wish to wed?"

Her heart leapt at the sight of him. "Yes! When?"

Simon pulled out a gold timepiece, studying it with mock seriousness. "How about … now? Unless you would prefer to wait?"

The past few weeks flashed through her mind, followed quickly by memories of their decade apart. "Truly? Right now?"

He grinned. "If it pleases you?"

She would like nothing more. Life had thrown so many obstacles in the way that she needed not a second more to tick away. Any future trouble they faced would be as man and wife, if they wed this evening.

Madeline glanced down at her silk dress. "Is this why Miss Moreau dressed me in my best evening gown?"

Her mother grinned across the table. "Of course."

"Have you made some sort of arrangements?"

"Why not collect your pelisse and we shall see?"

Madeline darted, knocking over her chair in her haste as Henri mumbled in complaint. Soon they were in the hall, Simon and a footman assisting them into their outer garments.

"You knew of this?" she asked her twin. Henri gave a knowing smile, indicating her assent. "You kept it a secret?"

"Henri is not good at keeping secrets," laughed their mother. "She was told this afternoon because she had to assist in the arrangements."

"Arrangements?" Madeline was elated at the possibilities.

"You shall see." Henri was smug, clearly pleased to be privy to information that Madeline was not.

Soon they were headed down the path to the hidden garden, with Madeline's arm tucked around Simon's. He felt so good; the muscles rippled beneath her fingertips while the silver moon shone down on them with an air of approval.

Entering the archway, she found people waiting for them along with fragrant hothouse flowers bedecking the ornate urn in the middle. Lord Blackwood was seated in an armchair that had been brought from the house. Nicholas was sitting on the bench next to Molly with his long legs sprawled out, and Lady and Lord Trafford along with Uncle Reggie were admiring the gods peering down at them, lit by lanterns throughout the garden.

Madeline greeted each in turn, until Simon drew her over to meet a rounded vicar in vestments, introducing him as

Reverend Stone. He seemed quite jolly as he introduced his smiling wife with a friendly chuckle.

Then they gathered together as Rev. Stone angled his pages to catch light from one of the lanterns, and in their celestial garden, Psyche and Eros were united in matrimony.

* * *

IN THE WEEKS since his mother's suicide, it had become increasingly clear to him how his malevolent parent had influenced his thoughts, using his guilt over Nicholas's accident to manipulate his decisions until he barely recognized the shadow of the man he had become.

He had sworn to do his duty ever since Nicholas had fallen from the window. The fear that failing to do so might cause some new, terrible event had been ever-present since that night.

But he was finding his footing, the boldness of his youth quietly seeping back, fleshing out his soul and restoring his spirits and energy. The journey to Scotland had helped him sort through his thoughts, and having the irrepressible Trafford as a confidant was certainly aiding the process of his return to himself.

Simon held Madeline's hand as they walked back to his home. It was not proper, but given recent events, he doubted anyone would complain—except perhaps the vicar, which was why they had fallen to the back of the group.

Her hand felt delicate in his grasp, and he was filled with relieved satisfaction that she had accepted his proposal. Despite their long history, he was surprised by how nerve-racking it had been to make the offer to the woman he admired above all others. If she had declined, his world would have shattered. But now, they were here, side by side.

The time for duty had passed and Madeline was now his duty. His obsession. His passion.

"We are wed!" Madeline's voice brimmed with wonder.

It was brilliant to be home. Being away in the north had only made him appreciate what he had waiting for him in London. Once he had confirmed the details of his inheritance and the responsibilities of his titles, he had rushed back, changing horses through the night to reach his beloved Psyche.

As part of his financial planning, he had invested in the manufactory, securing his place as an equal partner rather than a charity case for Eleanor Bigsby. This had been his most fervent wish—to unite with Madeline and guide Bigsby's into a new era. He had worried about making these decisions without consulting her, but he believed they had discussed their dreams enough over the years. Eleanor had even agreed to cancel the negotiation if Madeline was unhappy with the arrangement. Thankfully, she was more than satisfied with the direction their future was taking.

When they reached the house, Nicholas held the door open, his lips twitching as Simon let go of Madeline's hand. They followed their guests into the dining room, the space aglow with the shimmer of glass and silver reflecting the light from oil lamps. Tall candles flickered in a faint draught, cooling the room's heat. He and Mrs. Bigsby had timed their return so that Madeline had not eaten much earlier, ensuring her favorite foods would be enjoyed during their wedding supper.

Meanwhile, Duncan and Simon's valet were moving his belongings into her bedchamber so they could retire to their new home together. It might have been disloyal to admit, but Simon was thrilled to join the Bigsby household, which had been an oasis of peace during his youth. It was a relief to leave the past behind after the nightmarish events that had transpired during his last stay.

Dinner was warm and informal, with Trafford standing mid-meal to raise his glass.

"I propose a toast to new beginnings."

"Hear, hear!" John called out, echoed by Nicholas.

"To my new chum, Simon, who turns out to be an excellent chap, and his bride, Lady Campbell, for her iron stomach." The reference to Madeline's body, a topic typically taboo in mixed company, set off a gale of laughter around the table. Trafford waited for the laughter to subside before continuing, "May they enjoy a long and healthy union!"

"Huzza!"

John stood, and Simon was heartened to see his brother's improved vitality. In the glow of lamps and candlelight, John's complexion looked far healthier than when Simon had left. He lifted his glass.

"I can confirm that my brother Simon is indeed an excellent chap! Mrs. Bigsby, I am heartened that our families have united under such happy circumstances, and I look forward to enjoying your company in the years to come."

Eleanor smiled broadly, giving a nod of acknowledgment as the other guests tittered and sipped their wine.

Madeline's Uncle Reginald rose to speak next. A slim, elderly gentleman with a thick gray mustache, he had an amiable manner. Simon knew he had been instrumental in helping Eleanor establish her business in a male-dominated world.

"It seems just yesterday that young Eleanor arrived in London as a widow with twin babes in her arms. Witnessing my niece's nuptials this evening is a testament to the passage of time, marked by glorious success. All my nieces are impressive pioneers, and I could not be more proud. So, to

Madeline and her Lord Campbell, I wish a long and happy marriage!"

The room filled with the clinking of glasses. Simon leaned toward Madeline, pleased to see her smiling face and shining eyes.

"Are you happy, fair Psyche?"

"Ecstatic! But ..." Madeline leaned closer, her voice dropping to a whisper. "What happens next?" She looked up at him, her amber eyes shimmering with shy curiosity. Simon caught the hint in her gaze and knew exactly where her thoughts were drifting.

Grinning, he bent down, his breath warm against her ear. "What would you like to happen next?"

She blushed, and Simon watched in fascination as the color spread up her neck, tinting even the delicate shells of her ears. Her tongue darted out to moisten her lips, and a wave of desire surged through him. His thoughts wandered to later that evening, imagining the moment he would join her in bed. The scent of orange blossoms hung in the air, teasing his senses as he envisioned unveiling her beauty to his hungry gaze.

"Are you ... joining me?"

He could not help it; his lips curled into a predatory smile. "My men are working with your Miss Moreau to move my things. We are finally together, fair Psyche, and there will be no more interruptions to our destiny."

Madeline smiled, her bare hand slipping under the table to find his. Simon covered it, stroking his thumb over her soft knuckles.

"I am so grateful I went looking for my mother when I did. What if I had not discovered you lying in the drawing room?"

Madeline grimaced at the reminder of that dreadful day. "She did not account for Lady Trafford's presence, which only proves we were meant to be together. We are Eros and Psyche, are we not?"

Simon chuckled. "I wish we had not followed their path quite so closely. Venus attempting to be rid of you so thoroughly?"

Madeline inhaled deeply, then recited in a dramatic tone, "Even the gods shuddered at the sight of Venus's wrath, for no one could temper the fury of the goddess of love."

"Are you showing off your knowledge of Apulieus?" Simon teased.

Madeline flashed an impudent grin.

Simon stroked his thumb over her knuckles again and cleared his throat. "Love had conquered the god of love himself, and Eros, burning with passion, defied his mother's orders."

She winced playfully. "It has been a trial, but I'm glad we found a happy ending."

"Indeed. We have been victims of my mother's interference. I look forward to living without her shadow looming over us."

"And I ..." Madeline hesitated, a fresh blush warming her face. "I look forward to ... later this evening."

CHAPTER 17

"The god of love stood before her, radiant and divine, yet humbled by the strength of his love for her."

Lucius Apuleius, Metamorphoses

* * *

er lady's maid unbuttoned her bodice while Madeline huffed in impatience. Simon was in the next room, and he was sure to be disrobed far sooner than she. Finally, the gown was loose, and she wiggled out of it so that it dropped to the floor. It was quickly retrieved to be rehung.

Banking her frustration, she waited for her stays to be loosened, leaning down to untie her garters and remove her stockings. Miss Moreau brought over her best night rail, and helped her put it on. Soon the servant brushed her hair out and cleared all her things away, departing the bedchamber to leave Madeline fidgeting nervously as she tried to decide what to do next.

Mama, Henri, and Uncle Reginald had remained in the family drawing room downstairs. They wished to chat over tea, they had said, but Madeline was grateful to realize her mother and sister were delaying their retiring to their bedrooms in order to afford Simon and her some privacy, and Uncle Reginald was taking advantage of some leisure time with Mama.

A knock on the door made her flinch, startled at the loud interruption. She licked her lips, realizing the moment of truth had arrived and discovering she was unexpectedly reluctant to take this final step.

"Madeline?" His deep voice sent a shivering thrill chasing along her nerve endings to settle as a quivering sensation in her lower belly.

"One moment, please?" She winced at the alarm evident in her shrill tone. She had imagined this moment for longer than she could remember, but now that the moment had arrived, she—

A low chuckle emitted from the other side of the door. "Let me in, fair Psyche. This will be easier if we are in the same room."

Madeline bit her lip. She had not anticipated how nervous she would be. Perhaps waiting for this night for such a long time had built it up to agonizing levels. But Simon was her best friend, so perhaps she should let him in.

She crossed over, reaching out to turn the handle, then flinched at the crack of the latch disengaging. Cracking the door open, she peered up at him. He was dressed in a colorful banyan with loose-fitting trousers, the column of his throat and clavicle bared to reveal that he wore no shirt beneath the robe.

Simon's gaze dropped with appreciation to take in the curve of her bosom, returning to stare deep into her eyes. The blueness of his irises drew her in as she drowned in their depths. How was it he had his mother's eyes, but his were so warm while Isla's had been as icy as a glacier?

Madeline shoved the memory of the murderous baroness aside. The terror of Lady Blackwood had passed, and she was determined to be present in this moment with Simon, as soon as she recovered her courage.

"I have dreamt of this night."

It took a moment for Madeline to realize it was not her own thought, but something Simon had declared out loud in a mellifluous baritone.

"Me, too …" she admitted in a tremulous voice.

"Then … may I come in?"

She swallowed hard and stepped back to allow him in before shutting the door. "I was not expecting to be so shy."

Simon flashed a wide smile, revealing a pearly slash of teeth. He approached her slowly, bending his head to brush a kiss against her mouth. Madeline exhaled in sweet pleasure, her fears dissolving as she drew in his male fragrance of shaving soap, coffee, and leather. A muscled arm wrapped around her waist, drawing her in so that her soft curves were pressed against his hard body before his lips found hers again in a drugging kiss. His tongue found hers and tangled in hungry abandonment.

He was firm and hot as her arms stole up to encircle his neck, her head falling back to accept his ardor. Sensation fired up, rising from between her thighs to engulf her in flames as she kissed him back with all the love she had for him, had always had for him. Their kiss continued as Simon reached down to swoop her into his arms, striding over to the canopied bed.

Lowering her onto the counterpane, Simon dropped his knees to the floor so that they were at the same height when he raised his head to gaze at her with adoration.

"Is this real? Am I dreaming? Will I wake up to learn you are still in Scotland?"

* * *

Simon gave a crooked smile. "I am here and I am never leaving. I regret how much time I wasted."

Madeline reached up, her amber eyes enchanting him despite the desire raging through his starving body. She touched his cheek. "You are here now. We are together."

"Thank you for waiting for me. I thought I could let you go. Watch you marry another man, but I think—I think it would have killed me." It was the truth. Madeline was his best friend. How could he have considered a lifetime of estrangement? He was a fool to have allowed his parents to convince him to leave her behind.

She stared up at him, biting her lip and reaching up to clasp the back of his head. Pulling him back into a kiss, she whispered, "It is in the past."

Their mouths fused together, and Simon drowned in the vortex of fantasy realized, breathing in the scent of orange blossoms, savoring the taste of fruit upon her tongue, while he settled his touch on her waist. Slowly it glided up until he cupped one of the full breasts that had tantalized him these past years. He growled in approval at the firm roundness against his palm, as Madeline's head fell back. She moaned, arching into his palm in invitation as he glanced down to be nearly unmanned by the sight of his tanned hand plumping the cotton-covered globe.

Without conscious thought, he released his grasp so his mouth found its way to the hardened pink jutting against the thin fabric. Painting her with his tongue, he lost all sense of time as she undulated against him, keening as she gripped the counterpane in agonized pleasure.

Simon gripped the hem of her rail, yanking it up with impatience until it was gathered around her narrow waist as he continued to suckle on her heated flesh. Rising, he divested her of the garment to reveal the beauty of a goddess before him. She was curves and shadows. Her breasts, bountiful and pert, beckoned like a siren's call, but his gaze dipped lower to find her rounded hips, then settled on honey-blonde curls that shielded her womanhood from his eyes.

"You are more beautiful than I imagined."

His lips found the fragile skin of her nipple, and soon she was mewling like a kitten as she tried her best not to howl out loud. Simon swirled his tongue around and over, savoring the sweetness of his love and shifting to the neglected breast. She quivered and shook beneath him until he settled onto the bed over her to paint a path down her creamy abdomen. As he approached her lower belly, she bucked, and he swiftly sank lower to lash his tongue against her cleft and taste her essence. Her thighs fell open in invitation, her hips rising as he explored the swelling folds with the tip of his tongue. Hearing her passion mount up, while his own lust gathered to make him harder than he had ever been, he swiped his tongue over the pearl at the apex of her crease.

Madeline's commitment to keeping quiet broke as she squealed her tortured ecstasy, but Simon continued mercilessly to lap at the sensitive nub until the waves of climax broke across her dainty form.

Slowly, she sank back onto the mattress as he rose above her to take in her dazed expression. Amber eyes flickered open, amazement reflected in their depths as he lifted himself off the bed.

His fingers tugged at the knot before he cast his robe aside without regard to where it fell. Madeline gazed up at his chest in curiosity, and he realized she was cataloging the condition of his muscles. The sculptor in her was clearly fascinated by his masculine form.

"You *are* Eros," she declared in admiration, her eyes falling to the bulging front of his cotton trousers which were tied at the waist. "That is new."

Simon looked down at his hard length tenting the fabric and burst out laughing. "All that art you studied did not include any …" He winced, seeking an appropriate word.

"Erections? They did not."

He shook his head, shuddering with suppressed mirth. Madeline was such a strange mix of innocent and worldly because of the work she did.

"Are we going to finish this?"

"No longer nervous?"

She licked her lips. "I suppose … it is time?"

He grinned, divesting himself of the cotton trousers to move back to the bed. Her eyes dipped with fascination to his engorged shaft, but he was done waiting, so he moved to stretch over her, capturing her mouth in a searing melding of lips and tongues as he settled between her legs.

Taking hold of his cock, he guided himself to her slick entrance to tease her until Madeline's legs parted to wrap around his hips. With one decisive motion, he buried himself in her quivering heat as she hissed in brief pain, coming to a halt while she grew accustomed to him and panting at the discovery that paradise was being wrapped within her warm clasp.

Seconds ticked by and then Madeline gyrated against him. It was all the invitation he needed, reaching out an arm above her head for support as he began to thrust into her tight sheath over and over again, and she moaned and undulated beneath him. He could feel her passion mounting in new waves, so he slid his free hand between them to toy her into new peaks of pleasure. As he felt the quiver of her climax, he lost control to reach new heights of sensation hitherto unknown before spending in an agony of ecstasy.

* * *

AFTER SIMON HAD COLLECTED a cloth to clean the two of them, he lowered himself into the bed and drew her into his arms. Madeline cuddled her head into place beneath his chin, listening to the sound of his heart thudding within his rib cage.

"Are you well?" he drawled as one who was heading toward sleep.

"Very well. Can we do that every night?"

His chest heaved beneath her cheek in a huff of laughter. "We can try."

"Will there be a scandal, do you think? Your mother expired a few weeks ago, and now you have wed in the middle of the night."

"That is probable, but I think news of one of the renowned Bigsbys marrying a Scottish viscount will be the bigger event. The other will fade away."

Madeline considered this, trying to determine what she thought of it. "I suppose I do not care as long as we are together."

"Forever, fair Psyche."

It was at that moment when Madeline caught sight of a small sculpture of Eros sitting on a side table, positioned to stare toward the garden—their garden. It was the one she had carved for Simon more than a decade earlier, and this was not a dream. They had finally united, and he was here to stay.

They fell asleep wrapped in each other's arms, and Madeline was the happiest she had ever been. All their troubles of the past receded into nothing as the longed-for future of her dreams began.

EPILOGUE

"Take care, Psyche, for the road ahead is filled with more dangers than you can foresee."

Lucius Apuleius, Metamorphoses

* * *

NOVEMBER 29, 1821

Simon was working in his brother's study, reviewing correspondence from the estates. He looked forward to turning this all over, having suggested hiring a private secretary for John. He hoped that Marco Scott would make a competent replacement to whom he could turn these duties over, but an assistant would be of help no matter Marco's managerial talents.

He checked his timepiece. Earlier this morning, they had received word that the ship his nephews were sailing on had arrived in port, and Simon had dispatched two carriages to collect them and their two companions who had journeyed to England with them. The first carriage was for them, and the second for their trunks. The friends were to be house-guests, he supposed. It was fortunate he had vacated his bedroom to make room for such a large party, who would each require their own chamber.

But the carriages had departed hours earlier, and Simon was surprised by how long it was taking for them to return. Perhaps many ships had sailed into port this morning, causing traffic on the wharfs?

He returned to his work, sharpening his quill to scribble his responses.

When he raised his head again, the sun had moved low into the sky. Simon frowned, checking the time to discover another two hours had passed. He rose to ring the bell, wondering if he had missed their arrival.

Soon, one of their lower footmen arrived.

"Is there word of Mr. Scott's arrival?"

"I do not know, sir, but I was informed that the second carriage has returned. The luggage has been brought in, but we were not certain which trunks belong to whom, so we have been waiting for the gentlemen to arrive so we can sort it out."

Simon frowned again. How could the luggage have arrived before their guests?

"Have a carriage brought around for me." He had yet to make arrangements for his own cattle and vehicle, so he was still making use of John's. "I shall go down to the port to find out what the delay is."

He needed to see to their arrival so he could return home. Madeline would be expecting him for dinner, and he was looking forward to spending the evening with her. They had agreed they would host a feast for St. Andrew's Day with his nephews the next day, allowing them to rest after their long journey from Italy. It was his duty as a Scottish laird to mark the occasion, and his northern brethren belowstairs had proved to be excited about the festivities which his mother had been remiss in celebrating.

Twenty minutes later, Simon approached the front door just as Duncan appeared in the hall. The head footman looked worse for wear, his green and blue livery dirtied, and he had a scratch on his broad cheek.

"Duncan? What is this?"

The manservant was flushed as he responded, "I came to find you as soon as I could, milord. There has been an accident. A wheel came off the carriage, and the gentlemen were injured."

"What?"

Duncan swallowed hard, clearly unhappy about being a messenger of ill tidings. "They are well, just scuffed up. A doctor is attending them. I am to send a carriage to collect them, and a wagon so we might collect the damaged vehicle."

"What in tarnation happened?"

The weather was clear, and Simon could think of no reason why their fine and well-maintained vehicles should malfunction.

"Milord … there was a suggestion of foul play. The coachman wishes me to inform you that he believes the wheel was tampered with."

Simon groaned, raking his hair back in anguish. Weaving his fingers together to clasp the back of his head, his mind whirled at the terrible possibilities.

His mother—what had she said when she had slipped into the oblivion of infinite slumber? Simon cast his thoughts back, trying to recollect the dreadful scene by her bed which he had tried his best not to think about these past weeks.

"My journals are … my confession … to clear your name."

Simon approached the bed, still trying to make up his mind what to do. "Why, Mother?"

"You will be baron ... the greatest Campbell ... Papa would ... be so proud."

Simon frowned, attempting to unravel the words. "You mean my father?"

His mother's face creased into a euphoric smile. "Lord Campbell ... My papa ... I disappointed him so ... but ... not anymore. My son ... will be Baron ... of Blackwood."

"Mother, there are other heirs."

Her eyes drifted closed. "I ... have ... taken care of ..." With that, his mother slipped into unconsciousness.

He and Trafford had dismissed it as delusions of a dying woman, but ... Could his mother have left behind an accomplice?

It was too grotesque to consider. There had been nothing in her journals to suggest another person was involved. Surely the coachman must be mistaken, and the accident was merely a coincidence. His mother could not have arranged for someone to kill his nephews. It was madness to even contemplate it.

Even so, Simon would consult Trafford about hiring some of his guards for Madeline. Her safety was paramount. And he faced an unenviable task of rereading his mother's journals to make certain there was no hint of a third conspirator in her web of death and mayhem.

* * *

Discover if Lady Blackwood left someone to complete her evil deeds in Lord of Intrigue when Molly Carter meets the mysterious heir from Italy.

AFTERWORD

Growing up in the South African high veld, I have long been fascinated with the grandeur of a beautiful sunset. The sky is huge, the colors rich, while the stars sparkle with vivid vivacity in the darkening firmament. I can recall those moments, alighting from the bus to walk the final mile with a gorgeous sundown to make me pause in amazement as the last threads of light vanished over the wooded horizon, the diamond-studded heavens my only companion as darkness fell.

Today I may live in a city awash with artificial light, and the beauty of a big country sky may be something of a distant memory, but the ethereal moments from my youth have crept into this tale of fated love. I humbly propose that London may have had a much clearer sky more than two hundred years ago, from the vantage point of a secret garden, and with candles and gas lamps to light the night.

Eleanor Bigsby is loosely based on the highly successful businesswoman, Eleanor Choade. One can enjoy the overwhelmingly popular Choade stone products at Buckingham

Palace, The Royal Pavilion in Brighton, and the Royal Naval College in Greenwich.

Henrietta "Henri" Bigsby, too, is loosely based on a historical figure. Lady Hester Stanhope acted as the private secretary and political hostess for her uncle. She went on to become an antiquarian, writer, and adventurer after his death, and in 1815, she excavated Ascalon, an ancient city on the Mediterranean coast. She is believed to be the first to use modern archeological techniques.

For the arsenic poisoning and most of the symptoms, I used the 1821 case of Mary Biggadike, whose husband, James Cawthorn, poisoned her milk, for which he was tried and executed.

Scottish peerages, in the case of a lord having only daughters, pass to the eldest child, which is why Simon inherited titles from his mother.

Book Five of Inconvenient Scandals will bring the mystery to a close while introducing a thrilling adventure romance series, Inconvenient Ventures!

A mysterious heir is on his way to England. Will Molly be able to find her place in his household, or will a tragic fate befall one of them within the week?

When Molly Carter meets her de facto guardian, Marco Scott, she is horrified to find herself attracted to the gentleman who will run her trust. Her composure shatters in his presence, as she struggles to find *not* the words that fit, but the words that are fitting. She is quite aware that her mother would have been amused to witness her daughter's discombobulation.

Marco has troubles of his own, and he does not need to be distracted by a pretty English girl when his world is in turmoil. Since arriving in England, bizarre accidents dog his heels, and it doesn't seem too far-fetched to consider that foul play might be afoot.

Read Lord of Intrigue to learn if Molly and Marco can come to terms with their newfound passion and solve the mystery before one of them ends up in a grave.

ABOUT THE AUTHOR

Nina began crafting her own stories as a teenager but took a detour from writing after finishing school to pursue non-profit work with recovering drug addicts. Her journey took her into the heart of South Africa, where she encountered people from all walks of life, from the privileged to those in rural shanty towns.

Her own love story unfolded when she met a real-life romantic hero—a fellow bibliophile—whom she instantly married. Together, they moved to the USA, where Nina enjoyed a successful career as a sales coaching executive at an Inc. 500 company before returning to her first love: writing Regency romances.

Now living with her husband on the Florida Gulf Coast, Nina is passionate about kindness and the resilience of the human spirit. Inspired by the incredible people she's met around the world who dared to change their lives, she writes mischievous tales of life-altering decisions and transformative characters. When not writing, she can be found savoring excellent coffee and doing her best to resist cookies.

Join Nina's Newsletter at NinaJarrett.com for free books, fun Regency content, announcements, and exclusive discounts.

Follow Nina Jarrett on your favorite platform.

ALSO BY NINA JARRETT

INCONVENIENT BRIDES

Book 1: The Duke Wins a Bride

Book 2: To Redeem an Earl

Book 3: My Fair Bluestocking

Book 4: Sleepless in Saunton

Book 5: Caroline Saves the Blacksmith

INCONVENIENT SCANDALS

The Duke and Duchess of Halmesbury will return, along with the Balfours, Abbotts, and Lord Trafford in an all-new suspense romance series.

Book 1: Long Live the Baron

Book 2: Moonlight Encounter

Book 3: Lord Trafford's Folly

Book 4: The Trouble With Titles

Book 5: Lord of Intrigue

INCONVENIENT VENTURES

The duke's brother and his friends journey from Italy in a bid to right past wrongs through the pursuit of treasure.

Book 1: The Courtship Trap

* * *

BOOK 1: THE DUKE WINS A BRIDE

Her fiancé betrayed her. The duke steps in. Could a marriage of convenience transform into true love?

In this spicy historical romance, a sheltered baron's daughter and a celebrated duke agree on a marriage of convenience, but he has a secret that may ruin it all.

She is desperate to escape...

When Miss Annabel Ridley learns her betrothed has been unfaithful, she knows she must cancel the wedding. The problem is no one else seems to agree with her, least of all her father. With her wedding day approaching, she must find a way to escape her doomed marriage. She seeks out the Duke of Halmesbury to request he intercede with her rakish betrothed to break it off before the wedding day.

He is ready to try again...

Widower Philip Markham has decided it is time to search for a new wife. He hopes to find a bold bride to avoid the mistakes of his past. Fate seems to be favoring him when he finds a captivating young woman in his study begging for his help to disengage from a despised figure from his past. He astonishes her with a proposal of his own—a marriage of convenience to suit them both. If she accepts, he resolves to never reveal the truth of his past lest it ruin their chances of possibly finding love.

* * *

BOOK 2: TO REDEEM AN EARL

She planned to stay unmarried, but Lord Richard Balfour is determined to make her his countess.

In this steamy historical romance, a cynical debutante and a scandalous earl find themselves entangled in an undeniable attraction. Will they open their hearts to love or will his past destroy their future together?

She has vowed she will never marry...

Miss Sophia Hayward knows all about men and their immoral behavior. She has watched her father and older brother behave like reckless fools her entire life. All she wants is to avoid marriage to a lord until she reaches her majority because she has plans which do not include a husband. Until she meets the one peer who will not take a hint.

He must have her...

Lord Richard Balfour has engaged in many disgraceful activities with the women of his past. He had no regrets until he encounters a cheeky debutante who makes him want to be a better man. Only problem is, he has a lot of bad behavior to make amends for if he is ever going to persuade Sophia to take him seriously. Will he learn to be a better man before his mistakes catch up with him and ruin their chance at true love?

* * *

MY FAIR BLUESTOCKING: BOOK 3

A rebellious young woman. A spoilt buck. When passions ignite, will opposites attract?

She thinks he is arrogant and vain ...

The Davis family has ascended to the gentry due to their unusual connection to the Earl of Saunton. Now the earl wants Emma Davis and her sister to come to London for the Season. Emma relishes refusing, but her sister is excited to meet eligible gentlemen. Now she can't tell the earl's arrogant brother to go to hell when he shows up with the invitation. She will cooperate for her beloved sibling, but she is not allowing the handsome Perry to sway her mind ... or her heart.

He thinks she is disheveled, but intriguing ...

Peregrine Balfour cannot believe the errands his brother is making him do. Fetching a country mouse. Preparing her for polite society. Dancing lessons. He should be stealing into the beds of welcoming widows, not delivering finishing lessons to an unstylish shrew. Pity he can't help noticing the ravishing young woman that is being revealed by his tuition until the only schooling he wants to deliver is in the language of love.

Will these two conflicting personalities find a way to reconcile their unexpected attraction before Perry makes a grave mistake?

* * *

BOOK 4: SLEEPLESS IN SAUNTON

A sleepless debutante. A widowed architect. A lavish country house party might be perfect for new love to bloom.

In this steamy historical romance, a sleepless young woman yearns for love while a successful widower pines for his beloved wife. Hot summer nights at a lavish country house might be the perfect environment for new love to bloom.

She cannot sleep ...

Jane Davis went to London with her sister for a Season full of hope and excitement. Now her sister is married and Jane wanders the halls alone in the middle of the night. Disappointed with the gentlemen she has met, she misses her family and is desperate for a full night's sleep. Until she meets a sweet young girl who asks if Jane will be her new mother.

He misses his wife ...

It has been two years since Barclay Thompson's beloved wife passed away. Now the Earl of Saunton has claimed him as a brother and, for the sake of his young daughter, Barclay has acknowledged their relationship. But loneliness keeps him up at night until he encounters a young woman who might make his dead heart beat again. Honor demands he walk away rather than ruin the young lady's reputation. Associating with a by-blow like him will bar her from good society, no matter how badly his little girl wants him to make a match.

Can these three lonely souls take a chance on love and reconnect with the world together?

* * *

BOOK 5: CAROLINE SAVES THE BLACKSMITH

She helps injured the blacksmith on Christmas Eve, leading to a romantic attraction despite their aversion to love.

She has a dark past that she must keep a secret. He has a dark past he wishes to forget. The magic of the festive season might be the key to unlocking a fiery new passion.

She will not repeat her past mistakes ...

Caroline Brown once made an unforgivable mistake with a handsome earl, betraying a beloved friend in the process. Now she is rebuilding her life as the new owner of a dressmaker's shop in the busy town of Chatternwell. She is determined to guard her heart from all men, including the darkly handsome blacksmith, until the local doctor requests her help on the night before Christmas.

He can't stop thinking about her ...

William Jackson has avoided relationships since his battle wounds healed, but the new proprietress on his street is increasingly in his thoughts, which is why he is avoiding her at all costs. But an unexpected injury while his mother is away lays him up on Christmas Eve and now the chit is mothering him in the most irritating and delightful manner.

Can the magic of the holiday season help two broken souls overcome their dark pasts to form a blissful union?

* * *

BOOK 6: LONG LIVE THE BARON

After she clears his name of murder, a marriage of convenience

is the only way to save her reputation! Will their uneasy alliance spark a lasting passion?

A steamy historical suspense romance, about a young woman driven to do the right thing, a lord who does not quite appreciate the gesture, and a murder investigation that could end their new relationship before it begins.

Her conscience drives her to act ...

Miss Lily Abbott knows the new baron is innocent because she saw him entering the widow's home next door at the time of the crime. But when the widow refuses to assist him, this young woman who hoped to marry for love cannot stand idly by when she knows the truth. Lily risks everything to provide an alibi for the glib gentleman who barely remembers her name.

He can't believe he has to marry her ...

Lord Brendan Ridley stands accused of patricide to gain the title he now holds. Not even his close family connection to the powerful Duke of Halmesbury can help him. He prays his paramour will come forward to clear his name, but honor dictates he not reveal his whereabouts that night without her consent. When help comes from an unexpected quarter, he finds himself forced to marry an annoying chatterbox to save her from scandal.

When these two mismatched people are forced to marry, will they find a way to work together to reveal an enduring passion before the real murderer strikes again?

* * *

BOOK 7: MOONLIGHT ENCOUNTER

Lord Aidan Abbott investigates Mr. Smythe but compromises his daughter, Gwen, at a ball in front of a crowd of important guests.

In this steamy historical romance, the heir to a viscountcy is determined to protect his sister, accidentally ruining a young woman while searching her father's home. Now he will need to choose between his crusade and the growing love between them.

He feels guilty for failing his family ...

Lord Aidan Abbott neglected his duties as a chaperone when his parents left his little sister in his charge. Because of him, Lily was forced to wed under a cloud of scandal. Now Aidan must solve a murder to keep his sister and her new husband out of danger.

She is caught unawares ...

A mysterious lord interrupts Miss Gwendolyn Smythe while she is taking air on the terrace. Unfortunately, they are discovered together, so she is forced to marry a man she has never met before to quell the scandal. Now Gwen is determined to make the best of their new marriage, with or without his cooperation.

While Aidan continues to secretly investigate Gwendolyn's family, he realizes that the scholarly redhead now holds his heart in her hands. How can he reveal what he has been doing without shattering their only chance at love?

* * *

BOOK 8: LORD TRAFFORD'S FOLLY

A daring lord and a young woman find themselves in peril, igniting a possible romance as they escape to stay alive.

A steamy historical suspense romance, about a lord who agrees to help his friends with their quest to solve a murder. Now he must fend for himself while protecting the young lady he has endangered with his choices. Can he keep her safe from harm from both the enemy pursuing them, and his urge to kiss those plump lips?

He thought it would be a lark ...

When Lord Julius Trafford, the heir to an earl, agrees to help his friends in a quest to solve a murder, it was mostly because he was bored. Now he is in hot water, and he has dragged his father's delectable ward into danger with him. Together, they are forced on the run, and Lord Trafford must engage his wits before it's too late.

She is determined to keep him alive ...

Miss Audrey Gideon feels compelled to care for Lord Trafford when he is attacked by a murderous assailant. As they make their escape from London in search of safety, Julius begins to demonstrate his true potential and Audrey wonders if there is more to the foppish heir than meets the eye.

Can this unlikely pair rise to the challenge and discover true love along the way?

* * *

BOOK 9: THE TROUBLE WITH TITLES

She has loved him for years. In his darkest hour, she is determined to save him by uncovering the real killer.

In this steamy historical romance an heir stands to lose everything unless he can find the truth, and the girl next door is the only one standing by his side while danger lurks in the shadows.

He could lose his title and his life ...

Simon Scott is set to inherit a title and a fortune until powerful lords accuse him of murder. Now his betrothed has broken ties with him and he could be arrested at any moment. Trouble is he knows he is innocent, but who will believe him when all the evidence points to him?

She knows he is not a killer ...

Madeline Bigsby has been in love with Simon since they were children, but he was too self-absorbed to notice. In his darkest hour, she is determined to save him by uncovering the real killer.

The stakes are high and love has never been such a dangerous game. Can Simon accept help from the girl he left behind to discover who has framed him and perhaps learn the value of true love along the way?

* * *

BOOK 10: LORD OF INTRIGUE

A mysterious heir is on his way to England. Will Molly be able to find her place in his household, or will a tragic fate befall one of them within the week?

In this steamy mystery romance, two people are thrust together on the ashes of a disastrous murder plot. Now they must find a way to work together despite the unexpected attraction between them.

No one knows the new heir ...

Marco Scott has never been to England, but now he is next in line to a title. Surrounded by potential enemies, he must find his footing in this strange land. Learning he is to act as guardian to an enticing young woman only makes matters more complicated.

A ward stuck in a stranger's home ...

Molly Carter is handed over to the new heir, a man no one knew existed until it was revealed a peer was murdered to conceal his existence. To make matters worse, he might be the most beautiful man alive, which is making her blurt out the most embarrassing nonsense.

But someone is not happy that Marco will inherit. Danger lurks in the shadows, and he can't inherit if he's dead. Can Molly and Marco come to terms with their newfound passion to solve the mystery before one of them ends up in a grave?

* * *

BOOK 11: THE COURTSHIP TRAP

She wants to begin again. He wants to set things right. When goals collide, can a renewed courtship lead to a second chance at love?

A steamy historical adventure romance about the brother of a duke returning from Italy to retrieve a painting from the girl he once loved. He needs to solve an epic mystery, but soon he is trapped in a courtship that revives the attraction between them.

She wants to change her luck ...

After falling victim to a terrible curse from the bride of a former lover, widow Lady Slight no longer finds joy in her idle pursuits. So when a former love comes knocking on her door, she coerces him into a nostalgic courtship that reminds her of happier times when the future was full of possibility.

He is solving a mystery ...

Sebastian Markham departed England years ago after Harriet betrayed him. Now he is back and he needs the priceless painting he once gifted the girl he loved. But Harriet has changed, and Sebastian soon finds himself agreeing to spend time with the complex woman who has haunted his dreams.

With adventure afoot, Sebastian assures himself it is because he really needs that painting, but is it the promise of reawakened passion that beckons? Perhaps the timing is finally right, and perhaps Harriet is ready for a life not of high society comfort and status, but of high adventure and art.

Printed in Dunstable, United Kingdom